STAR WARS™

ADVENTURES IN WILD SPACE

THE RESCUE

TOM HUDDLESTON

D0032037

LOS ANGELES · NEW YORK

For information address Disney · Lucasfilm Press,
1200 Grand Central Avenue, Glendale, California 91201.
Printed in the United States of America
First United States Paperback Edition, April 2018
1 3 5 7 9 10 8 6 4 2
FAC-029261-18054
ISBN 978-1-368-00315-5
Library of Congress Control Number on file

Cover art by Lucy Ruth Cummins
Interior art by David Buisán

Visit the official *Star Wars* website at: www.starwars.com.

SUSTAINABLE
FORESTRY
INITIATIVE

Certified Chain of Custody
Promoting Sustainable Forestry

www.sfiprogram.org
SFI-01054

The SFI label applies to the text stock

CONTENTS

ADVENTURES IN WILD SPACE

THE RESCUE

It is a time of darkness. With the end of the Clone Wars and the destruction of the Jedi Order, the evil Emperor Palpatine rules the galaxy unopposed.

After months of searching, Milo and Lina Graf have learned that their parents, Rhyssa and Auric, are being held in an Imperial mining colony on the planet Agaris, deep in Wild Space.

Traveling in a stolen Imperial transport, Milo and Lina have reached Agaris determined to free their parents from the clutches of the Empire. But on this mist-shrouded world, nothing is as it seems. . . .

CHAPTER 1
AGARIS

THE ANCHORING SPIKE shot out from the *Star Herald*'s underside, burrowing deep into the surface of the tiny moon. The rock was barely worthy of that name, Lina thought. It wasn't so much a moon as a misshapen meteor, caught by the planet's gravity and doomed to orbit endlessly. But it should be enough to hide them.

Milo hit the recoil switch and the cable drew taut, securing the stolen Imperial ship in place. CR-8R cut the power and the cockpit was plunged into darkness. Morq burrowed down into Milo's lap, chittering softly.

"Nice move, Sis," Milo breathed. "Crate, did they see us?"

CR-8R shook his metal head. "There has been no detectable increase in Imperial chatter," he said. "It would appear that Mistress Lina's quick thinking has allowed us to arrive unnoticed."

Lina peered out through the viewport as the pale light of dawn leaked into the cockpit. "Now the question is, how do we get from here to there?"

Above the moon's desolate surface, the planet Agaris was rising. A gloomy, forbidding world, it was shrouded in shifting banks of murky clouds. But even in those small patches where the cloud cover broke, Lina could see none of the dazzling greens and blues she would've expected from a world like that. Agaris was teeming with life—all their sensors said so. But beneath the gray all she could see was more gray.

"The Imperial compound is located on the

northernmost continent," CR-8R said, pointing with a long metal finger. "Sensors read a powerful energy signal."

"Just one base?" Milo asked, surprised. "Mira and Ephraim said the Empire had been taking over whole worlds, setting up base after base so they could control the population."

"Maybe there's no population to control," Lina pointed out. "There's no sign of any cities or technology."

"Master Milo has a point, though," CR-8R said. "If Agaris is the site of an Imperial mining operation, why do the sensors pick up no drilling sites or auxiliary bases beyond the central compound? That said, it does help us in one important respect: there is only one place your parents could possibly be."

Milo reached for Lina's hand and together they gazed at the vast pale globe. Somewhere up there Rhyssa and Auric Graf were waiting, imprisoned and unsuspecting. Their long search was almost at an end.

Lina tried to picture her parents' faces, tried to summon up the smell of them and the sound of their voices. In recent weeks these things had begun to fade, her dreams of Rhyssa and Auric drowned out by darkness and danger. But no longer, she promised herself. Soon, somehow, they would all be back together. She and Milo would find a way. They had to.

A glimmer in the blackness caught her eye, and she felt Milo's grip tighten. The Star Destroyer *Executrix* glided from the planet's shadow like a sleek silver shark hunting for prey. The command tower emerged into the light, bristling with laser turrets and antennae.

"Are you absolutely *sure* they can't see us?" Milo asked nervously.

"All of the *Star Herald*'s systems have been powered down," CR-8R told him. "We are a gray ship on a gray moon. And they have no idea we are here."

"Let's hear them anyway, Crate," Lina suggested. "Just in case."

"I assure you, Mistress Lina," CR-8R said, a little defensively, "I am monitoring all Imperial transmissions. If anything out of the ordinary—"

"We trust you, Crater," Milo said. "It'll just make us feel better, is all."

"You'll feel better listening to the voices of your enemy?" CR-8R asked. "Sometimes I simply do not understand the two of you."

But he patched the signal through anyway, the hiss of static rattling through the *Star Herald*'s internal speakers. It had been an unwitting gift from the ship's previous owner, Captain Korda—a scanner pretuned to all the Imperial communication bands, even a few classified ones. When this was over, Lina thought, they could hand the ship over to Mira and Ephraim Bridger, back on Lothal. Perhaps their friends would forgive them for running away.

"Executrix, *this is transport three-six-six.*" A man's voice came through, distant and distorted. "*We're ready for departure.*"

"*Roger that, three-six-six,*" a second man

replied. *"Prepare to release docking clamps."*

A bulky haulage vessel emerged from the Star Destroyer's ventral hangar, flanked by a pair of TIE fighters. Engines flared and the three ships moved toward the planet, a trio of black specks silhouetted against the clouds.

"Agaris base, we have locked on to your beacon and are making our descent," the first man said as the transport vanished into the murky atmosphere. *"Escort, keep your eyes peeled for those stalks."*

Milo looked at Lina, confused. "Stalks?" he asked. "Like, plant stalks?"

"Or storks?" Lina suggested. "Maybe some kind of giant bird down there?"

"They'd have to be pretty huge to take down an Imperial transport," Milo said. "Either way, it's weird."

"*Executrix, this is C-patrol,*" a clearer voice cut in, and Lina ducked instinctively as a second pair of TIEs shrieked overhead, angling toward the Destroyer. *"We've finished our sweep. There* are no ships out here. Whatever happened to those men, it's the compound's problem, not ours."

"Stow that talk, C-patrol," someone replied abruptly. "Or I'll have you reassigned to planetary scout duty. How would you like that?"

"R-roger that, Executrix," the pilot replied. "Um, please inform Governor Tarkin that our sensors are clean. But we'll do another sweep just in case."

"That's better, C-patrol," the officer said. "Make this a double shift and perhaps we can forget about your . . . inappropriate comment."

"Tarkin," Milo said. "I've heard that name. Ephraim said he was a big shot in the Imperial high command."

"So what's he doing all the way out here?" Lina asked. "And what were they talking about? What happened to their men?"

"Maybe it's those giant storks," Milo mused. "Maybe they ate them!"

"The pilot implied that the incident was still a mystery," CR-8R added. "Clearly the situation on Agaris is far from satisfactory, from an Imperial standpoint."

"Which could be good for us," Lina said. "If they're distracted by these storks or whatever, it'll make it easier for us to sneak in."

"If this Tarkin is as important as Master Milo believes, he will be well guarded," the droid told her.

Milo nodded. "But if they're busy guarding him, maybe they won't pay as much attention to a couple of prisoners."

Lina grinned. "Right," she said. "Let's get down there and find out."

They watched in silence as the *Executrix* crossed the face of the planet, a black arrow against the swirling clouds. The moon drifted on an opposite orbit, taking them gradually out of range. Soon the Star Destroyer had been swallowed by the gray face of Agaris.

"Once we've detached I'll give her two seconds of thrust," Lina explained. "That should be enough to break the moon's orbit and enter the planet's gravity. Crater, leave all other systems shut down until we reach the cover of those clouds."

"All of them?" the droid asked. "But, Mistress Lina, with no way to navigate we will be in a blind spin. You will have no way to—"

"Let me worry about that, Crate," she said. "With luck, anyone watching will think we're just a hunk of debris. Milo, retract the anchor. Let's move before that Star Destroyer comes back around."

She felt the *Star Herald* lifting gently off the moon's surface, and heard a clunk as the cable snaked back into the ship. "Crater, bring the engines back online," Lina ordered. "Three, two . . ."

And she hit the thrusters, the little moon's gravity tugging them back in their seats as the *Star Herald* rose, its snub nose pointed directly at the dim world below.

Seconds later Lina cut the power, hoping no Imperial observers had spotted the brief flare of their engines. She felt the planet's gravity take hold, a steady downward pull. The *Star Herald* began to roll, Agaris sliding slowly out of view, replaced first by star-studded space then by the lumpy, uneven cylinder of the little moon, receding behind them.

Milo groaned. "I shouldn't have eaten the last of that icefish for breakfast."

"Try shutting your eyes," Lina suggested.

Milo tried it for a moment, then shook his head. "That just makes it worse."

They could see Agaris again, filling the screen with shifting masses of gray. Their spin was starting to speed up, the planet's gravity tugging them in every direction at once. Morq gave a sickly moan. Lina knew how he felt.

"Executrix, *this is C-patrol.*" The pilot's voice was suddenly back, and Lina jerked her head up. "Executrix, *come in please.*"

"*This is* Executrix," the officer replied. "*What is it now, C-patrol?*"

"*We're making our second pass,*" the pilot

said. *"We've picked up something on the scanners. Sending the report now."*

Lina looked back at Milo, not daring to speak. As the *Star Herald* rolled, they could see the fighters, distant but closing.

The officer sighed. *"We appreciate your diligence, C-patrol, but there's no need to report every meteorite your scanners pick up."*

"It's made of metal, sir," the pilot radioed back. *"I know there are no power readings but—"*

"So it's a meteorite with an iron core," the officer interrupted. *"Or it's a hunk of space debris, probably from last time we dumped the garbage. Ignore it, C-patrol, and continue your sweep."*

Lina sighed in relief. That had been way too close. If the Empire spotted them now, they'd be finished. Even if they managed to escape, they'd have lost the element of surprise.

The *Star Herald* rolled toward the planet, and she could see high cloud turrets reaching up toward them. Once they were safely inside the atmosphere, she'd fire up the thrusters and find somewhere to land. "Crater," she said, "get ready to—"

"Executrix, *we're going to check it out.*" The pilot's voice crashed back into the cockpit. "*You're probably right, but it's my neck if the governor finds out we missed something important.*"

Milo's face whitened. Lina gripped the armrests.

"*All right, C-patrol,*" the officer replied. "*But make it fast.*"

"Crater, get her started," Lina barked. "Milo, strap in tight."

She felt the engines rattle and catch and slammed the thrusters, turning that sickening roll into a twisting dive. She could imagine the look of surprise on the TIE pilot's face as the drifting hunk of space debris suddenly flared to life, rocketing toward the planet.

"They're coming after us," Milo warned her.

"I'm sure they are," Lina replied as they

plunged into the atmosphere, the air fading from black to blue.

Then the clouds swallowed them. One moment they were streaking down in bright sunlight, the next they were ploughing through a dense fog, trails of vapor streaming across the screen. Winds buffeted the *Star Herald*'s hull and the ship rattled as Lina hauled back on the steering bar, leveling them out.

They broke from the clouds into the gloom of a murky day. The sun was a watery glow

behind the clouds, and below them Lina could see a dark plain stretching to a range of jagged mountains on the distant horizon.

At first she thought the surface was bare—just smooth gray-brown rocks. Then, looking closer, she saw that it was covered with huge domes, like blisters on the skin of Agaris. "Are those . . . ?" she began, perplexed. "They look like . . ."

"Mushrooms," Milo finished for her. "A whole forest of them. And they're huge—look at that one, it's bigger than the ship."

"Giant fungi are not uncommon. They are found on many charted worlds," CR-8R pointed out.

"But there doesn't seem to be anything else," Milo said. "Where are the trees? Where's the grass? It's just mushrooms every—"

There was a roar, and the *Star Herald* shook violently. Morq shrieked, jumping from Milo's lap and shivering beneath the navigation console. Lina slammed the steering bar sideways and the next blast just missed them, a green bolt flashing past into the mushroom forest below.

"We cannot evade them, Mistress Lina," CR-8R said. "They are following too closely behind us."

Checking the rear viewport, Lina saw that he was right. The two TIEs were almost on them, their ion engines roaring. Evasive maneuvers would be no help at all at this range—so where were they going to go?

"What's that?" Milo asked, pointing up ahead. "It looks like a tower."

A tall shape was outlined against the sky. Milo was right; it did look like an artificial structure: a slender black skyscraper with a wide base.

"Imperial?" Lina asked.

"The Imperial compound is still some distance away, at the base of those mountains," CR-8R said. "And this structure does not correspond to any design I am familiar with."

Another blast hit the ship, sending them tumbling. Lina grappled for control, managing to right the *Star Herald*'s course but knowing another shot could finish them.

"We'll head for it anyway," she said. "We don't have a choice. Maybe whoever built it can help us somehow."

"Wait," Milo said in amazement. "Is it moving?"

Somehow the entire massive structure was angling toward them, the base rooted in the ground but the higher levels swinging to face them. As it did so, Lina realized it wasn't a tower at all; it wasn't even straight. The structure curved in the middle like a tall stem weighed down by a heavy, bulb-like cap.

"That's no building," Milo said. "It's another mushroom!"

"Is it . . . pointing at us?" Lina asked, their pursuers momentarily forgotten.

As they watched, a series of pale green folds peeled back along the mushroom's cap and the massive protuberance spread wide like a flower, revealing an opening in the center.

"It almost looks like . . . no, it can't be," Milo said.

"Like what?" Lina urged him.

"Well, it sort of looks like a cannon, doesn't it?" Milo asked. "Like a barrel, with the opening at the top and that massive stalk . . ." Then it hit him. "Lina, get us out of here. The stalks, remember? Watch out for the stalks!"

But it was too late. Lina saw a ripple building

at the base of the huge fungus, making its way up the stalk, picking up speed. When it reached the open bulb, something flew out, a gleaming red sphere as big as a TIE fighter's body, glistening with golden spikes.

Lina grabbed the steering bar with all her might, knowing they didn't stand a chance. The projectile slammed into the *Star Herald*'s starboard side, spines piercing the hull. Alarms wailed and sirens blared, but by then they were already going down, spinning helplessly toward the planet's surface.

CHAPTER 2
SCORCHED WORLD

GOVERNOR TARKIN removed one black leather glove and ran his finger along the steel railing of the balcony. His fingertip turned black. He shook his head in disgust, pulling a handkerchief from his pocket and wiping his hands clean before replacing the glove.

Everything about that planet was putrid. The air was damp and fetid, the ever-present clouds were gloomy and oppressive, and it seemed as though everything he owned—his clothes, his boots, his weapons, even his prized corvette starship, the *Carrion Spike*—had acquired an added layer of creeping black fungus. For a man who prized cleanliness, it was almost unbearable.

A flare of red light caught his eye and Tarkin peered into the gloom. From his vantage point high on the sloping side of the stone compound he could see out across the trackless mushroom forests of Agaris. It was a sight he had already come to loathe. He despised the huge gray domes and the smaller fungi clustered around them, their lurid markings like splashes of neon paint on a gray wall. But his deepest hatred was reserved for those giant stalks, with their infuriating habit of knocking his TIEs out of the sky with their ugly spiked seedlings. He would have ordered them all hacked down if it wasn't for more pressing problems.

The light flared again. He pulled a pair of macrobinoculars from his jacket. Two TIEs were tracking something. Could it be a ship? He gripped the railing, watching keenly. Could this be the answer he'd been seeking? Had rebels been there all along, stealing his men from under his nose?

Or could it be . . . yes. He'd heard the reports from Xala's moon, of the fall of Captain Korda and the flight of the Graf children. Where else would they go but Agaris? He smiled. It was almost too perfect.

He sharpened the focus, trying to make out the craft his fighters were pursuing. But the chase seemed to be over, the TIEs circling like rock vultures around a kill. Were the children dead, then? He hoped not; they would be a valuable tool to make their parents talk. Then again, if the droid was still with them, Tarkin would no longer need the Grafs, so maybe it would be cleaner if the children had perished.

The entry buzzer whined and Tarkin gestured. The shutter slid up to reveal a hulking figure almost too large to fit through the doorway. The KX security droid ducked his head and strode out onto the balcony, massive

metal arms swinging at his sides. K-4D8's black carapace had been polished to a fine sheen. On one shoulder the Imperial symbol was emblazoned in gold, a symbol of his enhanced status. Seeing that, Tarkin smiled thinly. The droid's loyalties may have been pledged to a man Tarkin despised utterly, but all three of them were merely servants to a much greater cause.

"Director Krennic sends his regards," the droid said, his voice like metal scraping on metal. "He has commanded me personally to oversee transportation of the first shipment of quadanium back to Sentinel Base. With your permission, Governor."

"Of course," Tarkin said softly, pursing his lips. "And those were Krennic's only orders, were they? Because a more suspicious man might suspect that you were sent to spy on me."

K-4D8 pulled himself upright, servos whirring. "My assignment was clear," he said. "To escort the first shipment as soon as the ore was prepared. And in the meantime, to place myself in Governor Tarkin's service and carry out any further assignments as he sees fit."

"Oh, so you're here to help?" Tarkin asked. "The director is too kind."

"He felt that one more pair of hands might speed things along," the droid explained.

Tarkin's eyes narrowed. "Yes, that sounds like him. Very well, droid, there's no sense hiding the truth. You know, and Director Krennic undoubtedly knows, that progress has been more than slow. In fact, our mining operations stalled before they even began."

He gestured down the sloping face of the compound to the courtyard at the bottom. The stone square was littered with the hulks of mining machines—drilling arms and ore extractors, rock pulverizers and drainage pumps, all of it lying idle, gathering fungus. Loadlifters shifted the equipment from one end of the square to the other, and groups of stormtroopers swarmed back and forth, but even from up there Tarkin could see that they had been ordered to look busy, to make it seem as though something was getting done. He knew better.

"The director was led to believe Agaris had some of the richest quadanium deposits in the galaxy," K-4D8 said. "Isn't this compound itself a former mining colony?"

Tarkin nodded. The Imperial base may have

looked from the outside like a single steep stone wall, leaning against the mountainside. But the miners had burrowed deep into the rock beneath them, leaving a complex network of dark, winding tunnels.

"Sadly, the seams here have been tapped out," he said. "And finding new drilling sites has proved . . . challenging."

A stormtrooper survey group was gathering in the courtyard, checking their sidearms and securing their helmets. As they turned to face the mushroom forest, the soldiers seemed to draw together, clearly reluctant to leave the safety of the compound. Their commander gestured firmly and the troopers moved off, blasters gripped tightly.

Tarkin could almost smell their fear.

"Is the problem one of equipment?" K-4D8 asked. "Do your scanners need recalibrating, or do—"

"The men keep disappearing," Tarkin

admitted abruptly. "We don't know why. We don't know if someone's taking them or if they're simply . . . getting lost. But sixteen patrols have vanished in the past eight days, a total of one hundred and eleven men."

K-4D8's surprise was evident in his pale metallic eyes. "One hundred and eleven," he repeated.

"The few who return have no clear recollection of what happened," Tarkin went on. "Some speak of shapes in the mist, eyeless figures ambushing them in the dark. Which is of course impossible. Agaris is devoid of sentient life—the old mining logs and our own sensors agree on that."

"You suspect outside interference?" K-4D8 asked.

"I have no idea what to suspect," Tarkin said. "This foul planet confounds us at every turn. But all is not lost. I have had a pair of prisoners brought here who know everything there is to know about the world of Agaris. They'll give me the answers I seek, or they'll suffer for it."

The droid leaned closer. "I am programmed in over ten thousand different methods of interrogation," he said coldly. "Please inform me if I can be of assistance."

Tarkin waved K-4D8 away. "That will not be necessary," he said. Then he smiled. "Though in fact, I do have a task for you. Moments ago, my fighters brought down a craft attempting to infiltrate Agaris airspace. On board there may be two children and a droid, who could be very useful in getting the answers I seek. Take a small squad. If the children survived, bring them to me. And either way, I want that droid's head."

"Won't your fighter pilots pick up the survivors?" K-4D8 asked.

"This is important to me," Tarkin told the droid, "and right now my men have a habit of vanishing. Whatever's out there, I imagine it would think twice about attacking you. And if you do not return . . . well, then I'll know this is serious."

The droid saluted briskly. "I shall report back," he promised, and strode off the balcony.

Tarkin pulled his comlink from his pocket. "Send up the prisoners," he ordered. "And bring a bottle of the Alderaanian white, with three glasses."

He leaned on the railing, wondering if that patrol was still out there or if it had already been taken like the others. He shook his head, frustration building in his gut. He refused to let this cursed planet defeat him.

Perhaps it was time for more extreme measures. His men had cut back the foliage surrounding the compound, but he could still see the wall of thick gray stems beyond the perimeter. They needed to cut farther, drive harder, burn the planet clean kilometer by kilometer.

For a moment the clouds broke and a shaft of

gold-tinged sunlight touched the fungus forest, sparkling on those huge domed carapaces and setting the smaller, colorful stalks agleam. For that instant, Tarkin mused, it could almost be considered beautiful.

Then the clouds closed and the gloom descended once more.

Rhyssa and Auric Graf were delivered to him in binders by a pair of stormtroopers. Tarkin ordered their bonds removed, showing his prisoners to a small table in the corner of the balcony where a bottle and three glasses had been placed. He poured the wine himself, settling into an upright chair and eyeing them intently.

The Grafs' incarceration had not been kind, he noted. Both were considerably thinner than their file pictures, their prison garb hanging loose on their bones. Auric had a blue-black bruise high on his cheek, and another on the back of his hand. Rhyssa, too, bore the scars of resistance, but her eyes flashed with anger as she regarded Tarkin, ignoring the glass he placed in front of her.

"Where are my children?" she asked. "I want to see them. Now."

Tarkin sipped his wine calmly. "You're in no position to make demands," he said. "And besides, you already know my terms. You tell me everything you know about this pitiful little backwater world—absolutely everything. If I like what I hear, I'll consider returning your children. If not, there's very little I can do. And I warn you, my patience is growing thin."

"Damn your patience," Auric growled, his fists clenched. "How do we know you have Milo and Lina? They evaded the Empire this long; what's to say they aren't still out there?"

"You don't," Tarkin admitted. "You are my prisoners. And if you ever want to see your children alive again, you'll do as I say."

"What will you do with the information we give you?" Rhyssa asked. "If we tell you what we know about Agaris, how much of this world will be left when you're done?"

"We know this is a mining operation," Auric said, gesturing to the machines in the courtyard below. "There's only one thing you'd be digging for on this world: quadanium. And there's only one thing you'd be building with it: weapons, so your vile Empire can ruin more lives, oppress more peaceful people. We won't be a part of that."

"Then your children will die," Tarkin said flatly, hiding the anger he was feeling. "It's that simple."

Auric sank back, biting his lip. But Rhyssa leaned closer, her pale face filled with defiance. "We won't doom an entire world to ruin, not on your word. You can threaten our children all you like."

"What's so special about this world?" Tarkin demanded. "I look out there and all I see is filth and fungus. I might understand your reluctance if there was any sentient life here . . . but there's nothing."

He broke off, glancing at Auric. Just for a moment, right as he said the word *sentient*, he thought he saw the man's eyelid twitch. It was only the faintest flicker, but Tarkin was sure it meant something. He had a sense for these things.

A bead of sweat ran down Auric's face and he brushed it away, reaching for his glass and gulping the wine. And with that, the governor's suspicion became a certainty.

He felt a tremor of excitement. A new species, hidden and uncharted. New recruits for the Empire—or new slaves for his mines, lowering the cost of the operation by orders of magnitude. All he had to do was find them.

"I'll give you one day to change your minds," he said. "Then I promise you, our next conversation will be over the bodies of your children."

He gestured to the stormtroopers guarding the doorway. "Get these people out of my sight."

Rhyssa drew close to Auric as they were marched back to their cell. The binders bit into her wrists and her legs were weak from hunger and exhaustion. But there was still strength inside her; she could feel it. She wasn't broken yet, whatever that foul Tarkin might think.

"I don't believe him," she whispered to her husband as they walked. "He's lying. He never had the kids."

"What if you're wrong?" Auric asked. His cheeks were hollow and she saw fear in his sunken eyes. "I won't risk their lives, Rhyss. Even for—"

"Neither will I," Rhyssa interrupted. "It won't come to that. I know it won't."

One of the troopers prodded her in the back with his blaster. "Move, scum," he said, shoving Rhyssa along the passageway.

The corridors in the compound were narrow and poorly lit, moisture glistening on patches of black fungus and green lichen. They descended a long flight of steps, passing a stone arch that echoed the sound of footsteps and machinery. Inside, Rhyssa could see a high-ceilinged hangar, with two rows of TIE fighters and a dagger-shaped starship bristling with weaponry. She'd lay bets that was Tarkin's personal craft; the ship had the same air of steely determination as its owner.

An MSE-6 repair droid skittered past, chattering to itself. Otherwise the hangar looked almost deserted. She could see a pair of troopers on duty by the entrance and another two taking apart a TIE engine, but that was all.

From the hangar to the cell she counted the turns. *The first corridor to the left, then twenty paces. Two right turns, a left, and another right.* Then the cell door was sliding open to admit them, and they were stepping through into their tiny black-walled enclosure.

The troopers removed the binders and retreated, closing the door. Auric lowered himself onto their bunk, stuffing a moldy blanket under his head.

"If we could just see them," he said. "If we could just know they were okay, for one second."

"They're okay," Rhyssa insisted. "I feel it. I believe it."

"You're just telling yourself that," Auric said, rolling over, his back to her. "You don't know."

Rhyssa knelt down beside him. "We can't give in to despair. We can't let him beat us."

Auric let out a short, bitter laugh. "He's already beaten us, love."

Rhyssa reached up and squeezed his shoulder. "No," she said. "He hasn't. Remember?"

And she gestured to the corner of the cell, into the shadows. There, buried in a tiny crack in the black stone wall, was just the faintest hint of color.

The mushroom's flat head was barely the size of Rhyssa's fingernail, but that was twice the

size it had been the day before. The shade was
richer, too—a burnished orange deepening to
red, like the first flush of sunrise.

One more day, Tarkin had said. She hoped
it'd be enough.

CHAPTER 3
IN THE FOG

"COME ON, CRATER," Milo insisted, almost pleading. "We have to go!"

The droid shook his metal head. "I'm afraid that is simply not possible, Master Milo. This blasted projectile has skewered me like a bladeback boar."

The spore had slammed into the *Star Herald*'s side, its gold-tipped spines tearing through the hull. Milo and Lina had been lucky; their seats were on the far side of the cockpit. But one of the spikes had plunged right through CR-8R's torso, pinning him in place. The crash had only made things worse, as the spore's weight brought the ship spiraling to the ground. CR-8R's attachments and appendages were now buried under a ton of crushed metal and oozing fungal matter.

"Those TIEs are coming," Lina said, shouldering her backpack and peering up through the cracked roof. The fighters had used their lasers to clear a landing site among the

building-sized mushrooms and were circling closer. "We really need to get out of here."

"Go," CR-8R urged Milo. "I have no time to cut myself free, and there's no sense in all of us being captured. You have to run."

"But where?" Milo asked him. "We're on an uncharted planet in some kind of weird fungus forest, and the Empire is everywhere."

"You'll be fine," CR-8R insisted, squeezing Milo's arm with his free hand. "Trust yourselves, and trust each other. And don't eat any funny-looking mushrooms."

Milo nodded. "We'll come back for you," he said. "I promise."

Then he tore himself away, clambering up through the collapsed cockpit, using the seat backs to push himself up. Morq followed, scampering up into the light. Lina reached down to pull her brother up, and the three of them perched for a moment on the ship's bruised and flattened nose.

"I wonder," Milo said, "if there's any class of starship you couldn't crash, if you really tried."

Lina punched his arm. "Watch it."

The TIEs had landed just beyond a dense clump of mushrooms. Milo could hear the chatter of comms as the pilots approached on foot. But a third craft was hovering, an armored dropship with open sides. He could see more troops inside, their blasters drawn.

As the ship descended, a tall black droid leaned from the hold, grasping the outer railing with one huge hand. It turned its head, spotting them. The droid held up a transmitter.

"Children," his voice boomed from the dropship's loudhailers. "You are safe now. There is no need to worry. Stay with your ship."

Lina snorted. "Not likely."

Milo turned to look over his shoulder. The mushroom forest stretched beyond them, all the way to the distant mountains. But just beyond the ship the ground sloped downward into a series of hollows dark with shifting gray mist.

"That way looks good," he said. "Maybe we can lose them in the fog."

They slid down the *Star Herald's* steep side, Morq springing ahead. Milo hit the ground running, making for the cover of the big stalks. The soil was spongy black mulch dotted with mushrooms of every shape and color, from hair-fine lichens to human-sized growths with spreading umbrella-like heads. But there was no dense foliage, nothing to impede them, and for that he was thankful.

They heard the troopers reaching the ship, the echo of blaster fire as they blew the outer hatch. Suddenly, Lina's communicator crackled to life. Milo's heart lifted. CR-8R had used this trick before, back on Xirl. He would patch his aural sensors through to the communicator so they could hear what the troopers were saying. Perhaps the droid could talk his way out of this, Milo thought. Or maybe he'd play dead and the troopers wouldn't bother with him at all.

"The ship's deserted but we've found a droid,"

a man said, and Milo recognized the voice of the TIE pilot they'd overheard above Agaris. "*It's trapped in the wreckage. We could cut it out, but it'd take a while.*"

"*The governor only needs the head,*" the black droid replied. "*Leave the rest.*"

"*No, please, wai–*" CR-8R managed—then a shot rang out.

The communicator went dead.

Milo looked at Lina, his heart pounding. She shook her head. "Worry later," she said. "Run now."

Milo did as he was told, sprinting over the marshy ground. *CR-8R might still be okay,* he told himself. This wasn't the first time the droid had lost his head.

They reached the first slope, scrambling down a rocky incline. The gloom deepened, the mist thickening as they descended. Around them, all was silent: no animal or bird calls, not even the sound of wind. But perhaps it was a good thing, Milo thought; in the stillness they could hear the troopers behind them, the crackle of comms as they marched in pursuit.

At the bottom of the hollow was a narrow stream, running over and beneath a tumble of moss-slick stones. They turned aside, following the flow of water deeper into the valley. The fog thickened, and soon they could hear a deep rushing sound, growing louder as they went. Milo grabbed Lina's hand and they skidded to a halt on the brink of a stony precipice, water tumbling into the darkness below. Morq crouched, peering over the edge and trembling.

Lina cursed under her breath. "Now what do we do?" They couldn't double back for fear of the troopers, and across the stream the rocks were heaped haphazardly, a tricky climb.

"We don't have a choice," Milo said. "We go over and up, right?"

"But there's no cover," Lina said, looking up. "If they see us, they'll blast us." She leaned over the edge. "We could jump, I guess. But we don't know what's down there."

Milo followed her gaze. The base of the falls was lost in the gloom. "No way," he said. "But wait, what about that?"

At the edge of the waterfall, a large rock jutted out, and beneath it was a shadowy cave. Milo squinted, trying to peer inside. But then he heard the mutter of voices and the splash of boots behind them and knew their time was up.

"It's the best we've got," he told Lina. "Come on."

They crossed the stream, dropping on the far side and swinging their legs over the edge. Then they clambered down, ducking beneath the shelf of rock—not a moment too soon. As they retreated into the darkness they heard voices above them, over the rushing of the water.

"There's no sign of them," the pilot said, his deep voice immediately recognizable. "The fog's too thick. Request permission to return to the ship."

"*Negative,*" the droid's voice crackled through the comlink. "*The governor wants those children found.*"

The pilot sighed, and Milo heard his comlink click off. "Since when does a droid get to give orders?"

"Since he was sent by Director Krennic," his companion replied. "I hear Krennic and Tarkin hate each other, and Krennic sent K-4D8 to find out what Tarkin's up to."

"Krennic sent a *droid* to check on Tarkin?" the pilot asked in amazement. "That's pretty insulting."

The footsteps stopped at the edge of the falls, right overhead.

"Those kids are long gone," the pilot sighed. "I'm guessing whatever took our men took them, too. And it'll get *us* if we stay out here much longer."

"You know DZ-372 and DX-491 got taken two days ago?" his companion said with a shiver. "They'd been with us since the Academy. I always figured there was some kind of creature out here, but now I'm hearing it's a secret rebel cell, picking us off one by one. Which would explain that ship back there."

Milo looked at Lina in surprise. Could it

be? The *Star Herald*'s sensors had found no evidence of technology outside the Imperial compound, but surely rebels would have some way of disguising themselves. For the first time since they'd crashed, he felt a glimmer of hope.

"Whatever it is, this whole planet gives me the creeps," the pilot said. "Let's check around those rocks, then head b— *What was that?*"

Milo's head snapped up. The fear in the man's voice had been unmistakable.

"What?" the second trooper asked. "I didn't see anything."

"In the fog," the pilot said. "Across the stream. There, I saw it again!"

Milo flinched as a trickle of pebbles rattled down into their little cave. Had the trooper kicked them loose, or was it something else?

"I saw it," the second trooper said shakily. "It looked . . . big. Bigger than a man, for sure."

"And it had more arms," the pilot replied. "Or were they legs?"

"I don't want to find out," his companion said. "Come on, let's get out of here before— *Hey!* Hey, something's got me!"

Lina grabbed Milo, pulling him back. Morq leapt into his lap, shivering fearfully.

"Get it off me!" the trooper bellowed. "Shoot it! *Shoot it!*"

They heard blaster fire, followed by a loud scraping like something being dragged over the stones.

"Where are you?" the pilot cried. "I can't . . . No. *No!* Stay back! Stay back, I'm armed!"

The blaster fired again, twice, three times. Then there was a scream, a crash, and silence.

CHAPTER 4
HUNTED

"WE DON'T HAVE A CHOICE," Lina insisted. "We can't stay here; they'll send more men. And there's no sense going back to the *Star Herald*. CR-8R's gone and the ship's finished anyway. We have to keep moving."

"But where?" Milo asked. "For a moment I really thought there might be rebels here, people who could help us. But you heard. Whatever took them, it wasn't rebels."

Lina shook her head. "No. But we're small. Maybe if we stay quiet it won't come after us."

"Maybe," Milo said. "Or maybe we'll make a perfect after-dinner snack."

"So what do you suggest?" Lina asked,

frustrated. "The way I see it, our only choice is to stick to the plan. Make for the Imperial compound and hope we don't run into anything on the way."

"It could take days," Milo said. "You saw how far those mountains were."

"So it takes days," Lina said. "We've got enough food in my pack, and we know exactly where we're going. We stay low, and we stay quiet."

Milo sighed. "Okay," he said. "But you can go in front."

Lina shrugged. "Fine. If I was a hungry monster I'd take the one at the back first, so the other didn't notice he was gone."

Milo frowned at her. "That's really, really not funny."

They scaled the rocks as quietly as they could, leaving the waterfall behind. Morq made himself useful, leaping ahead to show them the best footholds. Lina paused, scratching the little monkey-lizard under the chin. He might annoy her sometimes, but Milo's pet wasn't all bad. Morq clicked his beak happily, then scampered off into the fog.

As they reached the top of the rockfall, he returned, clutching something in his beak. It was a tiny creature, gray-black and moving slowly. Milo ordered him to drop it and Morq did so, springing back with his tail waving expectantly.

Lina crouched at her brother's side. The creature was like nothing she'd ever seen, a flat disc the size of her palm, covered with fine, sprouting fur. It seemed to have no arms or legs or even a head, but as they watched it rolled over and began to wriggle away, the fur on its belly rippling in waves.

Milo reached out, touching the creature lightly. It froze, then began to move sideways at precisely the same pace. "I know it sounds weird," Milo whispered in amazement, "but I think this is another mushroom. One that moves. In fact, I think this planet's entire ecosystem might have evolved from fungus. That's why

there's no trees or grass. Just mushrooms and
lichen and . . . this."

Lina looked around. The great wide-capped
growths loomed over them, and through a
crack in the canopy she could see one of those
cannon-shaped stalks jutting into the gray sky.
"The thing that took the troopers," she began.
"Could it be a big one of these?"

Milo shrugged. "Carnivorous fungi have
been recorded on several worlds. They trap and

consume microscopic organisms. Maybe this one's evolved to digest larger prey."

"Great," Lina sighed. "We're going to be eaten by a giant mushroom."

The black creature rippled toward Morq, hesitated, then moved in the opposite direction.

"Hey, it backed off," Lina said. "Like it saw him and moved away. But I don't see any eyes."

"Maybe it uses smell," Milo suggested. "Or that fur on its back could be sensitive to heat or moisture."

"So maybe it's actually a good thing we're both so cold and wet." Lina smiled. "Come on, let's keep moving."

The walk was steady at first as they trudged out of the valley beneath the cover of the spreading mushrooms. At the summit they found a rocky outcrop and took their bearings. The mountains were just a faint smudge on the horizon, a line of black beneath the descending sun.

"Two days," Lina said, shielding her eyes. "Three at the most."

But before long she was forced to revise that estimate. The next valley turned out to be more of a canyon, sheer-sided and so deep that when Milo kicked a pebble over the edge he counted to five before it hit the bottom. They had no choice but to go around, following the ravine as it wove and narrowed, slowly descending. At last they reached a place where the walls were low enough for them to climb down, but by then the sky had darkened, the sun sinking out of sight.

"We'll camp here," Lina said as they reached the bottom of the canyon at last. "We'll have walls on both sides and shelter if it rains."

"And look, firewood," Milo said, crossing to the far side. One of the big mushrooms had tumbled into the ravine and gotten wedged beneath a rock, its cap dry and cracking. "Well, not wood exactly. But it's carbon-based. I don't see why it shouldn't burn."

"Is that a good idea?" Lina asked. "The light could attract that . . . fungus monster."

"It's more likely to scare it away," Milo said. "If it does sense heat and moisture it'll definitely steer clear of fire."

He broke off several large fragments and stacked them, then Lina used her fusioncutter to set them alight. The mushroom burned brightly, sending a dense black smoke spiraling up through the ravine. But she welcomed the heat on her face, and the smell was surprisingly appealing.

"I don't suppose—" she started.

"No." Milo cut her off. "Crater said we shouldn't eat anything, and I agree. Loads of mushroom species are poisonous."

"You're right," Lina sighed. "I just wish it didn't smell so much like breakfast."

She rooted in her pack, pulling out a pair of Imperial ration packs and handing one to Milo. The food was dry and tasteless, but it filled her up. Soon her head was nodding, the heat of the fire and the warmth in her belly making her drowsy. She placed her pack on the floor, lying back and resting her head on it. But then she heard Milo's voice.

"Lina?" he asked, and somehow he sounded far away. "Lina, what's happening?"

She sat up, looking around. The smoke was thicker, billowing toward her in black waves. She coughed, covering her eyes. There was Milo, on the far side of the fire. His eyes were streaming, his face red. Lina felt so heavy . . . all she wanted to do was lie down.

"Milo!" she called, her voice echoing from the canyon sides. "What is it?"

He turned toward her, stumbling. For a moment the smoke rolled in, hiding him. Lina rubbed her eyes. Then, suddenly, Milo was at her side, gripping her arm.

"I saw something," he said urgently. "In the dark, I saw something."

"The creature?" Lina asked, her heartbeat quickening.

"I don't know," Milo admitted. "I couldn't see

straight. I think this smoke's done something to my eyes. And I feel really tired."

"Me too," Lina said. "Come on, let's get away from the fire."

Milo nodded, turning. But then he stopped dead, squeezing her hand.

Something was standing in the gloom just ahead of them, motionless and wreathed in smoke. At first Lina couldn't make it out; it was just a deeper black among shifting shadows. Then the smoke cleared and she saw a humanoid shape, with two long legs and a trunk topped with a domed head.

"Hello?" Milo called out. "Who's there?"

Another shape joined the first, smaller and less distinct. Beside it was another, and another. They drew silently closer, creeping over the rocks like shadows from a nightmare.

"Stay back," Lina warned them.

The first figure stepped toward her in the firelight, raising one slender arm. There was

something grasped in its hand, or claw, or whatever it was: a brightly colored mushroom, its red cap fringed with orange, like the first light of sunrise. The dark figure held it out, and for a moment Lina had the absurd notion that it was offering the mushroom to her, the way her father would sometimes give his wife flowers.

Then the cap exploded in a cloud of crimson gas. Lina looked down, confused. A red haze filled her head and she toppled to the ground.

CHAPTER 5
AGARIANS

"AURIC, RHYSSA, WAKE UP!"

The voice was soft and close, and he felt a gentle touch on his arm.

"Auric!" the voice repeated. "Rhyssa! Awake!"

Milo groaned. Why was someone calling his parents' names? His head was clouded, his memory foggy. But when he opened his eyes, things didn't really improve. All he could see were tendrils of gray mist and a high stone ceiling. There was a sound all around him, a rushing drone like a great beast breathing, somewhere in the dark.

Then with a start he remembered. The smoke in the air, the shapes around the campfire. He reached out and felt Lina beside him, just stirring. "Milo?" she asked blearily. "Is Dad here? What's going on?"

"I don't know," he hissed, sitting upright. "But we're not alone."

The dark figures stood in a circle around them, silent and watchful—or at least, as watchful as any creatures without eyes could be. That was the first thing Milo noticed about them. They had heads, or at least places where their tubelike bodies bulged at the top, often tipped by a fringed, toadstool-like cap. They even had mouths, dark slits beneath the cap's brim. But he could detect nothing on the creatures that might be used for seeing.

The walls of the cave were dotted with patches of luminescent fungus, and as his own eyes adjusted Milo could study the creatures more closely. The differences between them seemed greater than the similarities. They each had a roughly cylindrical body with limbs sprouting from it, but that was as far as it went.

Some were humanoid, with two limbs below and two above. But others seemed to have three legs and no arms, or six legs like an insect, or no legs and eight tiny arms arranged in a circle. One particularly large specimen close to Milo had four arms sprouting from the top of its head, and in place of legs, a single, twitching tentacle.

Then one stepped forward, and Milo recognized the manlike figure who had

approached them the night before. He crouched before them, his skin a pale, silvery gray.

"Auric and Rhyssa," he said, his soft voice rising above the hissing in the air, "it is good to have you back on Agaris."

Lina sat up. "W-Why do you keep calling us that?" she asked.

The creature seemed confused. "But that is what you told us to call you. Do you not remember? You told us many things on your last visit, and I cannot recall them all. But your names I could never forget, Auric and Rhyssa Graf!"

His mouth twitched, and to his surprise Milo found himself smiling back. There they were, stuck in a dark cave surrounded by the strangest bunch of freaks he'd ever seen, and somehow the creature's voice and manner made him feel . . . not safe, exactly, but certainly not as terrified as he had been.

"Auric and Rhyssa are our parents," he said. "Do we really look that much like them?"

The creature sat back. "Parents?" he wondered. "So you are children." He looked back at his companions, who all nodded and snuffled to one another. "That explains a great deal. We were wondering how you had become so much smaller and brighter."

"Brighter?" Lina asked.

"How to explain?" the creature mused. "Ah, yes. We Agarians—that was the name Auric and Rhyssa gave us, you understand. Agarians. A good name. We Agarians do not have eyes as you humans do. It is strange for us to even imagine it. After long discussions with your mother I had almost come to understand the concept of sight, but now I find it has slipped away again.

"So we cannot see, but we can sense the world. We smell and we hear. We feel the movement of air and the warmth you emit. And we feel the . . . what was the word Auric used? The vibrations, yes, the vibrations given off by all things. In this way do we see. So when we find a pair of creatures who smell and feel like

Auric and Rhyssa Graf, just a little smaller and more vivid with energy, we assume that they have simply changed their form, the way we sometimes do."

"We can't change our form," Milo said. "We're just kids. I'm Milo, and this is Lina."

He held out his hand and the Agarian did the same, extending a flat, flipper-like paw coated with rows of tiny fronds, all squashy and damp against Milo's palm. Suddenly, he realized.

"You're a mushroom," he said in amazement. "All of you—you're living mushrooms!"

The Agarian laughed, a thin wheezing sound. "In a manner of speaking," he said. "You humans have animal ancestors. We evolved, as you say, from fungi. My name is—" And he made a sort of damp purring noise, like Morq sometimes did when Milo scratched his chin.

With a start, Milo remembered his pet. But there he was, stretched out on the stone floor with his legs kicking in sleep. It made sense; if the Agarians had used some sort of gas to knock them out, it'd take longer for little Morq to sleep it off.

Lina tried to pronounce the Agarian's name, but all that came out was a wet huffing noise.

"*Hhhuuhhhffffffffrrrrrrr*," Milo managed, and the creature nodded, impressed.

"Good, Milo," he said. "Now just a little more swiftly. *Hffrr*."

"*Hffrr*," Milo said. "I like it."

Lina was still struggling, a look of frustration on her face.

"It was the same for your parents," Hffrr smiled. "Your mother became quite familiar with our speech in the time they were here, but your father decided it was easier to teach me yours. Which is good for us now, is it not?"

"When did they visit?" Milo asked. "It must have been a long time ago, before we were even born."

Hffrr seemed to shrug. "To me, it seems but a moment," he said. "But we Agarians measure time very differently. Tell me, Milo and Lina, where are your parents now? It would please me greatly to speak with them."

Lina's face darkened. "They're prisoners. Of the Empire."

Hffrr bowed his head. "Ah, this is a pity," he said. "To think of Auric and Rhyssa, so full of life and teachings, being held by those burning, destroying, metal-hearted—" He made a bitter, spitting noise that Milo could tell was an Agarian curse.

"We came to get them out," Milo explained. "But then we crashed."

"Tell me," Hffrr said. "I do not understand everything about your people, but . . . are human children not helpless creatures who must be protected by their parents? How is it you have come so far, all alone?"

Milo and Lina looked at each other and shrugged.

"You are no ordinary children, it seems," said Hffrr thoughtfully.

"We know where they are," Lina told him. "They're being held in the Imperial compound. But we don't know how to get to them. Do you know a way in, can you help us get to them?"

"No," Hffrr said flatly. "It is impossible."

Lina's face flushed. "I know the Empire has weapons—perhaps you are afraid to face them, but—"

"We are not afraid," Hffrr said. "But we cannot take you to the compound. There is an energy source deep inside that place. It was installed by the miners, and it is the only reason we did not drive them away as we should have done, before their discovery of quadanium brought the Empire. This generator powers the compound, the drills, the lights, the cooling systems, everything. We cannot go near it."

"But why?" Lina asked. "What's so terrible about it?"

"To even come close to the compound means sickness. The energy vibrations are so strong that our senses become confused; it brings on a kind of madness. There is no way to fight it. It is as though the very air itself is our enemy." Hffrr shook his head. "It is a problem, because our own efforts to fight the Empire have left us in a difficult position. This cave is getting too full."

He held up one arm and a jet of green gas rushed from his wrist, billowing out into the cavern. Everywhere it went the fog cleared, breaking up into fine droplets that clung to the walls of the cave. Seams of green lichen were revealed, lighting the place with a ghostly glow.

As the mist dissipated Milo could make out other shapes, strewn haphazardly in the base of the cave. He could see an arm here, a boot there. A white torso, a molded helmet. Stormtroopers! But all of them were motionless, sprawled on the banks of creeping moss that covered the floor of the cavern. He heard that rushing sound again, and realized it was the sound of a hundred men breathing in unison, hissing and droning in sleep.

"We keep them here," Hffrr explained. "We do not know what else to do."

Milo saw one of the shapes stirring and peered closer. A tiny gray tendril snaked under the trooper's helmet.

"We keep them fed," Hffrr said. "But we cannot return them. They would be back on patrol the next day. Still, we cannot hold them forever. It was our hope that losing so many soldiers might frighten these Imperials away, convince them that Agaris is not worth the effort."

Lina snorted. "You clearly don't have much experience with the Empire."

Hffrr shook his head. "They are new to us. But we have dealt with invaders before, and survived."

"Others have come here?" Milo asked, yawning. The effects of the gas had still not completely worn off.

"It is a long story," Hffrr said, "and forgive me, but you both seem very tired. You should sleep. Tomorrow I will take you as close as I can to the Imperial compound, and perhaps you will be able to find a way inside."

"It's a long walk," Milo said. "How many days will it take?"

"I know a swifter route," the Agarian promised. "I think you will like it. But for now, sleep."

He showed them to an alcove in the wall, layered with a thick bed of moss. Milo climbed inside, stifling another yawn. Lina turned back.

"If we did find a way in," she said. "If we switched that generator off, you could help us find our parents, couldn't you? You'd have no reason to fear the compound."

Hffrr nodded. "It might be possible," he agreed. "Though many of my people would be against it. We have always tried to avoid violence."

"I understand," Lina said. "But if you want to save your world, you might not have a choice."

CHAPTER 6
THE SPORE

WHEN THEY AWOKE, a pale light was filtering into the cavern through fine cracks in the rocky ceiling. The captive stormtroopers lay beneath a layer of mist, their only sign of life that constant breathy roar. Lina sat up beside Milo, rubbing her eyes with one grubby hand.

"Wow," she said, blearily. "So it wasn't a dream."

Milo smiled. "Afraid not."

"But we're okay. Aren't we?"

"Definitely," Milo agreed. "And we'll see Mom and Dad today. I know it."

As he sat on the edge of the alcove, a tiny

shape came bounding from the gloom, leaping into his lap. Morq was bright-eyed and wide awake, waving his scaly tail and nuzzling his beak affectionately against Milo's belly. Milo stroked the little monkey-lizard's head, feeding him scraps from his ration pack. Morq coughed and spat them out.

Hffrr appeared soon after, striding through the cave. Milo couldn't help noticing that the Agarian's legs were longer than they had been the night before, his head just a little more humanlike.

"Come, Milo, come, Lina," Hffrr said brightly. "We have far to travel."

He led them on winding paths through the caves, passing from halls the size of hangar bays into tiny, burrowing tunnels where even Milo was forced to duck. The underground system was thronged with Agarians of all shapes and sizes. He saw bulging bodies like great gray Hutts, using arms and tentacles to drag themselves along. But others barely reached Milo's knee, hurrying through the tunnels in little chattering packs. At first he thought they were children, until Hffrr led them past a nursery cave where tiny, gray-capped Agarians came sprouting from the soil, babbling and laughing merrily.

"This is all one system, isn't it?" Milo asked.

"Your people, the big stalks, the flat mushrooms on the surface, even the moss in the cave. It's all connected."

"It is the same on any world," Hffrr agreed. "Every planet is a sealed system. Every part depends on every other part. But you are right, on Agaris the connections are . . . closer." He tilted his head, gesturing beneath the cap-like brim, and Milo saw tiny colored fungi clinging to the gray skin. Looking down he saw others on Hffrr's back, and patches of fungus covering his trunk and legs.

"They feed on you?" Milo asked.

"They are part of me," Hffrr told him. "These ones resonate on different frequencies and enable me to hear a whole range of sounds. The moss on my back cools me and keeps me from drying out. In exchange I enable them to reach sunlight, to collect nutrients from the air as I move."

"You can change shape, as well, can't you?" Milo asked.

"Yes," Hffrr admitted. "Our basic form remains the same—one body, one what you would call 'head'—but we can alter our size and the number of our limbs."

"You changed in the night," Lina said. "You look more like a person now."

"That is true," Hffrr said. "Where we are going, I need you to trust me."

They climbed through a last, sloping tunnel and emerged onto the side of a steep hill surrounded by branching stalks. The sun was up, but Milo couldn't see it through the clouds. Lina covered her eyes, gazing off toward the distant mountains.

"I thought you were taking us to the compound," she said suspiciously. "But I think we're farther away. Look, there's our ship." She pointed to a thin trail of smoke on the horizon.

"I said we were going to the compound," Hffrr agreed. "I did not say we would walk there. Come."

He led them to the crest of the hill, where

the mushroom forest broke into a stony clearing. In the center stood a vast cylindrical shape, reaching to the sky. Milo recognized it right away.

"That's the thing that knocked us out of the sky," he said. "It nearly killed us!"

Hffrr nodded. "That was unfortunate," he said. "The stalks have an . . . instinct of their own, and love to take shots at Imperial ships. How were they to know?"

Milo peered up at the vast bulb-like protrusion overhead, almost lost in the clouds. The stalk bowed under its weight, the sinewy roots dug deep into the rocks. Hffrr crossed toward it, laying both palms flat. Beneath his fingerless hands the stalk rippled gently, responding to his touch. Hffrr stepped back as a section of it peeled away, folding outward to reveal a dark passageway.

He beckoned. "This way."

"Uh-uh," Lina said, standing firm. "No way I'm going in there."

"You must," Hffrr insisted. "The only other way is to walk for three days. We do not know what may happen to Auric and Rhyssa in that time."

"He's right, Sis," Milo said. "We don't really have a choice."

He ducked through the opening. The walls inside were cold and clammy, but he could feel life pulsing within. Morq jumped up to crouch on Milo's shoulder, shivering nervously.

Suddenly, the walls were gone and he was standing in an open space enclosed by smooth red skin. The chamber was twice Milo's height and seemed to be perfectly spherical. From the base of the sphere sprouted a golden cylinder topped with unevenly shaped branches. Hffrr gestured to it.

"Take hold of the core, Milo," he said. "And you, too, Lina. Hang on tight."

"Why?" Lina asked worriedly, following them in. "What will happen?"

Milo looked up at the ceiling, and gulped.

"I think we're . . ." he managed. "I think we're inside . . ."

"No," Lina said, turning. "No, we can't . . ." But the entrance had already sealed up behind them, the walls of the sphere closing seamlessly.

Milo perched on one of the branches, wrapping his arms around the central structure. It was soft but solid in his grip, and the branch beneath him felt equally secure. But still he felt fear in his throat as the sphere began to rise, slowly at first, then with increasing speed. It was like being in a turbolift, he thought, only there were no controls to make it stop, and no upper level. Up they went, faster and faster. Lina screamed and Morq joined her, squawking in terror as they shot up through the stem.

Then there was a loud popping sound, and they were flying free. The wind roared and the walls around them turned a paler red. The spore rocketed upward in a great smooth arc.

"Can you control it?" Lina yelled to Hffrr. "Or do we just hope for the best?"

Hffrr took hold of the central branch, sliding his palms over the surface. Milo felt the sphere shifting subtly, its direction altering.

"How does it work?" Lina asked.

"Minute flaps in the outer skin," Hffrr explained. "They open or close, directing the flow of air."

"How do you see where we're going?" Milo wondered. "Or don't I want to know?"

Hffrr smiled, and Milo felt a lurch as they reached the top of the arc. For a moment they were weightless, clinging to the branching structure. Then there was a cracking, ripping sound and the chamber was flooded with light.

Milo cried out as the walls of the spore peeled away, whipping off in the wind that tore at their hair and clothes. Something spiraled from the center: a long tendril that snapped in the breeze. But as it lengthened it began to unravel, widening to form a flat, almost cloth-like sail. The tether snapped taut and the spore began to descend.

Milo felt his heart thundering, wrapping his arms around the core and trying not to look down. The clouds were far below them, the sun a blazing disc above the curve of the planet.

Lina laughed, her cheeks flushed, her eyes streaming. She reached for Milo's hand, grabbing it tight. He tried to smile back but his stomach rolled, his head spinning. Morq crept inside Milo's jacket, shivering against his chest. He gritted his teeth and clung on.

"There," Hffrr said, pointing. Toward the horizon, the mountain peaks broke through the clouds like a line of jagged teeth. The sail shifted and they drifted down, buffeted by air currents.

"Can I try?" Lina asked, placing her hands on the core.

Hffrr nodded. "Be gentle. You will feel it respond."

The sail jerked and the spore shuddered.

"Are you sure that's a good idea?" Milo asked.

"Don't be silly," Lina said defensively. "I can fly anything."

"You can *crash* anything," he muttered.

They were descending quickly now, the clouds rushing up to swallow them. For a long time they could see nothing, just swirling gray. Milo shivered, feeling condensation gather on his skin. Then they broke through and the surface of Agaris was revealed.

"I see it," Lina said, pointing. "Look!"

Milo followed her finger. There on the side of the nearest mountain he saw the outline of the Imperial compound, a sloping stone structure topped with antenna spikes and gun turrets. At its base was a courtyard filled with the dark shapes of men and machinery.

Hffrr cried out, wrapping his hands around the central stalk. "What is it?" Lina asked.

Hffrr gestured. At the base of the compound the forest had been cleared, cut back for several klicks in every direction. Milo could see troopers on the perimeter, smoke rising as they blasted the undergrowth.

The parachute twisted and the spore began to bank, but their turn was too shallow. Hffrr clutched his head in pain. "We are too close," he said. "I was careless. I brought us in too close. I thought we could take cover in the forest. I did not know they had managed to cut so far."

In the clearing ahead Milo could see the

scorched shapes of giant mushrooms being dragged away by Imperial machinery. "We have to jump," Hffrr said. "They will catch us."

Lina looked down. "We're not all squishy like you," she said. "We've got bones and they break."

Hffrr clutched his head in agony. "We are too close," he repeated. "I cannot . . . the pain, it is too much. I cannot . . ."

Lina grabbed his hand. "Go," she said. "We'll find a way inside and we'll shut that generator down. Then you can come and rescue us. Okay?"

Hffrr nodded. "I am sorry."

Then he let go, toppling backward. Milo saw him plummet to the ground, turning as he fell. He landed spread-eagled on a broad mushroom cap and vanished into the undergrowth.

Milo looked up. The spore drifted slowly down, taking them closer to the clearing, to the compound, and to capture.

CHAPTER 7
THE PLAN

RHYSSA STARED IN horror at the head on the desk. There was no light in those metallic eyes.

"Crater," she said, clutching Auric's arm. "No."

Tarkin smiled thinly. "You asked for proof. Here it is."

Auric drew himself up. "And the children?"

"They are safe," Tarkin said. "And they will stay that way. You, on the other hand . . ."

Rhyssa nodded. "Everything you needed was inside Crater's head."

"Precisely," Tarkin said. "The maps of Wild

Space, all your notes on your previous trip to
Agaris. I'll admit, it made for fascinating reading.
These Agarians, I can scarcely believe they
exist. Sentient fungus. They'll have to be wiped
out, of course. Unless they could be put to work
in our mines."

"Never," Auric told him. "They're too proud."

Tarkin nodded. "As I suspected. Ah, well,
it cannot be helped. They will work, or they
will die."

He lifted CR-8R's head, turning it in his hands. Then he crossed the room, opening a hatch in the wall and dropping it inside. Rhyssa heard a descending rattle as CR-8R's head vanished into the garbage chute.

"Take us to our children," she pleaded, taking a step toward Tarkin. "There's no reason for you to keep them from us now."

He did not turn around. "It's quite impossible," he said. "If you had agreed to my terms, if you had told me what I wanted to know, then perhaps . . . But there must be penalties for defying the Empire, surely you understand that. You will never see your children again."

He gestured and a pair of uniformed officers strode into the room, laying their hands on Auric and Rhyssa. They tried to struggle but the men were too strong, hauling them back toward the door.

"Please," Auric cried. "Whatever you're going to do, just let us see them."

"No," Tarkin replied flatly, and the door hissed shut.

They were shoved along the corridor and down the steps. It was all over, Rhyssa knew. She wondered if Tarkin would come in person to see them executed. Somehow, she doubted it.

She reached inside her jacket, her fingers wrapping around the stalk hidden there. They reached the base of the steps, passing the hangar doorway. The whine of machinery echoed within, and she heard the sound of voices.

Then they were past, moving through the poorly lit corridor. The officer behind Rhyssa gave her a shove and she staggered forward. This was it, her best chance.

In a single motion she turned, drawing the stalk from her jacket and pointing it at the two startled officers. The cap was as wide as her palm now, gleaming blood red.

The guards stopped abruptly, blasters drawn. Auric had halted, looking at her fearfully.

The officers looked down at the mushroom in her hand. One of them gave a snort.

"Look, she's got a mushroom," he said, grinning.

"I'm so scared," his companion chuckled, gesturing with his blaster. "Enough jokes. Move."

Rhyssa covered her face with her sleeve as the cap exploded, letting out a burst of crimson gas. The officers were still laughing when they hit the floor, grins pasted on their unconscious faces.

Rhyssa reached down, grabbing their blasters and handing one to Auric. He took it, glaring at her over his sleeve. "You could've warned me you were going to do that."

"It was our best chance," she said. "If we'd gone back to that cell we'd never have come out alive."

"So what do we do now?" Auric asked as the red gas dissipated. "They've got Milo and Lina, remember? We can't just leave them here."

Rhyssa shook her head. "I still don't believe

it. He'd have let us see them. He wouldn't have been able to resist the chance to gloat."

"But what about Crater?" Auric protested. "How could they find him without getting Milo and Lina?"

"I can think of a thousand ways," Rhyssa said. "They might've been split up. Crater could've sacrificed himself to save them. And even if they were here we'd have no way to find them. This compound is huge. We need help."

"The Agarians," Auric realized. "You want to go to Hffrr."

"We have to warn him," Rhyssa said. "The Empire knows about his people now. They're coming after them."

Auric pursed his lips. "Okay," he said. "So what's your plan?"

Rhyssa frowned awkwardly. "This was as far as I got," she admitted. "From here we'll just have to improvise."

They crept back to the hangar, peering

through the arched doorway. Rhyssa counted five stormtroopers and three uniformed officers inside, plus a tall black droid who seemed to be giving orders. She gestured to a stack of crates by the doorway and they slipped behind it, keeping low.

"We've searched the area thoroughly," one of the troopers was saying. "If there were any rebels on that ship they're gone, along with twelve of my men."

"Very well," the black droid replied. "I will inform the governor. Rejoin your units."

He marched toward the door and Rhyssa ducked, her heart thumping.

An alarm blared suddenly, cutting through the din. The droid froze, turning. Then it unslung a large assault rifle from its back and began to stride toward the mouth of the hangar, where the huge cavern opened onto the stone courtyard beyond.

"With me," the droid ordered, and Rhyssa

saw men hurrying to obey, following the tall black figure out into the daylight.

"Well that's convenient," she whispered, getting to her feet. "Come on—while they're distracted."

They hurried toward the nearest TIE. Above them the hatch was raised, a ladder extending down from the fighter's spherical body.

"Can you even fly one of these?" Auric asked as Rhyssa began to climb.

"I can fly anything," she told him over her shoulder.

Auric shook his head and started up. From the courtyard he could hear shouts and footsteps. Whatever was going on out there, he was thankful for it.

Then another sound caught his ear, and he froze. It was a high-pitched, chattering cry, clearly animal in nature, and strangely familiar. For a moment he was confused. There were no monkey-lizards on Agaris. Why would the Empire have brought one?

A tiny shape came hurtling into view, skittering over the smooth stone floor of the hangar. A pair of troopers sprinted after it, blasting indiscriminately. The monkey-lizard ducked behind an open container, looking around in terror. Then it lifted its head, sniffing the air, and looked directly at Auric.

The creature sprang from hiding, scampering madly toward them. "No," Auric whispered, waving desperately. "Morq, no."

But it was too late. The troopers saw them and raised their blasters. "Hey," one of them barked. "Get down from there!"

Auric looked up, seeing Rhyssa at the top of the ladder. But she wasn't looking at him, or at Morq, or even at the troopers. She was staring out into the courtyard, where a gaggle of figures came striding toward them, led by the black droid. Auric could see four stormtroopers and three green-clad officers. And there in the center was a pair of prisoners, their heads hanging, their hands bound.

"Lina!" Rhyssa cried, her voice ringing from the rocky ceiling high above. "Milo! We're here!"

The prisoners raised their heads, and Auric almost dropped from the ladder in shock.

In the hours that followed, Lina could barely recall how she broke free of the men surrounding them. All she remembered were the shouts behind her, and the sight of her father's face as she sprinted toward him across the hangar. And the joy in her heart, most of all.

Auric dropped from the ladder, pulling his daughter close in disbelief. Rhyssa clambered down as Milo joined them, weeping as he buried himself in his mother's embrace. Auric spread his arms, enclosing them. They huddled together, sobbing and laughing, ignoring the big black droid as it told them to stand back, line up, obey orders. For that brief moment, the Empire was a million light-years away.

Then Lina heard the men snap to attention, and the air around them seemed to grow colder. Auric disentangled himself, keeping one hand on his son's shoulder as he turned to face the trim, gray-haired figure marching toward them. Lina and Milo wiped their eyes, their hands still locked together.

"Well, isn't this touching," the man said, regarding them with slate-gray eyes. "The family Graf, reunited at last."

Rhyssa pulled her children close. "You never had them, Tarkin," she said. "You were lying all along."

The governor tilted his head. "True," he admitted. "But none of that matters now, does it? And finally, you understand. You cannot escape the grip of the Empire."

"We already have. Like, four times," Lina said, thrusting out her chin. "Once more shouldn't be too hard."

Tarkin looked down in disgust, as though he'd seen something foul on his boot. "You're no longer dealing with a rank incompetent like Captain Korda. And you have no rebel friends to help you this time. Yes, I know where you have been hiding. And you're going to tell me everything you know, the name of every rebel spy and the location of every safe house."

"Forget it," Lina said, ignoring her father's warning hand on her arm. "We're saying nothing."

"We shall see," Tarkin snapped. "You're lucky you arrived when you did. Each of your parents still has both their eyes, and both their arms. Their hearts continue to beat. It doesn't have to be that way." He smiled thinly. "Rest tonight. Tomorrow you will tell me everything."

He strode away, followed by the black droid. Lina felt her hands shake as one of the troopers took her wrists, locking them behind her back.

"This way," he barked, and she was shoved forward. But even as they dragged her away, even as she was driven out into the low, dark corridor, still she felt like she was floating on air.

She glanced back and saw her parents following, a stormtrooper gesturing with his blaster. Milo walked a few steps ahead, driven by a big trooper with a stun stick clipped to his belt. But when he caught Lina's eye, a grin spread across his features. They'd been through so much. They'd been chased and caught, imprisoned and beaten, shot at and blasted from the sky, and they'd come through all of it. They were still in one piece, and they had achieved what they set out to do.

"Wipe that smirk off your face," the trooper growled, "or I'll wipe it off for you."

But however hard she tried, Lina couldn't stop smiling.

CHAPTER 8
MEAT AND METAL

THE SMELL was driving him wild. It had to be coming from behind one of those doors. But which one? Every time he tried to peek inside, the steel would slide shut in his face, or a human in huge boots would barge out and almost step on him. One had even spotted him and given chase, but he had managed to scramble up a rocky wall and hide in a tiny tunnel filled with cold air and echoes.

He didn't know where they'd gone, his boy and his girl. He had vague memories of men in white shooting fire at him, and a friendly face he remembered from the very distant past. He had fled in panic, diving into the darkness, eager to escape all the noise and the blasting. But now he was lost and hungry and alone.

A door at the end of the hallway slid open, emitting a blast of steam. Morq began to salivate. The smell was so strong, that must be the place. He crept closer, alert for any sign of the white men and their big boots. He hunched in the shadows, waiting, and the moment the door moved, so did he.

Morq darted inside, dodging feet, scrambling under a low counter. The room was big and hot and bright, but there appeared to be only one man inside it—a big one with stains on his coat. He was stirring something in a pan, something rich and meaty.

Morq shook his head. Hunger was making him dizzy. He couldn't risk going near the man, but he had to get to the food. He darted from one shadow to the next, freezing at the first sign of movement. Then he realized—it was no use being down there. Humans never put their food on the floor unless they were giving it to you. He had to climb higher.

He scaled a rack of shelves, using his claws to drag himself up. Then it was just a case of jumping across to the counter, a short, easy leap. The surface was smooth and slippery so his landing was far from graceful. But there was his reward—a platter of freshly cut meat, just waiting for him.

Morq looked around cautiously. The big man was still stirring, his back turned.

Morq shot forward, grabbing a slice of meat and scarfing it down. The taste was almost too much. After the dry rations this was a luxury beyond imagination. He gobbled another piece, and another.

He was going for a fourth when a hand grabbed his tail. Morq twisted around, cursing his own foolishness.

The big man had hold of him with one huge fist. And the other was coming down, a sharp knife glinting as it swung toward Morq's head.

He squawked and turned, sinking his beak into the man's hand. The man roared furiously, and the cleaver thudded into the countertop.

Morq yanked free, leaping from the counter and bolting toward the door. But then, disaster—there was someone in the doorway, striding through with a stack of metal trays. The newcomer saw him and yelled, dropping the trays with a crash and a clatter. Morq doubled back, looking desperately for another way out. There, up on the wall, stood an open hatch. It would be quite a leap, but he might just make it.

He crouched, ready to spring. On one side the big man came striding in, his butcher knife raised. On the other the newcomer raced toward him, hands outstretched. Morq jumped, kicking as hard as he could with his legs.

He hit the wall, scrabbling desperately with his claws. For a moment he thought he'd missed his shot, that he was going to fall to the floor and be chopped to bits. Then he felt his long claw catch, the muscles in his arm tightening as he scrambled up and over and into the hatch.

He fell for a long time, slamming into the sides of the metal shaft before plummeting into something warm and sticky and foul. The smells there were overpowering—rotting food and filth, all coming from the slimy pool into which he'd dropped. But there were dry places around the edge. He spotted a tangled heap of scrap metal and machine parts and paddled toward it, dragging himself out of the pool.

He crouched, surveying his surroundings. His boy was not there. In fact, he could see no life at all, not even a nice tasty rat. But something was making a sound: he could hear it echoing from the walls and the low rocky ceiling. It was a familiar sound—not a human sound but one he knew.

It was calling his name. Morq darted around, confused. He could see no people, just a strange domed object with glowing eyes. He moved closer, and that's when he recognized it.

Somehow, the Floating Man's head had

become separated from the rest of him—an accident that would have killed Morq, but the Floating Man had survived. He was speaking very insistently, and he seemed to want something. Morq recognized the tone if not the words. Then the Floating Man spoke one syllable that the little monkey-lizard recognized: "Fetch."

Morq looked around eagerly. What could the Floating Man possibly want in all this rot and junk? He had no way to explain himself. He was just a head. Morq would have to work it out on his own.

It would probably be something metal, because the Floating Man was metal. Perhaps he was hungry? No, he never seemed to eat. What else would the Floating Man need? What didn't he have?

Then he saw it. Reaching up from the tangle of scrap, a flat disc with five extended fingers. Morq leapt toward it, locking his beak on to the longest digit.

Behind him he could hear the Floating Man

still talking. "Yes, Morq!" he was saying. "Good Morq! Good!"

Morq felt a flush of warm pride down in his belly and set to work.

Milo woke to the sound of voices, looking up to see the black droid looming through the cell doorway. Rhyssa and Auric waited in the corridor under guard, their hands bound. Lina sat up, rubbing her eyes.

"Move," K-4D8 demanded. "The governor wants to see you."

"And what if we don't want to see him?" Lina asked.

The droid turned toward Rhyssa, raising his heavy assault rifle. Lina leapt to her feet. "We're coming," she said. "Don't do that. Please."

Milo ran to his mother's side, unable to hug her because of the binders on his wrists. She bent down, nuzzling the top of his head with her nose. "Get any sleep?" she whispered.

Milo shook his head. "Not really. I'm feeling sort of tense for some reason."

Rhyssa laughed.

"Quiet," K-4D8 snapped. "No fraternizing."

They marched along the corridor in pairs, Milo and his mother followed by Lina and Auric, and last the two stormtroopers. The tunnel divided and they took the left-hand way, ducking into a clammy corridor with flickering lights in the ceiling.

"Where are you taking us?" Auric demanded.

"This isn't the way to the governor's quarters."

"We are not going to his quarters," K-4D8 retorted, ducking to avoid a clump of lichen hanging from the rocky ceiling. "Filthy planet," he muttered. "So much . . . life."

Looking around, Milo saw patches of black fungus on the tunnel walls, similar to the stuff that grew on Hffrr's back. He wondered where the Agarian was now. Was he out there somewhere, making a plan to rescue them? Or had he fled back to his caves, leaving them to their fate?

He blinked. For the briefest moment he'd thought he saw the fungus moving—a faint ripple catching the light. There was a strange low humming in the air.

K-4D8 halted, turning. The troopers drew their blasters. The sound grew louder, a steady drone throbbing from the walls of the tunnel. Again Milo thought he saw the black fungus writhing, like algae on the surface of the sea.

Then suddenly the noise changed pitch, and

he could hear words within it. "*Miiiilllloooooo . . .*" it said. "*Liiiiiinnnnaaaaaaa . . .*"

They looked at each other in amazement. The droid pushed toward them.

"What is that?" he demanded. "Who is making those sounds?"

"*We're comiiiiiiiing,*" the voice said, and Milo recognized Hffrr's gentle tones. "*Have nooooo feeeeaaaaaaaarrr. . . .*"

Lina grinned, clapping her hands. "They're coming," she said. Then she looked up at K-4D8. "You're in big trouble now."

That was when the shots rang out.

Milo ducked as blaster bolts exploded in the tunnel, sparks flying from the stone walls. The troopers returned fire, the roar deafening in the narrow space. K-4D8 raised his assault rifle, squeezing off six shots in quick succession.

Milo looked up, trying to see what they were firing at. The lights had been shot out, but at the far end of the hall he could make out a massive moving shape, ducking its head and striding toward them. The troopers crouched, firing back. Blaster bolts struck the figure's monstrous torso and it reeled. Then it started at them again, the floor shaking as it lumbered through the tunnel.

"Identify yourself," K-4D8 demanded. "That's an order."

"I don't take orders from you," the shape replied, and Milo's mind spun. *It couldn't be . . . could it?*

The monstrous figure fired at K-4D8, forcing him to duck. Then it paused, beckoning with one massive fist. "Mistress Lina," it said, "come quickly. You, too, Master Milo. I'll cover you."

"C-Crater?" Lina asked in amazement, getting to her feet. "Is that you?"

"It's me," the huge shape said, impossibly. "Now run."

Lina did as she was told, jumping to her feet. The troopers were still firing, their blasts striking CR-8R's enormous chassis.

K-4D8 roared "Stop!" and strode forward,

reaching for Lina, missing her by a hair. He took hold of Milo before he could follow, forcing him roughly to the ground. Then he raised his rifle above his head, blasting at the ceiling.

The tunnel collapsed inward, dust and smoke pouring into the narrow space. Milo heard rocks crashing down, saw one of the troopers buried by the rubble.

"Lina!" Rhyssa cried. But the second stormtrooper was already shoving them back along the tunnel.

K-4D8 followed, holstering his rifle. "Move, prisoners. The governor will not wait forever."

They staggered through the smoke and dust. Milo saw tears on his mother's cheeks.

"Lina's okay," he whispered. "She knows what she's doing. She'll be okay."

Rhyssa gritted her teeth. "I hope you're right."

CHAPTER 9
ATTACK

FROM END TO END the courtyard was filled with men, all standing smartly at attention. Stormtroopers stood in straight rows, their blasters clasped to their chests. The officers lined up beside them, motionless in the red light of the rising sun. At their backs, across a wide expanse of stony ground, the mushroom forest lay gray and misty in the morning haze.

"Ah, K-4," Governor Tarkin said as the black droid marched from the compound, leading Milo and his parents. "There were reports of firing in the tunnels. I wondered if you ran into trouble."

"It was nothing," the droid reported. "A

blaster malfunction. The Graf girl was injured. I had her sent back to her cell with a medical droid."

Tarkin's eyes narrowed. "A pity," he said. "I would have liked her to be here for this."

Why had the droid lied? Milo wondered. He must be ashamed to admit his mistake, frightened of the consequences if Tarkin discovered the truth. The realization that even a gleaming brute like K-4D8 was afraid of something made Milo feel oddly hopeful. The Imperials might seem unstoppable; they might act like the universe belonged to them—but deep down they had the same fears as everyone else.

Tarkin turned to Auric and Rhyssa, gesturing out into the courtyard. "Impressive, isn't it? I wanted to inspect my troops one last time before we begin."

"Begin what?" Rhyssa asked through gritted teeth.

"Why, my takeover of Agaris, of course."
Tarkin smiled cruelly. He nodded to one of
his men, who hurried forward to remove
their binders. "You know, you made all of this
possible, you and your children. The records we
found in your droid's head told us everything we
needed to know about these Agarians, including
how to kill them. My troopers have had new air
filters fitted into their helmets. They won't be
breathing any more of that filthy gas."

He gestured up into the sky, where a phalanx
of black shapes came screaming through the
clouds. Shielding his eyes, Milo saw the familiar
twin-pod shapes of TIE bombers.

"They've been fitted with special mining
charges," Tarkin went on. "Cave crackers,
they call them. They'll tear this planet open
like a rotten fruit, and my men will mop up
the remains. In a matter of days, Agaris will
be mine."

He turned away, raising a comlink to his

mouth. The men in the courtyard fell silent. The air was perfectly still; all Milo could hear was the screech of engines as the bombers sped closer. Agaris held its breath.

Governor Tarkin drew himself upright. "Today—" he began.

Then everything fell apart.

The front-most TIE bomber roared, black smoke pouring from the starboard pod. It began to spin madly, dropping out of formation. Milo saw a spiked spore jutting from one wing panel.

Tarkin looked up, his face white with fury. The men in the courtyard began to turn, their ranks breaking. Milo saw one of the huge stalks way off in the distance, its barrel-like stem raised.

The bomber tumbled, screeching toward the courtyard. The pilot tried to pull up, but it was no use. The ship slammed into the face of the compound like an insect on a speeder's windshield. Hunks of twisted metal came tumbling down the sloping stones, shattering in the courtyard to either side of them. Troopers and officers alike scrambled back, all order collapsing.

"Hold formation!" K-4D8 barked, his vocabulator at maximum.

Then Milo heard a cry, and he raised his head. Above the gray line of the mushroom forest a line of dark specks was rising. They arced toward the compound, cutting a smooth course. Milo was confused; the red spores would be no use against solid stone. They'd splatter on the compound wall just like that bomber.

But these spores were black, not red. And as they curved toward the courtyard they exploded in midair, popping like a row of fireworks. Crimson smoke burst from them, descending in a thick cloud. "Helmet filters on!" K-4D8 ordered.

But many of the officers and compound staff had no helmets, and as the gas settled

Milo saw them slumping to the ground, some laughing and twitching, others just dropping on the stones. One of Tarkin's men approached with a case of breath masks, handing them out hurriedly. The governor clamped the mask to his face, breathing through the clear plastic air pipe.

"Give them to the prisoners," he said. "I want them to witness my response."

Milo took the offered mask, tying the strap around his head and trying to breathe calmly. The red gas had begun to dissipate, leaving a trail of unconscious figures sprawled on the stones. In the silence he heard cries of pain and confusion, the crackle of comms, and men barking orders.

Then another sound rose, faint and distant but impossible to ignore. It came from beyond the courtyard, beyond the expanse of cleared ground. It came from deep within the mushroom forest itself. It was the sound of voices, hundreds of them, raised in anger. Their cry was wordless, but the defiance in it was unmistakable. Milo felt his hopes rise. The Agarians were coming.

A second line of spheres appeared on the horizon, spiraling toward them. They pulsed with a sickly purple light, as though something inside was glowing. Then, like the first set of spores, they exploded in midair, sending thousands upon thousands of tiny, glistening pellets raining down on the men in the courtyard.

Milo ducked, hearing a clanking hiss like hailstones on a tin roof. But when he looked again the stormtroopers were picking themselves up, their armor dented but not pierced by the rain of seedlings.

Tarkin smiled grimly. "Is that the best these Agarians have got?" he spat. Then he raised his voice. "K-4, wipe them out!"

The black droid nodded, striding out into the courtyard. The troopers were beginning to reorganize, their weapons pointed back toward the forest. The droid marched among them, issuing commands. The remaining TIE bombers circled back, and Milo saw gouts of fire blossoming along the line of giant stems, a curtain of orange flame exploding from the fog. He heard distant cries, lifted on the hot wind that swept toward them.

The first line of stormtroopers moved

forward, flamethrowers raised. At a signal from K-4D8 they hit their triggers simultaneously, scorching the ground ahead of them. The bombers returned, unleashing another wall of fire. Milo saw huge mushrooms in flames, their caps cracking and crumbling in the inferno. And he saw other shapes, too, scrambling clear of the raging firestorm and disappearing into cracks in the ground.

The Agarians were out there, withstanding the Imperial assault. But unless the generator was taken out of action, they were stuck where they were, unable to close in on the compound. At any moment the first stormtroopers would engage them, and Milo had no idea how that fight would play out. The Agarians were many, but the troopers were better armed, better trained, and had no doubts when it came to killing.

He wondered desperately where Lina was. As far as he could tell, there were two possibilities—either she was lying injured under a rockfall, or she and Crater were on their way to find the generator. For all their sakes, he prayed it was the latter.

CHAPTER 10
THE GENERATOR

"AND THEN I THINK the fall must have triggered my reactivation response, because when I came to my senses I was in a garbage pile," CR-8R was saying. "Truly, Mistress Lina, you can't imagine how I've suffered. It's a miracle that I'm here at all. In one piece, or near enough."

In one very big piece, Lina thought. She was finding it impossible to come to terms with CR-8R's new body as he stomped alongside, kicking up clouds of dust with every crashing footstep. Lina had seen loadlifters at work; she'd almost been flattened by one in a mining yard on Cedonne. This one was battered and bent, its one remaining arm grasping a bulky blaster. The torso was almost as wide as the tunnel itself, terminating in a pair of massive, tree-trunk legs. Perched off-center atop this vast cube, CR-8R's head looked like a bolo-ball balanced on a scout walker.

Lina didn't know where the other arm had originated, but she suspected it was from some kind of lumber droid. The long, slender limb terminated in a toothed power saw that kept starting up at the worst moments, like when Lina had pulled CR-8R in for a hug after the shootout in the tunnel. He'd meant to comfort her, and ended up almost taking her head off.

"It wasn't a miracle that saved you," she reminded him. "It was a monkey-lizard."

"I suppose so," CR-8R agreed reluctantly. "This . . . animal proved himself useful after all."

"And after all the mean things you've said about him." Lina grinned. "You should apologize, Crate."

CR-8R sighed. "Morq, I am sorry I did not appreciate your worth sooner. Thank you for rescuing me."

Morq purred, clambering onto CR-8R's massive shoulder and rubbing his beak lovingly against the droid's metal cheek. CR-8R gave a reluctant purr of his own, and Morq sat back happily.

"According to the schematics I accessed in the compound's mainframe," CR-8R said, "the generator should be at the end of this hallway."

"It'll be guarded," Lina warned. "They can't all have gone off to this inspection thing."

The corridors had been mercifully empty, but they had overheard a pair of mechanics bickering over whose fault it was that they were late for the governor's personnel review.

"I hope Milo's okay," Lina went on. "That ceiling came down pretty hard."

"I'm sure he was clear of the impact zone," CR-8R told her. "That KX droid would not risk both of his governor's prized prisoners. He hasn't had the chance to question you yet."

"I wouldn't tell him anything anyway," Lina muttered.

"You'd tell him whatever he wanted to know," CR-8R said. "You would not risk your life or that of Master Milo or your parents simply for some information that might already be out of date."

"But he wanted to know about Mira and Ephraim," Lina protested. "And their whole network."

"And if the Bridgers were here, they would tell you the same," CR-8R said. "They can look after themselves."

There was a rumbling overhead and the walls shook. The lights in the ceiling flickered, and far away Lina heard a dull, rolling crash. "It's started," she said. "We need to move." She picked up the pace, hurrying along the tunnel.

"*Hey!*" A shout froze her in her tracks. "What do you think you're doing?"

At the end of the corridor a steel door stood

wide. A pair of young crewmen huddled in the entranceway, awkwardly clutching blasters.

"Halt!" the nearest one cried. "Or we'll open fire."

"Crater," Lina hissed. "What are we going to do now?"

"Fear not, Mistress Lina," CR-8R said. "I have it under control."

He began to run, his huge feet slamming on the stones. To Lina's amazement he roared, charging down the corridor toward the startled guards. One of them fired, the blast ricocheting off CR-8R's armored torso. But still he kept charging, Morq clinging to his shoulder and screeching.

The crewmen looked at each other in surprise and terror. They were barely more than cadets, Lina saw, left on guard while their superiors attended the inspection. She could only imagine their terror as they saw that massive shape thundering from the shadows.

The lead crewman broke first, bolting back

through the doorway and pulling his companion with him. He slammed the door controls as he fled, but CR-8R reached the door before it could slide shut, grabbing it in his massive fist. The steel tore like paper as the droid charged through.

Lina hurried after him, pushing past the twisted door and into the generator room. On the far side she saw another panel hissing shut.

"You let them go," she objected.

CR-8R nodded. "I may look like a monster, Mistress Lina, but that does not mean I have become one."

The ground shook again, dust drifting down into the room.

"They'll be back," Lina said. "And they'll bring reinforcements."

"Then we should do what we came to do," CR-8R said. "And quickly."

The generator towered over them, a black cylinder shimmering with colored lights. Lina could feel its power. The air was greasy with electricity, and blue sparks danced overhead.

"Do you think there's an off switch?" she asked.

"Perhaps," CR-8R told her. "But it could take time to find it. This will be quicker." He fired up his power-saw attachment, swinging it down on the console in front of them. Sparks flew, shards of metal and plastic hissing through the air.

Lina ducked. "Hey, careful," she protested. "We're not all covered in armor."

"My apologies," CR-8R said. "Take shelter behind me, Mistress Lina."

He drove his saw into the center of the console, the blade whining as the teeth dug in. With the other hand he aimed his blaster, hammering the console with four quick shots.

"Hit it again!" Lina cried. "I think it's working!"

Steel melted and hissed. The generator shuddered, sparks of electricity showering down on the shattered console. Morq ran for cover as electric bolts arced through the air.

Then, with a cough and a groan, the generator gave out and they were plunged into darkness.

"Nice work, Crate," Lina said. "Now all we have to do is find our way out again."

"I'm afraid my new body does not seem to possess any glowlamps," CR-8R said apologetically. "However, I can see by infrared. I will attempt to locate a light source. Ah, what's this?"

Lina heard a click, followed by a hiss of static. "That doesn't sound like a flashlight to me," she said.

"Very astute," CR-8R said. "It's a radio. Perhaps we can get some news of Master Milo, or at least find out what is causing these groundquakes." He scanned through the Imperial bands. Suddenly, a voice leapt from the darkness.

"*The creatures are moving toward us,*" it crackled. "*I can't . . . I can't quite make them out.*"

Between the words Lina could hear explosions and blaster fire, and troopers barking orders. "*Wait,*" the man went on, his voice trembling. "*The smoke's lifting. I see . . . I see them. They're coming this way. Sir, there are hundreds of them!*"

"*Hold your position!*" a second voice snapped, and Lina recognized K-4D8's cold tones. "*Use flamethrowers and blasters, but hold them back.*"

"*There are too many of them!*" the trooper cried out. "*They're everywhere! They're coming out of the fog! Aieeeee . . . !*"

His scream trailed off, and for a moment there was silence. Then the droid's voice cut back in.

"*Hangar, this is K-4D8,*" he said. "*Prepare the* Carrion Spike *for immediate liftoff. And have the brig prepared. The governor is taking his prisoners with him.*"

"*Right away,*" someone responded.

"They're taking them to the hangar," Lina said. "Do you know the way?"

"Of course," CR-8R said, and in the darkness she heard his servos whirring. "Follow my voice."

"Right with you, Crate," Lina called out, holding up her hands. She felt the ragged edge of the busted door and pushed through. In the corridor the air was cooler, but just as dark.

"Reach out to your left, Mistress Lina," CR-8R said, and Lina did so. She felt something smooth and round, then wrapped her hand around it.

"It feels like a pipe," she said, lifting it. "What do I need it for?"

"To defend yourself, if need be," CR-8R replied. "Between us, we should now be equipped to repel any Imperial attacks."

Lina laughed.

"What is so amusing?" the droid asked.

"You," Lina said, hefting the cold steel and

feeling a bit braver. "I remember when you were scared of everything, always telling us to be careful, go slow, don't take any risks. Now you're telling me to take on the Empire with a metal pipe."

"Maybe this new body has gone to my head," CR-8R admitted.

"It's not just that," Lina said. "It started before we even landed on Agaris. You've gotten tougher, Crate."

"Perhaps," CR-8R agreed. "But so have you, and Master Milo. We have been forced to confront situations that none of us could have imagined before your parents were taken. We have all changed."

"I guess you're right," Lina sighed. "But it's a good thing, right?"

"For the most part," CR-8R agreed. "You and Master Milo can take care of yourselves now. If such a disaster should happen again, you would be well equipped to deal with it."

"But?" Lina asked.

"But you are still so young," CR-8R said. "Children your age should not have to fight for their lives. They should not have to make the choices you have been forced to make."

"I doubt we're the only ones," Lina pointed out. "This must be happening all across the Empire. Kids losing their parents and their families, having to struggle like we did."

"Indeed," CR-8R said sadly. "I think of them often." Then he picked up the pace. "Come, Mistress Lina. We must be swift. If Governor Tarkin achieves liftoff, this has all been for nothing."

CHAPTER 11
THE BATTLE

"MOVE, BOY," K-4D8 BARKED, shoving Milo forward. He stumbled, grabbing his father's hand. Auric turned, glaring at the droid and the stormtroopers marching behind.

"Knocking my son down won't make us go any faster," he said angrily.

"He's right," Tarkin agreed, turning in the tunnel. "There is no need to be rough. Just know that the faster you move, the faster you'll be safe on my ship."

"We're not getting on your ship," Rhyssa spat. "You'll have to kill us first."

"As you will," Tarkin said. He marched ahead, leading them out into the hangar.

The *Carrion Spike* stood on the far side
of the cavernous space, gun turrets gleaming.
Power droids buzzed around the ship's landing
gear, and Milo saw a pair of officers hurrying
down the gangway, making their final checks.
Inside, all was black.

"Milo, look," Auric hissed, and Milo turned to
follow his father's gaze.

Out beyond the hangar's open entranceway,
all was chaos. The red gas rolled in waves,
hiding much of the courtyard from view. But
Milo could see enough.

He could see bodies littering the ground,
some motionless, some slowly moving. Most
were Imperial officers, the ones who'd gone
down when the gas first descended. But he saw
a few stormtroopers, too, and here and there a
large gray shape.

An explosion sounded, waves of heat
driving the red smoke back. As the noise
faded Milo saw the front line of the Agarian

attack, driving raggedly toward the compound. A misshapen wall of gray, they came rushing and rolling across open ground to the edge of the courtyard. The stormtroopers retreated, attempting to repel the enemy with blasters and flamethrowers. But the Agarians were too many; they overwhelmed the troopers, returning fire with gas guns and fleshy slings that shot pods filled with dagger-sharp pellets.

Governor Tarkin watched silently; if he was in any way troubled by what he saw, he refused to show it. "Get them on board," he told K-4D8. "Quickly, now."

The droid took hold of Milo's shoulder, almost lifting the boy off his feet as he marched toward the waiting ship. The troopers shoved Auric and Rhyssa forward as the officers from the *Carrion Spike* crossed the hangar toward them. "She's prepped and ready, sir."

"Good," Tarkin said. "Secure the prisoners. I will pilot the ship myself."

Milo heard blaster fire, closer now. He turned as the smoke in the hangar's mouth parted, revealing a group of dark figures.

"Stop," the closest Agarian demanded. "Let them go." Milo knew that voice.

Tarkin turned at the foot of the gangway. The stormtroopers closed ranks, shielding the governor. K-4D8 froze, holding Milo by the collar.

"Let them go," Hffrr repeated, his soft voice echoing. "Now."

His companions halted. There were seven of them, ranging from a waist-high sproutling to a pair of four-armed monsters half the size of a TIE fighter.

Tarkin peered at the Agarians with disgust, as though they were the embodiment of all he loathed about that planet. "These people are my prisoners," he said. "They're coming with me."

Hffrr took a step forward. "You are in command here?"

"I am the authority on Agaris," the governor agreed. "My name is Tarkin."

"Taaah-kin," Hffrr said. "Yes. Your name is known to us. We have your men."

The governor pursed his lips. "I thought as much. Are they dead?"

"No," Hffrr said. "They are simply sleeping. If you leave this planet, they will be returned to you."

Tarkin gave a dismissive wave. "If those men were foolish enough to get captured, I have no use for them."

Hffrr took another step. "That is your choice," he said. "But you will not take these people."

Tarkin sighed. "I grow tired of this," he said. "K-4D8! Kill them, would you?"

The black droid nodded once. "With pleasure," he said, and opened fire.

One of the Agarians toppled back, green gas erupting from his body. The rest took cover behind a stack of crates as the stormtroopers blasted them. Sparks flew, lighting up the hangar.

"Auric and Rhyssa, take cover!" Hffrr yelled, and something rolled toward the troopers, a tiny round seedling. The Grafs ducked as the fungus grenade exploded, darts thudding into the stormtroopers' armor and knocking them to the floor. Milo was protected by K-4D8's metal body; the droid barely flinched as three of the darts pierced his black chassis.

The Agarians advanced, Hffrr leading the charge as they ran and rolled toward the shuttle. Tarkin stood for a moment, looking down at his fallen troopers and up at the approaching Agarians. Then he turned and marched up the gangway, raising it behind him.

K-4D8 backed into the hangar, dragging Milo by the collar, the boy's feet scraping on the stones. He kicked, trying to twist free, but K-4D8 barely seemed to notice. Milo saw two troopers staggering to their feet, firing wildly. One of the big Agarians fell, shrouded in green gas.

Rhyssa grabbed the nearest trooper around the waist, relieving him of his blaster. Auric took hold of the other and they wrestled on the stones. Milo saw his father wrap his hands around the trooper's throat.

Then there was a roar and a wave of heat, and the *Carrion Spike* began to rise. Through the cockpit window Milo could make out the back of Tarkin's head, bent over the controls as he piloted the ship out of the hangar. The thrusters roared and the cavern was bathed in light and heat. Then the ship was gone, tearing through the clouds and vanishing into the murky sky.

"Let Milo go," Hffrr ordered, taking a step toward K-4D8. In his hand he held a blaster, taken from one of the fallen troopers. "Let him go, and you will live."

The droid pulled himself upright. Milo

crouched at his feet, K-4D8's hand still tight on his collar.

"Stop where you are," the black droid ordered. "Stop or I'll kill your precious boy."

"I will destroy you first." Hffrr raised the blaster, aiming it at K-4D8's gleaming head. They were the same height, the metal monster and the slender Agarian. "Release him, or I will use your own weapon to finish you."

"I don't believe it," K-4D8 replied. "You are weak. You will not kill me."

Hffrr said nothing, his hand trembling as he gripped the gun tighter.

"It's a machine," Rhyssa urged him. "It's not alive. Take the shot."

Hffrr glanced at her, confused. "It speaks," he said. "It thinks."

"It's not the same." Auric joined his wife. "Do it. Save Milo."

Hffrr looked down at the blaster, then up at the droid. Milo could see the conflict on his smooth gray face. Then slowly, he lowered the gun. "This is a sentient being. I cannot kill it."

"I, however, do not have that problem." The voice boomed from the back of the hangar, deep in shadow.

K-4D8 spun around, pulling Milo with him. Something was emerging from the darkness. He heard the whine of a power saw.

"Put him down," CR-8R demanded, striding forward on massive metal legs. "Now."

Lina hurried behind him. She saw Milo and froze, one hand on her mouth, the other gripping a rusty piece of pipe.

"You look . . . different," K-4D8 said, raising his assault rifle.

"I feel different," CR-8R agreed.

Then he fired and ducked simultaneously, K-4D8's blast missing him by a hair. The black droid was not so quick; CR-8R's shot struck him in the shoulder, sending sparks flying. His hand snapped open inadvertently, releasing Milo.

K-4D8 roared in frustration, reaching for the boy. But before he could take hold, CR-8R went storming in, the power saw raised. He swung it down, the steel teeth grinding into K-4D8's

arm. The black droid turned, grabbing CR-8R with one huge metal fist. They wrestled, servos grinding and sparks flying. Their feet slammed into the floor of the hangar, cracking the stones.

First CR-8R had the advantage, his saw biting deep into K-4D8's exposed shoulder wiring. Then the black droid went low, jamming his rifle into CR-8R's torso and firing twice. CR-8R's armor was solid, but the blasts drove him back. He put his head down and charged again, grabbing K-4D8's rifle arm. The next shot went wild, barely missing Lina as she ran to her brother's side.

They took shelter behind the wing of a TIE fighter, watching as the droids grappled furiously. "What happened to Crater?" Milo asked, amazed.

"Long story," Lina said. "It sort of suits him, though, right?"

"I think he's winning," Milo said. Then he raised his voice. "Come on, Crater! Rip his arms off!"

"I'm trying, Master Milo," CR-8R called back, striking a blow that sent K-4D8 flying. The black droid landed on his back with a crunch.

"Stay down," CR-8R ordered, marching toward him. "Or I will crush you. Nobody touches Master Milo and gets away with it."

K-4D8 pulled himself up. One arm was crooked, sheared cables sparking in the hollow of his shoulder. "I fight for the Empire," he said. His vocabulator had been damaged, making his voice sound slow and mean. "I fight!"

He lumbered forward, lowering his head. CR-8R staggered back with the impact. K-4D8 swung wildly, his huge fist pummeling CR-8R again and again in the same weakening spot. To Milo's horror K-4D8 managed to punch through, and sparks flew as he twisted and tore with his fingers. CR-8R let out an electronic whine, falling back with oil gushing from his chest.

"No!" Lina cried, jumping to her feet. She sprinted from the TIE's shadow, wielding her pipe.

CR-8R struggled on his back like an insect, trying to stand, but the bulky body was too heavy. K-4D8 put a foot on his torso, holding him down. He lowered his assault rifle, pressing it to CR-8R's head. Milo knew that if he destroyed those cranial circuits, there'd be no coming back. CR-8R would be gone forever. He jumped to his feet, following his sister.

"Kids, no!" Auric yelled, and Milo glanced back to see his parents hurrying toward them, hands raised. Hffrr was with them, striding across the hangar.

But Milo and Lina ignored them, running at K-4D8, yelling like animals. Lina swung her pipe, smacking the droid in his articulated back. There was a loud metallic clang. She hit him again and again, swinging as hard as she could. Milo ran in, grabbing K-4D8's gun arm.

The droid growled in frustration. "Children," he drawled. "Foolish."

"We won't let you touch him!" Milo yelled. "We won't!"

K-4D8 leaned in until his cruel face was just centimeters from Milo's. "Kill you first," he growled. "Then finish your friend."

And he raised his gun arm, lifting Milo right off his feet. Milo clung on, trying to pull the droid down, but he simply wasn't heavy enough. The rifle swung back toward Lina. Dimly, Milo could make out something moving on the edge of his vision, something rising from the floor.

Lina took a step back as K-4D8 turned on her. She held the pipe in front of her defiantly, and Milo was reminded of his parents' old

bedtime stories about the Jedi and their lightsabers. Lina faced the droid, her face firm, the pipe raised. K-4D8 laughed and took aim.

There was a screeching metallic whine, and Milo felt hot sparks spraying the side of his face. K-4D8 staggered and Milo dropped, turning to see the tall black droid still upright, an expression of shock on his face. His head began to vibrate, as if it was about to explode. Fragments of steel and plastic erupted from his neck.

Then there was a clunk and a hiss and K-4D8's head slumped forward. It struck his chest and rolled to the floor, landing with a hard metallic thud. The black droid fell to his knees, and Milo jumped back as the decapitated body dropped like a tree.

Behind him CR-8R was revealed, his power saw raised victoriously. Then his knee joints weakened and he, too, staggered, sitting down hard on his armored backside.

Lina ran to him, wrapping her arms around

his head. Morq leapt onto CR-8R's shoulder, licking his face excitedly.

Milo grinned. "That was without a doubt the most awesome thing I have ever seen."

CR-8R looked up at him. "I am glad to be of service, as always."

Rhyssa joined them, looking down at K-4D8's motionless form. "I don't think I ever programmed you for battle, Crater," she said.

He nodded weakly. "You'll find a lot has changed, Mistress Rhyssa."

Auric crossed to join Hffrr. He was gazing out at the courtyard, his arms crossed. The battle was over, and through the drifting smoke Milo could see the Agarians lifting the unconscious officers and lining them up on the stones. The surviving stormtroopers sat in a square, their arms crossed over their heads. The Agarians had collected their blasters, throwing them into a tangled heap beyond the courtyard. As Milo watched, the ground cracked open and the weapons toppled into it, vanishing from sight.

"Tarkin will return," Auric said to Hffrr. "You know that, right?"

"I do," Hffrr agreed. "I saw it in his eyes. He will come back, and he will destroy everything."

"So what are you going to do?" Auric asked. "You can't fight him. He'll bomb you from orbit if he has to."

"It is time for us to leave," Hffrr said. "We have suspected this for some time. The preparations are already in place."

"Leave?" Milo asked, joining them. "Leave how? You don't have any ships."

Hffrr smiled at him. "You will see, young Milo," he said. "You will see."

CHAPTER 12
EVACUATION

LINA BUCKLED INTO the copilot's seat as Auric made a final check of the *Star Herald's* flight controls. Lights rippled across the freshly soldered console as Milo took his seat behind her, checking the navigation array.

"How we doing back there?" Auric called, and Lina twisted to peer into the darkened hold. She saw a spray of sparks, and heard her mother curse loudly.

"We're almost there!" Rhyssa shouted back. "Crate, hand me the hydrospanner."

The Agarians had delivered the ship at sunrise, hauling it through the mushroom forest using ropes and rollers. Rhyssa had set to work right away, patching up the *Star Herald*'s smashed side and refitting the cables that ran from the cockpit to the engine. Fortunately, the thrusters were undamaged, and once CR-8R had reconnected with his old chassis he was able to help her make the final repairs.

"This bucket of bolts had better hold together," Auric muttered, reaching to trigger the fuel feeds.

"She will," Lina told him. "She's not bad, for an Imperial ship. She's just had a few knocks."

"We should've asked to borrow one of those," her father said, pointing. "I'd feel safer."

Through the viewport they could see an Imperial transport lifting off from the compound, soaring up toward the Star Destroyer waiting in orbit. A handful of stormtroopers still huddled in the courtyard, waiting to be evacuated.

"I can't believe Hffrr's just letting them go," Lina said. "If they'd held on to their prisoners the Agarians would've had something to bargain with."

"It wouldn't make any difference," Auric told her as the transport vanished into the clouds. "Tarkin wouldn't think twice about bombing this planet to smithereens, whether or not his men were still on the surface."

Lina felt sick. "That's horrible," she said. "He's a monster."

"He is," Auric agreed. "But Hffrr isn't. He'd rather let them go, even though he knows they'll rejoin their units. I admire that."

Lina nodded. The thought of all those Imperial soldiers getting away free made her furious, but she knew her father was right. If the Agarians left them to die, they were no better than the Empire.

"So what do *you* think's going to happen?" Milo asked, leaning between the seats. "What did Hffrr mean when he said it was time to leave?"

Auric shrugged. "Your guess is as good as mine," he said. "On our last trip, we never saw any sign that the Agarians had interplanetary technology. But there's so much we don't know about them. I mean, Hffrr looks basically the same as he did thirteen years ago. He hasn't aged."

The Agarians had been busy all night making preparations, but what it all meant Lina couldn't begin to guess. New growths had sprouted from the mushroom forest, vast bowl-shaped fungi that towered over even the highest stalks. Since dawn there had been no sign of Hffrr or his people; they had delivered the *Star Herald* and retreated underground. She wondered if he would come to say good-bye.

Another Imperial ship landed, wings folding as it touched lightly on the stones of the courtyard. Auric's eyes narrowed. "That has to be the last one," he muttered. "We really need to go. What are they doing back there?"

"I can hear you, you know," CR-8R called from the hold. "We are working as fast as we can."

"I know," Auric said. "Work faster."

"Hey," Rhyssa snapped, coming to the cockpit door. Her hands were black with grease. "When Crate says we're working as fast as we can, then we're—"

"Quiet," Auric said, holding up a hand.

Rhyssa's face reddened. "Don't you tell me to—wait, what's that noise?"

A hiss had begun to fill the cockpit, seeming to come from all around them. For a moment Lina was perplexed. Had something gone wrong with the ship? Then she remembered the incident in the tunnel, that strange moment when the walls had seemed to speak.

"Hffrr?" she asked. "Is that you?"

"*It issssss....*" The Agarian's voice was faint, but growing clearer. "Are you ready to lifffft offfff?"

Milo reached up to touch a patch of black fungus on the wall. The fungus vibrated beneath his fingers. Lina saw another patch on the console, and a larger one on the floor beneath the pilot's seat.

"We're almost there," Auric said, not sure which direction to talk in.

"Good," Hffrr said. "Your ship should not be damaged when it happens, but you should make yourselves as secure as possible."

"When what happens?" Milo asked. "What are you up to?"

Hffrr laughed silkily. "Young Milo," he said, "I will miss your curious mind. Very well, since we have a moment to spare. You call us Agarians, but this world is not our true home. We colonized it the same way you humans would colonize an uninhabited world. When I first arrived, Agaris was nothing but a rock. All the life you see around you came with us."

"But how?" Milo asked. "How did you travel here without ships?"

"In spores," Hffrr explained. "We are not like you. We do not require oxygen to survive, only a little light. We can survive in the vacuum, journeying long and far until we find a world fit for our needs. Then we settle, and this is the result."

"Wait, go back," Auric said. "You said when you first arrived. But it must have taken thousands of years for all this life to flourish. How old are you, Hffrr?"

The Agarian laughed again. "We do not measure time the way you do," he said. "But I have seen stars born and die."

There was a sudden, low rumble, and Lina felt the ground beneath them shake.

"It has begun," Hffrr said. "It is time for you to leave."

"We're ready," CR-8R called from the back of the ship. "The connections are secure. I can make the final repairs to the hyperdrive once we are in orbit."

Rhyssa nodded. "Good enough for me," she said, strapping herself in beside Milo as the ship rattled around them. "Let's get moving."

"We will not see each other again," Hffrr's

disembodied voice said sadly. "But it has been a joy getting to know all of you. Lina, be brave. Milo, keep exploring. Rhyssa and Auric, look after one another. If there's one thing I've learned in my long life, it's that family is the most important thing in the universe."

"Thank you," Auric said, firing up the engines. "For everything."

"We won't forget you," Milo added.

"Good-bye, Hffrr," Lina said. "Thanks for saving us."

"*It wassss...my pleassssure...*" Hffrr hissed as his voice faded away.

Auric hit the thrusters and the *Star Herald* began to lift. A wind was rising. Lina could feel it buffeting the ship as they ascended toward the clouds.

"What's happening?" Milo asked, peering out of the side window as the ship banked. The ground had begun to shift and shake, geological waves rippling outward across the planet's surface. As the groundquakes increased in intensity, Lina saw the mountains beginning to subside, boulders tumbling into the plain below. The Imperial compound split open down the center, smoke billowing out as the courtyard heaved and tipped. And at the center of each wave was one of those massive new growths, a vast circular bowl of gray-green fungus with a dark opening in the center.

"What *are* those things?" Milo asked as the *Star Herald* tore through the churning clouds. "What are they d—"

There was a deafening *WHOOMPH*.

Agaris shook from pole to pole, as though a massive explosion had gone off in the heart of the planet. The *Star Herald* rattled, walls and windows vibrating. Through the glass Lina could see the entire world shudder, as though an invisible hand had taken hold and was shaking it roughly.

And like a giant puffball ejecting its seeds, Agaris shed its skin. The clouds shredded, billowing out into space. Lina saw the mushroom forest sloughing away from the planet's surface, fountains of black soil churning up toward them. The great round caps tumbled and rolled, huge root systems dragging behind them. The slender stalks shot up like arrows, driven by the force of the groundquake. One of them swept toward the *Star Herald*, its bulbous head clipping the ship and knocking it aside.

"Get us out of here," Rhyssa ordered as the cloud of debris swallowed them. Auric nodded.

It was like steering through an asteroid field, Lina thought, except the projectiles were smaller and squashier, drifting outward into space. The ship would still suffer serious damage if one of the big ones slammed into it, though.

Then something shot past the viewport, traveling faster than any of the loose stalks. It was a black sphere half the size of the *Star Herald*, moving at blinding speed into the darkness beyond. Another followed, and another.

"It's them!" Milo said excitedly, craning his head to look back at the planet.

The black spheres came bursting from the center of those giant funnels like bolts from an ion cannon, punching through the debris field and out into empty space. The planet shook with every violent discharge.

"What do you mean, them?" Auric asked, watching in wonder.

"The Agarians," Milo said. "These must be the seedlings Hffrr was talking about, the ones that can survive in space. Look, they're headed for the sun."

He was right. The spores moved in formation, curving toward the distant star.

"Won't they burn up?" Lina wondered.

"They must use the star's gravity," Rhyssa suggested. "A slingshot, to give them speed. They need to cross interstellar distances, after all."

"Okay, that's now the most awesome thing I've ever seen," Milo said. "Sorry, Crate."

"Not at all," the droid called from the hold. "I quite agree."

"Even the Empire is getting out of their way," Auric said, and Lina saw the Star Destroyer taking evasive action, angling out of Agaris's orbit as the debris cloud expanded toward it.

"Let's listen in," Rhyssa said, flicking on the radio. Static filled the cockpit.

An Imperial voice broke through. "*Should we open fire?*"

"*Let them go,*" Tarkin replied in clipped tones. "*The planet is ours.*"

"*I'm picking up a ship leaving Agaris,*" the first voice continued. "*It's an Imperial craft, but all our ships are accounted for.*"

"*The family Graf,*" Tarkin sneered. "*Good. Send a fighter squadron to intercept.*"

Rhyssa flicked off the radio. "I really can't stand that man." She turned, raising her voice. "Crater, how's that hyperdrive coming along?"

"Almost there," the droid replied. "Two minutes."

Lina saw four TIE fighters emerge from the *Executrix* and turn toward them. "We might not have two minutes."

"I'll plot a course," Auric said, bending over the console. "We can make the jump to light speed the second Crater gives the all-clear."

"Do we know where we're going?" Rhyssa asked.

"Somewhere safe," Auric said. "We still have the maps, remember? We'll find a nice, quiet

world, somewhere green and peaceful, far away from stormtroopers and Star Destroyers."

An image flashed into Lina's head. A house in the woods, by a fast-flowing river. A plantation filled with lush, fruit-bearing plants. A place where she and Milo could grow up strong and healthy, where their parents could teach them all they needed to know to survive. Her whole family, together, light-years from danger. It was perfect.

But it was impossible.

"No," she said. "No, we can't."

Auric turned to her. "What do you mean?" he asked. "Lina, I won't put you both in danger again."

Lina put her hand on his arm. "The whole galaxy's in danger, Dad. The Empire won't stop until it's all theirs, every single world. And we won't be able to live with ourselves if we run away."

"We're not running away," Rhyssa argued. "This isn't our fight."

"It's everyone's fight," Milo said, facing his mother. "Lina's right. There are people out there who risked everything for us. We were lost and alone and we didn't know what we were doing, and they helped us. Now it's our turn to help them."

"The rebels?" Auric asked. "We'll never be able to thank them for all they did. But they chose to put their lives in danger. They made a decision to fight the Empire. We never had a choice."

"But now we do," Lina said. "And we have to go back."

"I agree." CR-8R floated in the doorway, watching them.

Rhyssa looked up. "You too, Crate?" she asked. "You're programmed to protect Milo and Lina, not lead them into danger."

"That is not quite correct, Mistress Rhyssa," CR-8R said. "If you recall, you were the one who installed my primary programming. You designed me to protect children, knowing that

I would begin with yours. But Milo and Lina are not the only children in the galaxy. There are billions more under threat. The Empire does not care about children. It does not care about anything except power. If we join this fight, who knows how many lives we could save?"

For a moment there was silence. Lina looked from her mother's face to her father's. Auric's eyes were on the floor, and he was shaking his head slowly.

Then a laser blast slammed into the *Star Herald*'s side and Milo cried out. The TIEs screamed toward them, blasting as they rocketed overhead.

"Crater, I hope you fixed the hyperdrive before you decided to come and lecture us," Rhyssa said.

"Of course," the droid replied. "And I also took the liberty of plotting a course for Lothal."

Auric looked up at him. "You did . . . what?"

Milo laughed. "Crater, you're a genius."

Another blast rocked the ship. Ahead of

them, Lina could see the Agarian spores circling toward the sun, gleaming as they picked up speed. She hoped Hffrr and his people would make it to safe harbor. But for her, there was no such place. It was time to go back and continue the fight.

"Punch it, Dad," she said, reaching for Milo's hand and squeezing it tight.

Auric hit the hyperdrive. The stars streaked toward them, and they were gone.

TWO KIDS TAKE ON THE EMPIRE

Milo and Lina Graf have located the mysterious Wild Space planet where their parents are being held. Milo and Lina must infiltrate a secret base to free them. With an entire legion of Imperial troops to contend with, can the children at last succeed in THE RESCUE?

ISBN 978-136800315-5

$5.99 US / $6.50 CAN

50599

9 781368 003155

0418

EAN

Disney

LUCASFILM
P R E S S

© & TM 2018 LUCASFILM LTD.
VISIT THE OFFICIAL *STAR WARS* WEBSITE AT:
WWW.STARWARS.COM.

THE BEST CHICAGO SPORTS ARGUMENTS

CHICAGO SPORTS

ARGUMENTS

THE 100 MOST
CONTROVERSIAL, DEBATABLE
QUESTIONS FOR DIE-HARD
CHICAGO FANS

JOHN "MOON" MULLIN

SOURCEBOOKS, INC.®
NAPERVILLE, ILLINOIS

Published by Sourcebooks, Inc.
P.O. Box 4410, Naperville, Illinois 60567-4410
(630) 961-3900
Fax: (630) 961-2168
www.sourcebooks.com

Library of Congress Cataloging-in-Publication Data

Mullin, John,
  The best Chicago sports arguments : the 100 most controversial, debatable
questions for die-hard Chicago fans / John Mullin.
      p. cm.
  Includes index.
  ISBN-13: 978-1-4022-0821-8
  ISBN-10: 1-4022-0821-9
  1. Sports--Illinois--Chicago--Miscellanea. 2. Athletes--Rating of--Illinois--
Chicago--Miscellanea. I. Title.

GV584.5.C4M85 2006
796.09773'11--dc22

                                                     2006024097

Printed and bound in the United States of America.
CH 10 9 8 7 6 5 4 3

Also by John Mullin

*The Rise and Self-Destruction of the Greatest Football Team
in History: The Chicago Bears and Super Bowl XX*

Tales from the Chicago Bears Sidelines

Tennis and Kids: The Family Connection (with Jim Fannin)

CONTENTS

ACKNOWLEDGMENTS

First thanks go to every reader, fan, media colleague, occasional friend, and buddy who shared an opinion, however misguided, with me on the questions contained in this book and many, many more.

Special thanks go to some of the true legends in the sports "debates" business, the ones who have left their marks on Chicago sports with their reporting, commentary, and opinions. Chet Coppock pioneered sports talk radio in Chicago and has been a news maker and news reporter for many colorful years in Chicago, New York, Las Vegas, and elsewhere.

Les Grobstein was there for so many of the epic moments in Chicago sports, reported on them, and had an opinion on every one of them. The Grobber is a walking encyclopedia of sports history and no one has ever done overnight sports talk radio like Les.

Dan Bernstein, Doug Buffone, Lissa Druss, Reid Hanley, Bryan Harlan, David Haugh, Melissa Isaacson, Dan Jiggetts, K.C. Johnson, Jeff Joniak, Rich King, Peggy Kusinski, Torjus Lundevall, Larry Mayer, Bruce Miles, Brad Palmer, Ken Paxson, Don Pierson, Dan Roan, Ed Sherman, Tom Thayer, and Mike Wolf.

The project never happens without my agents Greg Dinkin and Frank Scatoni at Venture Literary.

The support of my daughter, Jenny, and of my family are the treasures of my life. I can never repay my Dad in particular for all the games attended and played and talked about, and whose guidance helped me not only to play the games that were part of my growing up but also to appreciate those who played them. Of course, he did take his autographed Babe Ruth ball out and play with it, but hey, there was a depression going on, and love of the game came first.

The editing of my wife, Kathleen, has helped three books achieve at least a marginal level of coherence and the end results have been far better than I ever could have achieved by myself, even if she doesn't grasp the inherent silliness of soccer. Add in the love and patience I was given every day and you have a work by a very lucky writer.

– J. M.

INTRODUCTION

Sports are certainly jobs for those who play, coach, and cover it for a living. They are more than entertainment for a lot of those who watch and follow the games. But sports are something more, too.

Strangely, they are things that provide a way for people to get together, to have some common ground or interest besides the weather. From the mailroom to the board room, everybody has an opinion on the Bears game yesterday, the Cubs game last week, the Sox game...and so on.

In many of the debates, I spent time and space detailing some of the possibilities that did not make it into a best or worst category. Those were the by-products of thinking through the debate, and in case someone thinks all the decisions were simple, those accounts should lay that suspicion to rest.

I've been lucky enough to cover some of those games for the *Chicago Tribune* and analyze both the games and the personalities who play them. More than that, I've been fortunate to spend time talking to readers and listeners as well, whether at sports functions or on the air with friends at WGN, WSCR, ESPN, and other sports talk venues.

Along the way I have had challenges to what I've written, said, or thought. From those discussions have come ideas, many of which are incorporated in these pages. The beauty here is that I can lay out my side of the debates, which of course is the correct side.

The true fun of this book, however, was not only what I wrote, but also what I learned, and my real hope is that reading it will be some of the same for you as well. More than once I began with one point of view and, after I researched and reconsidered, came away with a completely opposite conclusion.

I have no doubt that more than once you'll probably mutter, "What is this guy thinking?" I'll take that as a compliment, and I'll pay one in return: we're both thinking and that's when the debates on our games become the most interesting, and above all, fun.

MYTHICAL MATCHUP:

Dick Butkus vs. Walter Payton

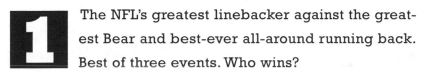 The NFL's greatest linebacker against the greatest Bear and best-ever all-around running back. Best of three events. Who wins?

We'll look at three different scenarios: 1) blitz vs. blitz pickup; 2) pass coverage vs. pass receiver; 3) third-and-one, linebacker vs. ball carrier.

THE CASE: Walter Payton

He was the greatest running back the game has ever seen. He was not necessarily the greatest runner; that debate can be left to supporters of Gale Sayers, Barry Sanders, Emmitt Smith, and O. J. Simpson, or maybe Jim Brown.

Walter was the number four pick in the 1975 draft, the genius find of Jim Finks and Bill Tobin, who preferred the more easily assessed talent of bigger schools but knew there was something special in this undersized back from predominantly African-American Jackson State. When Walter got to training camp, it did not take the Bears long to see it either.

At the start of camp, backfield coach Fred O'Connor looked over at Walter and figured this kid came from someplace other than just Jackson State.

"God one day decided He was finally going to do it right and make the perfect football player," O'Connor said. "So He made Walter Payton."

And one day He figured He needed the perfect guy to stop Walter. So He made Butkus.

THE CASE: Dick Butkus

Hall of Famer Bill George invented the middle linebacker position when George Halas had him stand up from his spot as middle guard in the Bears' 5-2 and take a couple steps back from the line of scrimmage. The middle linebacker position was born that day, along with the 4-3 that is an NFL staple to this day. George was the only man that Johnny Morris and a number of Bears admitted to being truly afraid of.

But the Bears chose Dick Butkus in the 1965 draft and on the first day of camp that year, George watched the rookie trot out of the locker room. He confided in friends that he felt a chill watching the malevolent specter move and knew at that moment that he was no longer going to be the middle linebacker for the Chicago Bears.

Walter Payton is forever "Walter" to fans in Chicago and elsewhere. Michael Jordan was on a first-name basis with the world as well. Dan Hampton was "Danimal" or "Hamp." Mike Singletary was "Samurai." Dick Butkus was just... "Butkus." Perfect. And when Rocky Balboa named his hulking dog, he named him...Butkus. Of course.

Minnesota Vikings running back Dave Osborne ran a sweep against the Bears. Butkus destroyed the play and Osborne. Afterwards Osborne was asked what had become of his lead blocker on the play. "I don't know," Osborne mused. "Maybe Butkus ate him."

Gale Sayers, drafted one pick behind Butkus in the '65 draft, once was asked to name the toughest player he had ever faced. Sayers said nothing, simply turned toward the practice field and pointed. To Butkus.

Butkus was the greatest linebacker to ever play the game. Not just the best middle linebacker; the best linebacker. His only peers were perhaps Ray Nitschke in Green Bay or Lawrence Taylor, the best pass-rushing linebacker of all time. But Nitschke was nowhere near Butkus as a pass defender or spreader of pure fear, and L.T. spent most of his NFL life lining up on the outside and destroying all he faced. Butkus was in the middle. Where the action was. Because he *was* the action.

The defensive lines in front of him, like Payton's on offense, are largely forgotten. Only Doug Atkins in his final

5

Chicago season went to a Pro Bowl with Butkus.

Chicago can count itself fortunate in both producing Butkus and in keeping him. He was a South Side guy, went to the University of Illinois, then was drafted by the Bears as well as the Denver Broncos in the AFL-versus-NFL era. The Broncos were too cash-poor at the time and the New York Jets ended up with the rights to Butkus. The Jets had beaten the NFL to Joe Namath the year before but Butkus was a Chicago guy. He was meant to be a Bear.

"To play this game you need a Neanderthal gene," linebacker and Butkus teammate Doug Buffone said. "Butkus had two."

MATCHUP NO. 1:
Butkus on the blitz, Walter on blitz pickup

The mythical 1985 season probably would have ended for the Bears in Minnesota, during game three, with no McMahon Miracle comeback. That is, if Walter did not pick up Vikings linebacker Dennis Johnson coming free on a blitz and threatening to end McMahon's night on the very first play, before McMahon ever let loose a throw to Willie Gault that changed Bears history forever.

Few running backs hit with Walter's ferocity and perfect technique. Blocking for a 205-pound back going against defensive ends and linebackers is a matter of "want-to." No one had more want-to in any part of the game.

Except perhaps, Butkus. Beginning in warm-ups he worked at building a rage, remarking that if a rival player was laughing, Butkus imagined himself as the one the opponent was laughing at.

In 1967, Butkus had 18 sacks, not an official NFL stat at the time. He was too much for most centers to handle head-up—a combination of too fast, too mean, and just plain too good.

So it's first-and-10 and Butkus is reading pass in the formation and fear in the quarterback. He is coming and Walter is staying in to pass-protect, because he is reading too. The snap comes and Butkus is already in motion, under the center's pads and closing on Walter's quarterback almost as fast as the signal-caller is taking his drop. Walter takes a step and sets his sights on Butkus.

The Decision

Walter could go low but he knows that Butkus knows that he knows that Butkus knows that nobody wants to take on Butkus high. So Walter, a contrarian if ever one existed in the NFL, coils and explodes, not at Butkus's knees, but right at spot between the 5 and the 1 on Butkus's jersey.

The impact is epic. But it is all Butkus in the end. He is 245 pounds to Walter's 205, has a full charge, and he didn't like the last time Walter carried and straight-armed him to the facemask. Without breaking stride he explodes right into Walter's block, firing a frightening forearm into Walter's chest that sends Sweetness flying backwards, and practically into a now-completely-terrified Gary Huff/Bob Avellini/Mike Phipps/Vince Evans, who ducks his head just in time to join the list of Butkus victims. Winner: Butkus.

MATCHUP NO. 2:

Walter on a pass route, Butkus in coverage

Butkus led the Bears with five interceptions as a rookie in 1965. He is tied for 10th in career interceptions with 22, with he and teammate Doug Buffone the only non-DBs on the Bears' all-time list. He was nimble and instinctive, one of the great linebackers in short coverage, and could make a one-handed pick as easily as deliver monster hits on receivers coming across the middle. He ranks third in NFL history with 25 fumble recoveries and is second among Bears all-time in combined interceptions-fumble recoveries.

Walter caught no fewer than 27 passes in 12 of his 13 seasons. Six times he led the Bears in receptions and his 492 catches are 136 more than Johnny Morris's number two total in franchise history. His 4,538 receiving yards are third all-time for the Bears. He is the only running back in the top 15. The short pass to Walter was simply a long handoff and served to get him out in space, in matchups that the Bears would take all afternoon against defensive backs and linebackers.

But against Butkus?

After the 7-yard sack on first down, the Bears break the huddle and come to the line, with Roland Harper or Matt Suhey in front of Walter, second-and-17. Butkus is calling out signals, pointing everywhere, but never taking his eyes off Walter.

The Decision

Bob Avellini fakes to Harper as Walter loops quickly out into the right flat. The fake freezes the defense; all except Butkus, who is in full rage and running to his left. He is bent on reaching Walter about the same time as the ball he knows is going there.

The pass is made. Walter, five yards outside the right tackle, takes it in stride and easily breaks the tackle of a nameless cornerback coming up fast. But it isn't the corner that Walter is looking for; it's Butkus. And Butkus is coming.

Walter is upfield several yards and Butkus takes an angle to stop the play after just those few yards. But Walter slows ever so slightly, throwing Butkus a fraction off stride, then gives Butkus the legendary high-step move as Butkus closes for the stop. Butkus gets a massive arm on Walter, but Walter repays the blitz forearm of a play ago with one of his own as he puts the hammer down and breaks free of Butkus. Buffone, pursuing on the play, brings Walter down after a gain of 16. Winner: Walter.

MATCHUP NO. 3:
Butkus square in the middle, Walter behind Harper/Suhey: third-and-one

No long build-up this time. Everybody in America knows who's getting the ball and knows exactly who will be somewhere around the ball when Walter has it. Quick count: ball to Walter coming straight up behind his fullback and center. Butkus is again in motion before the snap, this time attacking the center and standing him straight up.

Harper/Suhey hits Butkus, but he is off the center so fast that the block does nothing more than move him a step back but not off balance. Butkus slides, eyes on Walter, who is now three feet away, now two, now one. Butkus roars, spit flies, and Walter drives into Butkus full-speed. Butkus grabs Walter in a head-tackle and twists him to the ground. But Walter is driving the whole time, churning those legs forged on his hill of hell in Barrington.

The Decision

The bodies unpile. The referee signals for the chains and stretches out the 10-yard measure. Soldier Field is on its feet and.....

You make the call. I'm not dissing Walter even for a fantasy play, but if I say he made it, Butkus will hunt me down and find me.

HOOPING IT UP

The NBA's Greatest Game: Kobe, Michael, or...?

2 What is the NBA's greatest one-night stand? The debate started in earnest in early 2006 when Kobe Bryant rained 81 points on the Toronto Raptors. That topped every other single-game total in NBA history except the century mark Wilt Chamberlain posted against the New York Knicks on March 2, 1962.

Well, neither was the best ever in the history of pro basketball. That came in a Bulls uniform, to *the* Bull. Michael. He had so many great games, but nothing like the 63 points he lit up the Boston Garden with in 1986.

There's no shortage of stunning NBA performances. The best of the best are all by players on a one-name basis with not just Chicago, not just America, but the world: Kobe, Magic, Wilt, Michael. No last names needed; just an appreciation of greatness.

4. KOBE: 81 points against the Toronto Raptors, January 22, 2006

The 81 is just a number. It is a blip, what any number of NBA greats could have put up anytime their teams wanted to become so unbalanced. This is the mark of someone who said afterward that the best part was just getting "the W," but who cared so much about Ws that he wanted to be rid of Shaq rather than keep winning NBA titles. This performance not only isn't the best offensive performance ever, it's not even one of the top three.

Wilt put his 100 up against a team with four All-Stars. Magic did his magic in an NBA championship game. Michael did his against three Hall of Fame big men and one of the great defensive guards in NBA history, and in a playoff game.

Kobe's 81 came against a team whose fans were wearing bags over their heads through a 1–15 start, who threw a lineup of Chris Bosh, Mike James, Charlie Villanueva, Jose Calderon, and Joey Graham against him. Magic, Michael, and Wilt got their nights of history without a three-pointer. Kobe had 7. "We were just watching him shoot" was Bosh's comment afterwards. Now there is certainly some memorable NBA basketball, and don't you forget it.

Kobe did have a game for the NBA ages. He put in 28 of 46 shots and hit 7 of his 13 threes. He shot 20 free throws and hit 18. The Lakers were down at one point by 15 to one of the NBA doormats and Kobe brought them back. That's nice. And he had 6 rebounds, 3 steals, 2 assists, and a blocked shot.

It's just that it wasn't basketball. It was a 48-minute game of H-O-R-S-E. It was against a team that was 20–37 after Kobe set them on fire, and the Lakers reached .500 (29–29) with that win. That game doesn't even register on the "insignificant" list in the 2005–06 season.

This is in the group of games that includes David Thompson's 73, which was just the Denver Nuggets' attempt to let him get the scoring title ahead of George Gervin. David Robinson's 71 points weren't much better; those were also in the last game of a season when Robinson was trying just to take the scoring title away from Shaq. Robinson's 71 were in 1994 against the Los Angeles Clippers.

So what.

3. MAGIC: 42 against the Philadelphia 76ers, May 16, 1980

It was the second-greatest performance in NBA playoffs history, and nobody saw it. Well, almost nobody; the NBA had spiraled so far down in the drug-bitten 1970s that the Finals were no longer televised live to most of the country. So only the fans in Philly saw what Magic did to the Sixers.

You have to remember how great this series was. It was in Game 4 that Julius Erving drove the baseline, went under the basket, and reached back and out for one of the legendary highlight plays in a legendary career.

Kareem had gone down with a severely sprained ankle while scoring 40 points in Game 5 of the championship

13

series and he wasn't able to play in the possible clincher with the Lakers up 3–2 in Philadelphia. Magic was a twenty-year-old rookie and had played the season at guard, but coach Paul Westhead went with Magic in the middle against Philadelphia strongman Darryl Dawkins and his partner on the back line, Dr. J.

Magic jumped center and went from there to play every position on the floor. He scored 42 points, grabbed 15 rebounds, handed out 7 assists, and made 3 steals in a 123–107 Lakers blowout across the country from their home court.

This was the true birth of the Magic legend at the NBA level. It made him the first rookie ever named MVP of the Finals. Basketball Digest named it the greatest single NBA playoff game, one ahead of Michael's "The Shot" game over Craig Ehlo.

When Magic stepped into the circle for the opening tip, Sixers center Caldwell Jones looked at Magic and said, "Really?" I say, really.

2. WILT: 100 points against the New York Knickerbockers, March 2, 1962

One hundred points. Not 101 or 103. No, a perfect 100. If there's an NBA mark that will never be matched, this is it. And it is the second-greatest single performance in NBA history.

A couple of stupid misperceptions hang over Wilt's accomplishment. One is that he was against a bunch of

14

stiffs and runts, led by center Darrall Imhoff at 6'10". Not quite right. Imhoff was 6'10" and only in the second season of a generally mediocre NBA career, but he would make an NBA All-Star squad. And swarming around Wilt that night were a bunch of 6'5"/6'6" types that included Richie Guerin, who averaged 29.5 points a game that season and was a member of six All-Star teams; Willie Naulls, who was good for 25 points a night and four All-Star appearances; and Johnny Green, a four-time All-Star. Green, Guerin, and Naulls were All-Stars in that 1962 season.

OK, fine, so there were only four teams in the East. But, hey, c'mon, the guys could play. And besides Imhoff, the Knicks had Cleveland Buckner at 6'9" and Phil Jordon at 6'10". In any case, it was a lineup a whole lot more formidable than the cast of characters that Kobe dealt with in Toronto.

The other myth is that Wilt was nothing more than the Shaq of his day, a mauler who simply backed in and muscled balls down in an endless succession of rim-rattling dunks. Not true.

Early Wilt was an athlete not all that far removed from the one who ran track at Overbrook High School in Philadelphia and was so fast at 7'1", 275 pounds that no teammates could run with him in conditioning at Kansas. Far from just a dunker, Wilt had a fallaway shot that was as unblockable as Kareem's skyhook because it started along the left side of the lane and finished somewhere in the mezzanine seats after his release.

15

Wilt's fourth-quarter hoops that night at Hershey included a 20-foot fallaway in the fourth quarter. And he did it on the road in a town that gives you a great cocoa smell when you get within 10 miles of it.

If there's one thing that makes Wilt's night a little harder to put in context, it's the game itself. The NBA averaged 118.7 points per game per team in 1962, so shots were flying up at a rate that dwarfs anything "Showtime" was getting off a quarter-century later. Wilt put up 63 shots of his own that night in Hershey, but he made 36. That's 57 percent, or about what Shaq shoots now with all his hammer throwdowns.

The NBA also allowed mauling. That was something Imhoff did very well, and that every center did against Wilt because of his legendary problems at the free-throw line. Wilt shot 32 free throws that night, making an unheralded-for-him 28.

What also makes the 100 hard to grasp is that it was done by a guy who for the entire 1961–62 season averaged 48.5 minutes in a 48-minute game. Wilt played all but 8 of the Warriors' 3,890 minutes that season, never fouled out, and endured a level of pushing and grabbing that would turn modern NBA games into brawls every night. Celtic Hall of Fame forward Tommy Heinsohn told the Philadelphia Daily News in 1991 that the way Boston devised to "defend" Wilt was simply to put him on the line: "He took the most brutal pounding ever. I hear people today talk about hard fouls. Half the fouls against him were hard fouls." So when he's putting in 100, he's doing it in a street fight.

Ironically, when Chamberlain was traded from the Warriors to the Los Angeles Lakers in 1968 for the final stop in his career, one of the players going from West to East in the deal was Imhoff.

1. MICHAEL: 63 against the Boston Celtics, April 20, 1986

Bob Condor, sports editor at the *Chicago Tribune*, put together a marvelous book titled *Michael Jordan's 50 Greatest Games* that recounts a big block of Michael's head-shakers. It's a great read. But it's a little off at the top. Bob puts Game 6 and Game 5 of the 1998 Utah series one and two and the Boston game number three. Those two against the Jazz were great but they are way, way behind the Boston game, for a couple obvious reasons.

The Utah games were games in a series that was over; the Bulls were just working out the final 4-2 games tally. But in 1986 Michael was convinced that if the Bulls could win that game at the Garden, they would upset the mighty Celtics, who went on to win the NBA championship in six games over the Houston Rockets. He was playing to win, not just for the points.

Need proof? Michael had missed most of the season with a broken foot that had management pressing him to sit out the entire year, possibly for purposes of getting the Bulls a better shot at a higher draft spot. So this game was accomplished by someone who had missed 64 games in the season. Not bad.

The numbers are obvious. Or are they? Michael didn't just score 63; he hit 22 of 41 shots from the floor and 19 of 21 from the line. Do the math: Not one of his points came on a three-point basket. And he pulled down 5 rebounds, passed out 6 assists, picked up 3 steals, and blocked 2 shots.

And somebody is saying that Kobe had 6 boards, 3 steals, 2 assists, and a block himself?

Michael got those rebounds against a Boston back line that included four Hall of Famers: Larry Bird, Kevin McHale, Robert Parish, and Bill Walton. Only Parish (9) had fewer than 12 rebounds, and Charles Oakley was grabbing 14 for the Bulls.

It's notable that so many of the photos from that game are Michael shooting against Bird. Where were the Boston guards? Interesting question, since one of them was Dennis Johnson, who belongs in the NBA Hall of Fame and was all-NBA defensive first- or second-team every year from 1979–87. And Danny Ainge was first team all-NBA Most Annoying. Jordan lost both of them all night.

Ainge had gone out golfing with Michael after the first game, when Michael scored 49. Ainge beat him at golf and Michael advised him, "I'm going to score 50 on you." Years later, Ainge mused, "I should have let him win."

The convenient out is to say that Michael had six quarters in which to pile up his 63. Considering that Boston was running its roster at him, that just makes the 63 all that more remarkable.

The clincher, however, was the reactions of the Celtics. Coach K. C. Jones said that usually in situations like that, he could look down the bench and players are making eye contact with him hoping he'll go to them to stop the hot guy. Not that night. "I'd look down the bench and they were all leaning way back," Jones said.

Bird, who'd dismissed the 49 Michael scored in the first game because the Bulls just kept feeding him, marveled at the 63 because it came in the flow of an incredible game. If the Bulls had been feeding him the way the Warriors fed Wilt or the Lakers tilted toward Kobe, Michael might have scored 200 and done it against one of the great lineups in NBA history.

No, 63 points by a guy who was playing defense, hitting the boards despite a huge height disadvantage, stealing the ball, and dishing off assists....this wasn't the greatest Michael game, or the greatest Bulls game. This was the greatest individual game in NBA history.

THE "FIX" IS IN—OR IT SHOULD BE

3 There's so much that's right with sports, so why not fix these glitches and improve the games?

There's enough wrong with the players and teams of Chicago. There's no need for basic things to be wrong with the games and sports they play. So here are the main things that should be changed to make drastic improvements in the action we watch:

1. ONE FOOT DOWN

The standard rant is that the NFL is about slanting its game to favor the offense. If it really wants to do that without directly favoring either offense or defense, eliminate the requirement that a player catching a ball have both feet down in bounds for the catch to count.

Colleges use the one-and-in rule, and wasn't it colleges, after all, that gave the AFL and then the NFL the two-point conversion? And the forward pass? And the T formation?

So there's no reason to snub the farm system; it has produced more than players.

As long as the player clearly establishes possession, whether on a reception or interception, and gets one foot cleanly down in bounds while in possession of the ball, it's a catch. Seems fair; he only needs one foot out of bounds to be out, so why not make it one foot in bounds to be in?

2. SAVING FACE(OFFS)

Hockey is a fabulously fast game, which is why the on-the-fly subs are necessary. Part of what kills it, besides labor-management problems, is how often that great action is brought to a complete stop for no good reason.

If a team ices the puck, which is a violation, the other team isn't given possession of the puck; there's a faceoff, which the offending team has a definite chance of winning. If the puck flips up into the stands, regardless of whose stick it caromed off of, there's a face-off. A team commits a penalty and the offending player leaves the ice, but why does his team then have a chance to win a face-off when action resumes?

In basketball or soccer, if it's off you, you lose possession. At one point there was a jump ball after every basket. Basketball came up with a better way and hockey desperately needs to.

The solution is to create a drop spot similar to the point on a soccer field where a player inbounds the ball. A player from the team awarded the puck skates to that spot, the

21

official skates right over, drops the puck the way a basketball referee hands the ball to the inbounding team, and the action goes on.

3. ALTERNATE SCHMALTERNATE

The possession arrow is one of the curses of twentieth-century basketball and it somehow has been allowed to infect another century. Time to end the stupidity.

The joke of this invention is that it was set up to eliminate jump balls and speed up the game a little. Since when has the NCAA been seriously concerned about saving a few seconds, at least ones that couldn't be sold?

The way it works now is that a team can mishandle a ball and be tied up, and still get the ball back uncontested, often at a critical juncture of a game. No penalty. No loss of point or possession. The only jump ball is at the start of the game. If you're going to carry NCAA logic all the way through, why not just have the team captains meet at the center circle and do a coin flip football-style?

One of two things should happen in a jump-ball situation:

Either the ball goes to the defense as a reward for compromising the offense's control of the ball, or reward the offense for making such an issue out of a rebound off one of its shots.

Or there is a procedure reflective of what happened, contested control in which neither team had enough to possess the ball. In other words, a jump ball. At least then the team that hustled for a tie-up has a chance at getting the ball it worked so hard to get a piece of. But don't just hand it to anybody.

4. JUST CALL IT!

Even though most of Chicago delighted in MJ being allowed to carry the ball nearly as efficiently as if it were in a sack, that's just wrong. Even though there'd be a short-fall of highlight footage if traveling was enforced, it's time to rein in the game. Even though a tight strike zone favors the hitter and helps offense, it slows the game down to have anything above a batter's waist be called a ball.

Players will always adjust to officiating and it is laugh-able to see the jury-rigging of the rules that has been allowed, even fostered. You know perfectly well there's been a violation and no amount of gee-whizzing by announcers over the resulting basket makes it OK. It's wrong and in its own small, everyday way, it makes a little more of a travesty of the game involved.

Start making the calls that are required by the rules. For one thing, players will adapt; they always have. For another, it reduces the chances of bad officiating, where one umpire has one strike zone and another has a different one, where one referee calls X and the other doesn't. Nothing sets players off more than inconsistency, which frustrates them and ultimately pisses them off. When things aren't called, they expand the range of their actions accordingly.

The answer: Let officials know that they will be graded on the accuracy of their calls, not simply on whether the game went smoothly or not. Call it right and call it the same for everybody and our games get a whole lot better.

SHOWTIME

The Greatest Chicago Sports Movies of All Time

4 Sports movies are typically pretty bad, which is especially stupid considering how obvious some of their operating assumptions are. Most of the viewers will be fans of the sport involved, or will be with someone who is, when they go to see the film. People who don't like baseball, for instance, are hardly going to put down cash to go see a movie about it, right?

So then why are the sports scenes themselves so bad or ridiculous? You go see DeNiro and Snipes in *The Fan* and the climax of the movie happens in a downpour so drowning that the game would have been called long, long before the cops have to gun down Bobby (sorry to give the ending away if you haven't already seen it, but I'm saving you from a stupid sports movie).

When the actors and directors don't grasp that the sports have to be authentic or at the very least very credible, you get an inane movie in which the story and its lines are no more believable than the action between the lines.

But every so often they get it right, with a good story and good characters. Three greatest sports movies of all time happen to have hugely significant Chicago connections. More on that in a minute.

First, we need to cut the list of the "greatest" down to three, which is an incredibly difficult task. Here are the ones that didn't make it:

• *Eight Men Out* is an all-timer because of the actors and action and because it was such a pivotal moment in American sports. But where Eight falls short of my top three is in the fact that it is so intricately about Chicago baseball; it helps to know what a skinflint Charles Comiskey really was and you need to be from Chicago to appreciate that completely.

- *Field of Dreams* gets lots of votes in the list of great sports movies, but it's distracting that Joe Jackson is batting right-handed. Plus, I got so sick of Kevin Costner's wife shrieking instead of speaking that not even James Earl Jones intoning, "We'll always have baseball," can save it.

- Most of *Slap Shot* is so tremendous that it works into the top ten. It's pure farce and is as much fun now as it was twenty-five years ago. I don't care if it's low-brow. It's hilarious, and if you can't love the Hanson brothers, get help. The movie won the Hochi Film Award for Best Foreign Language Film in 1977. That's a Japanese award obviously, and they probably picked it in that category because they couldn't really tell what language the Hansons were speaking. For that matter, it should've walked with the Oscar in this country for the same reason.

- I'll always watch *It Happens Every Spring* when it comes on, which isn't often enough. The professor discovering a chemical substance that makes baseballs repellant from wood is a non-Disney version of Flubber but with a lot more to it. If you're from Chicago you don't like it because he plays for the Cardinals. It's actually a documentary, come to think of it; Greg Maddux has been making baseballs wood-avoidant for years.

- *Any Given Sunday* was complete nonsense, and some of the football choreography and sequencing at the end were particularly inane, not to mention just plain wrong. Frankly, if I want to be really entertained with a football movie, *I'll take The Longest Yard*.

- *Raging Bull* was a tour de force for DeNiro but there is no greater boxing movie, besides *Rocky*, than *The Harder They Fall*. The first time I saw *Harder* was pure chance, when I needed a break from late-night studying and happened to flip it on. What I saw from Humphrey Bogart, Rod Steiger, and that story was a look into the darkest side of humanity as well as the sport of boxing. Bogie giving his check to the gutted South American and then sitting down at his typewriter to tap out the tale was memorable.

- I liked *The Pride of the Yankees* and so did quite a few people, judging from its 11 Academy Award nominations. I just didn't like it as much as others up on the list.

- *Hoosiers* gets votes, particularly when you realize that it's another of those movies where you know the ending and are still glued to the screen anyway. Plus, Milan High School is Indiana's Hebron, which deserves its own place in history.

27

Enough about the ones that didn't make it.

The two most difficult to leave out of the top three were *Rocky* and *Bull Durham*, which would be five and four on my list. If they'd had a Chicago hook, maybe that would put them over the top and ahead of these top three:

3. THE NATURAL

I know I said I need credibility and I know Bump Bailey dies crashing through a fence. I know every light in a stadium is knocked out by a homer into one light standard. But there's enough credibility in knowing that Robert Redford actually can play the game and is good-looking enough to have made it with Kim Basinger.

You have Wilford Brimley's Pops Fisher shaving and he says talking to Richard Farnsworth's Red Blow, about how he should've gotten out and bought a farm. Roy Hobbs is standing in the doorway and agrees that there's nothing like being out on a farm.

"You know," Pops says, "my mama always wanted me to be a farmer."

"My dad wanted me to be a baseball player," Roy says.

"Well, you're better'n any player I ever had," Pops says, turning to him. "And you're the best goddamn hitter I ever saw."

Then: "Suit up."

Oh, come on. Roy Hobbs right then is every one of us.

So many times movies fall way, way short of the books

they were based on. In this case, the movie is far superior to Bernard Malamud's novel, which depressed and bored me. But you put a fun script with that cast and you have something epic: Redford, Brimley, Basinger, Farnsworth, Glenn Close, Darren McGavin, Joe Don Baker, Robert Duvall. It works.

When Pops tells Roy, "You don't start playing baseball at your age, fella, you retire," deep down inside, don't we all kinda know we could do it? Roy Hobbs is me, and you.

The movie was nominated for four Academy Awards (it didn't win any), including Close for Best Supporting Actress and Randy Newman for Best Original Score

It's one of those movies, like *Apollo 13*, where you know how it's going to end and you still have to watch it and lean a little forward in your seat, like the kids in the ballpark, when Roy Hobbs stands in against the big John Rhoades, that big Nebraska farmboy with a blinding fastball.

You know Roy isn't going to whiff against some big Nebraska farmboy (are there any little Nebraska farmboys?). He knocks out all the lights with a shot to one standard (never mind that back then a playoff game would have been played in the daytime; so what, gimme the dream anytime).

The Chicago connection? Are you kidding? Where do you think the Knights are playing when Roy gets down 0-2 in the count, is flailing and sinking into the Memo Paris quicksand, and Iris stands up? It's Chicago. Why did she stand up?

29

"Because I didn't want to see you fail." Do you love that woman or what? OK, so she was a little dicey in *Fatal Attraction* but I gotta think that was because she was a little down not knowing what'd become of Roy all those years.

And where do Roy and Iris get together for lemonade? At a great little place under the El tracks.

Of course, one minor gaffe here also involves Chicago. When Iris stands up and Roy jacks one through the clock in centerfield, it's the deciding blow of the game the stands empty and the cameramen are firing away.

Except that Roy was a Knight. For that blast to have ended the game, he'd have had to have been a Cub.

No matter. Down inside, we're all Roy Hobbs in our dreams.

2. NORTH DALLAS FORTY

Easily the best football movie ever made, in part because it was from a book written by a football player, Pete Gent, who was a tight end for the Dallas Cowboys. In the book "Dallas" becomes "North Dallas" and players like Don Meredith become Seth Maxwell—still a quarterback and still singing "Turn out the lights, the party's over" just like Dandy did in real life and on Monday Night Football.

What makes the movie so great is that it is a time capsule, as well as a study of a sport, unlike any other film offers of any other sport. To watch it now is to travel back in time, into the late '60s and early '70s and into a mystical team as Gent lays its guts open for all to see. By the way, the book ends a whole lot differently than the movie. Nick Nolte's Phil Elliott goes through his nightmare with Conrad Hunter and the front office, but in the movie at least he leaves on his terms, more or less; the book ends with....nope, you gotta read this one. It's worth it.

The movie is notable also because it was directed by a Canadian, Ted Kotcheff, not a Yank who grew up with or in football. He did a magnificent job of capturing pretty much everything, except for fans; the seats at the final championship game didn't have people in them. Oops. The Dallas Cowboys become the North Dallas Bulls and the other teams are changed but that's not important; Gent titled the book *North Dallas Forty* because that's where the Cowboys were headquartered.

And the Chicago connection? It's a huge one. In Gent's final game in the novel, when Delma Huddle fumbles rather than having his face mutilated as in the movie, North Dallas is playing, not the New York Giants of the book, but Chicago. All of the sordid football world plays out there and all in a game we join in the final two minutes. The Bo Svenson and John Matuszak characters cripple defensive tackle Alcie Weeks; Huddle has his face destroyed after he pulls up lame when the xylocaine wears off in his hamstring; Elliott makes the catch to apparently win the game, and then the snap for the tying PAT is fumbled and North Dallas loses.

To Chicago.

1. A LEAGUE OF THEIR OWN

This isn't the best Chicago movie. It isn't the best baseball movie. It is, pure and simple, the best sports movie of any kind ever put to film. Period.

If you don't need a tissue when the telegram comes for Betty Spaghetti; if you don't pretend you've got something in your eye when Madonna sings "This Used to Be My Playground" at the end of the movie; if you are dry-eyed all the way through the museum scene, you need to have yourself checked for feelings and have some installed. When Marla's dad takes Ernie Capadino aside and pleads for him to give his daughter—who "isn't pretty like them other girls"—a chance, and when he puts Marla on the train, with the American flag reflected waving in the window of the train as Marla waves.... hold on, I need a Kleenex.

This is a movie every young kid should see, and they oughta watch it with their folks. I made a Saturday ice cream party out of having my daughter's softball team watch the movie and its showing of young women running, diving, hitting the dirt, colliding, trying, and not being afraid to let it all go. And it just doesn't matter that the baseball itself wasn't superb.

Look at the cast of the movie, which some of the major female performers harangued their agents to get them in: Geena Davis, Madonna ("All the Way Mae"), Rosie O'Donnell. You have Penny Marshall directing it. Tom

Hanks as Jimmy Dugan. David Strathairn. Jon Lovitz. Bill Pullman. Garry Marshall.

This is the movie that gave us "There's no crying in baseball," which has become part of our lexicon, with substitutions for baseball accepted. The Rockford Peaches. The Kenosha Comets. The Racine Belles. The South Bend Blue Sox. Later they added more teams because the whole thing in real life was successful.

And the Chicago connection? Remember the tryouts, where Davis and Lori Petty walk out of the tunnel in their Lukash Dairy uniforms? In the movie it was Harvey Field. In life it was none other than Wrigley Field. Lovitz had one of the great lines of the film as they're walking out: "Hey, cowgirls, see the grass? Don't eat it."

But the connection is a lot bigger than that. The All-American Girls Professional Baseball Association (AAGP-BL) wasn't started by the owner of Harvey Candy Bars ("Yeah, we feed 'em to the cows; it keeps 'em regular"). It was started by P. K. Wrigley, who was afraid baseball would be closed down as the players went off to WWII.

Oh, and you think it's just a movie? Take this from the actual AAGPBL website: "We do not stop playing because we grow old, but we grow old because we stop playing."

GIVE 'EM A BREAK

They Don't Deserve All That Criticism

5 Chicago has had its allotments of villains, good guys, underachievers, jerks, and athletes of every stripe. And it also has had a number of performers who were the objects of public and media scorn or dislike.

But not all of those deserved the raps they took. Three in particular deserve a break:

3. ALONZO SPELLMAN, BEARS

'Zo's biggest fault was looking the way he did. Because he was one of the all-time natural physical specimens, Spellman was expected to play like the Superman he looked like. And when he didn't, the rant against him became that he wasn't giving all his effort, wasn't smart enough, wasn't whatever.

But his Bears career pretty much matched his Ohio State career in terms of production, so if there was disappointment in his play, he was really just playing the way he always did.

The source of real public rage with him came in 1996, however, and was completely the fault of others. He and agent Leigh Steinberg sought a contract extension worth $2 million a year from the Bears. The Bears refused to go to that figure and instead let him test free agency, but with a transition-player tag attached. That meant the Bears had the right to match any offer to him.

Almost the minute free agency started, the Jacksonville Jaguars signed him to an offer sheet worth not $2 million a season, but $3 million. The Bears then proceeded to match the offer, one of the more head-shaking moves by the team: they didn't think he was worth $2 million but were now going to pay him $3 million?

But the one who really paid was Spellman, who was now blasted as being overpaid despite never seeking the kind of money that was foisted on him. What was he supposed to do, give it back?

Spellman's legacy unfortunately would be his problems with bipolar disorder beginning in 1997. He became the object of ridicule, not sympathy. It was patently unfair to an athlete who was rarely anything but pleasant to deal with in my own years covering the team, which included being around Spellman from draft to departure.

2. FRANK THOMAS, WHITE SOX

The Big Hurt was too often dubbed the Big Blurt for some of his ill-thought comments on top of unpopular episodes ranging from leaving an All-Star game early, to appearing petulant and moody, to having some blowups with popular teammates like Paul Konerko and Robin Ventura. He could be unresponsive at times with fans, charming and accomodating at others.

He had bumps in his personal and professional life and eventually moved to Las Vegas to be away from the constant sniping that he experienced in Chicago. Thomas didn't have a good relationship with Ozzie Guillen, and when Guillen became Sox manager, Thomas's time in Chicago was heading for a close.

The way it ended, with the bitterness coming out toward the Sox and how they treated him after 15 years in Chicago, was regrettable.

But a number of other scribes I consulted and I all found Thomas to be pretty consistently a decent guy. He enjoyed the history of the game and talking about his possible place in all that. When he didn't feel like talking, he told you so. He was a proud player and took perceived slights harshly at times.

Thomas was the A.L. MVP in 1993 and 1994. He led the league in batting in 1997. And yet he was annually dealing with a public that seemed to never be satisfied with whatever he did. The best example: while he was establishing himself as possibly one of the greatest right-handed hitters in baseball history, with one of the greatest batting eyes since Ted Williams, some critics began to pick at him for not hitting more home runs. Williams wasn't well liked by the media but he never was tagged with that kind of inane criticism.

As Wilt Chamberlain once said, "No one likes or roots for Goliath." Thomas was Goliath and paid for it. Unfairly.

1. DAVE WANNSTEDT, BEARS COACH

No one ever deserved less of the vilification that he received than the Wanndog. Only Halas and Ditka won more games as Bears head coach. But Wannstedt will always be the brunt of jokes, caricatures, and ridicule despite getting the Bears to the playoffs and winning a round in only his second season.

If you're the "Man Who Replaced Ditka," and McCaskey's Man, you simply make the list of targets in Chicago—that's all there is to it. At one point in the 1996 season Wannstedt was concerned at the venom being directed at the team. He told me he understood that much of the fans' rage was directed at his boss, but McCaskey was nowhere to be seen on game days, meaning his team took the verbal abuse for him.

The irony is that Wannstedt was the hot coaching hire in 1993. The New York Giants and George Young wanted him and made him a serious offer. He had that Dallas Cowboys pixie dust dripping off him from the 'Boys' ravaging of the

Buffalo Bills and came in with the personnel authority that McCaskey had taken away from Bill Tobin, one of the men pivotal in the building of the 1980s Bears.

When Wannstedt made his immortal "All the pieces are in place" comment to the Tribune's Don Pierson, he was forever doomed to Chicago lore. The phrase has endured long after his departure in 1999.

The reality of Wannie is that he was above .500 in both his second and third seasons, something Ditka didn't manage until his third season. He won a playoff game on the road and then was given a contract extension that McCaskey would rue as the team was wracked with injuries like Erik Kramer's broken neck in 1996 and Curtis Conway's shoulder in 1997. The Bears spiraled downward with consecutive 4-12's in 1997–98 before Wannie headed down to Miami for a coaching reunion with Jimmy Johnson. That extension, a few short years later, would play into the debacle of Dave McGinnis that forever altered the course of the franchise.

The poor guy even achieved lofty villain status in Miami, where by 2002 there was a firedavewannstedt.com website.

Wannstedt did struggle as a game coach. He struggled even more as a talent evaluator. And he was put in the worst possible spot: precisely the wrong man and precisely the wrong spot at precisely the wrong time. Johnson was the personnel maven, not Wannie, but McCaskey still took personnel power away from Tobin and gave it to Wannstedt.

Worse, he was making his debut as the man in charge of personnel in 1993—the dawn of free agency, meaning it wasn't going to be enough just to scout college guys. And the Bears at the time had the second-smallest scouting department in the NFL, behind only the woeful Bengals. Wannstedt was in way, way over his head with a boss who was so badly overmatched himself. The marvel may have been not that he did as poorly as he did, but that he did as well as he did.

Wannstedt didn't particularly like defensive end Trace Armstrong so he traded Armstrong to Miami for draft choices that turned into Todd Sauerbrun and Evan Pilgrim, both busts in Chicago. Armstrong ultimately made a Pro Bowl. Wannstedt cut Super Bowl kicker Kevin Butler to go with Carlos Huerta; fortunately he fixed that with Jeff Jaeger several games into '96. The franchise paid heavily for Bryan Cox, who blew up in Chicago, and there was the matter of the Rick Mirer trade, giving up a No. 1 draft pick for a bust of a quarterback.

So many busts, so little time. Not a bad guy, just a bad coach, and one that will always draw eye-rolls and epithets in a Bears town. But he doesn't deserve all the venom.

THE STUPIDEST WORD IN SPORTS

6 It's always good for a chuckle when some sports performer is labeled an "overachiever." An overachiever. What in the name of whatever is that? And how can you "overachieve?"

You know who the overachievers are. They're short guys, slow guys, scrappy guys, and they're usually always guys because apparently women can't overachieve, or nobody pays enough attention to know it when it supposedly happens. Overachievers are of course always plucky, gutty, and occasionally lucky, but naturally that's just because the luck is the result of all their overachiever hard work.

And they're pretty much always white guys, which is a big point here. More on that in a minute.

Here are traditional Chicago "overachievers":

• Tom Waddle, Bears wide receiver—undrafted, went on to a very nice NFL career

- Steve Larmer, Blackhawks forward—undersized, plucky, heck of a scorer
- Jay Hilgenberg, Bears center—not real fast, not real big, definitely plucky
- Nellie Fox, Sox second baseman—small, gritty, scrappy, plucky

The first step toward becoming an overachiever is to be dismissed or written off. If people think you're really talented, you'll never be an overachiever because people will just figure you're being what you were supposed to be anyway.

And that's the key here. One of the reasons you're an "overachiever" is because some so-called experts decided how good you should be and when you went beyond that, you became an embarrassment. People were wrong in the evaluation, whether because of a draft round or size or whatever, and so rather than say they were completely off in their expert evaluation, you become an "overachiever."

Rare is the NFL scout who would like to be pressed too hard on why it was that they passed on Hilgy, annual Pro Bowl player but undrafted out of Iowa. Couldn't be a personnel screw-up; must be an overachiever.

But as Tom Waddle once said to me, you achieve what you achieve, period. Waddle or any other overachiever didn't do anything that wasn't within their abilities to do in the first place. The one huge exception to me is Sosa; he was a certain level of good and then...oh, you know.

So really there aren't overachievers, only underachievers.

Everybody has a certain amount of talent and if one person squeezes the last drop out of the tube, that's just being the best they could. If someone with more talent doesn't work as hard, maybe they have the same level of success, but aren't they really underachieving?

If you really have to have "overachievers," try these:

1. MICHAEL

Nobody should be that good. He developed himself a jump shot. He committed to being the best defensive player he could be. As his career went along, he got himself to a professional trainer and with that guy, Tim Grover, Michael made over his body, made it as strong as it was talented. Think he was all just talent? Wrong.

2. WALTER

Same as Michael. The guy was 5'10", 205 pounds, and made himself the most dominant running back in the game while he played it. He had the "want-to" to be a great blocker (just ask Jim McMahon) and to be a great receiver. The reason he never missed a game in his career (the one he sat out wasn't his choice) wasn't because he didn't get hit hard enough to sideline; it was because he put himself through hell on his hill in Barrington and became the toughest he could possibly be. If that isn't "over" achieving…

3. GREG MADDUX

Who knew? Certainly not the Tribune Co. when it let one of the greatest pitchers of any era leave for the Atlanta Braves. Didn't have great power pitches. Didn't have freeze-'em breaking stuff. All he had was game. He just learned how to play the game, respected it, and as a result reached the pinnacle of his profession. Overachiever? Or just a guy who did it right every single day?

4. BRIAN URLACHER

The guy is a freak: 260 pounds, runs like a scared deer, athletic enough to be a safety. Just pure ability? Think again. He adopted a different training regimen to improve his strength, and trained at high altitude to improve his conditioning. He was X-level good and took himself to the Y- and Z-levels of good by working like Michael and Walter did.

5. DICK BUTKUS

Butkus was also a freak. He was a center at Illinois besides a middle linebacker. He worked himself up into a self-generated rage at an opponent and it made him better. Actually, that's wrong; it made him what he was: the best.

No, there are no actual overachievers. Only true achievers. But there definitely are underachievers, ones who had something, some talent plus opportunity, and did exactly zero with it.

My five great Chicago underachievers:

43

1. CADE MCNOWN

He wasn't as talented as his 12th-overall draft slot suggested, but then he didn't study, didn't put in the practice time to know his receivers, and just coasted through one of the worst and mercifully short Bears careers ever.

2. KERRY WOOD

The injuries were one thing. Sticking to pitching mechanics accounted for some of those and that was Wood's doing. So was his flipping back and forth between being a pitcher and a thrower, which was just plain stubborn and dumb, pitching with his arm instead of his head. That 20-K game may have been the worst thing that could've happened to him as a young guy.

3. CURTIS ENIS

Everybody wanted Enis coming into the '98 draft. And before he suffered what turned out to be a career-turning knee injury, he was up to averaging 4 yards a carry. But his attitude about blocking and unwillingness to work at the whole of the game set back his development and never made up for what he lost in his holdout.

4. LA MARR HOYT

He was standing at the precipice of greatness, a Cy Young Award with a brilliant White Sox team coming off the '83 divisional win, and what did he do? Nada. A little dope, a little dopey, and he becomes one of the great whatever-happened-to's in Chicago sports history.

5. QUENTIN DAILEY

Dailey was so talented that the Bulls spent a first-round draft choice on one of the great character questions ever in Chicago sports. He wasted it all, and managed to be a jerk in the process. To call him a "tool" is to insult hammers.

ON THE RUN
Gale or Walter?

7 Gale or Walter: For one down? One game? One year? For a career?

Obviously Gale Sayers and Walter Payton are guys you win because of, not simply win with. Walter held 16 NFL records when he retired and still holds 27 Bears records. Gale went to 5 Pro Bowls and was the MVP in three of them.

Walter started 184 NFL games and had 100 rushing yards in 77 of them. Gale's career was only 68 games but in 20 of those he rushed for 100 yards, not to mention the return yardage or receiving yards for either of them.

But it's Draft Day for your Fantasy Football League and you have to choose one as the absolute best the Bears have ever put in a uniform.

GALE

It's too easy, and wrong, to dismiss Gale Sayers as just a great open-field runner; when Gale had the ball the whole field was open. It didn't matter where he was. The 6 touchdowns against the San Francisco 49ers that December 12 were staggering enough, but realize that one of them was on an 85-yard punt return, another was an 80-yard screen pass, plus runs of 21 yards, 50 yards, 7 yards, and 1 yard. Down by the goal line, Barry Sanders came out. Not Gale.

Not a bad day, and as Y. A. Tittle, then a 49er assistant coach said, "I just wonder how many that Sayers would have scored if we hadn't set our defense to stop him." If George Halas hadn't pulled him in the 61-20 laugher, Sayers figured maybe eight. And remember how muddy that day was? And that must have helped Sayers? Forget it. He didn't like playing in mud.

Try to grasp this: rookie year, 14-game season, 22 touchdowns, NFL record. Average of 5.2 yards per carry, 867 rushing yards, 660 yards on 21 kickoff returns, 507 yards on 27 pass catches. The guy had 2,440 total yards in 14 games.

Then he runs for 197 yards the next year against the Minnesota Vikings. That's right, the Vikings. Carl Eller, Jim Marshall, Matt Blair, Paul Krause. Those guys. That record lasted all of two years when he put 205 on the Packers—the Super Bowl II-winning Packers.

And tough? He takes a screen pass 80 yards for six against the Rams his rookie year. He gets drilled early in the play by Rosey Grier—yes, that Rosey Grier, the Fearsome Foursome one, 290 pounds, Hall of Fame—who said, "I hit him so hard I thought my shoulder must have busted him in two. I heard a roar from the crowd and figured he had fumbled. Then there he was, 15 yards downfield, heading for the end zone."

Try this for putting Gale in perspective: In 1968 he has 856 rushing yards, is averaging 6.2 yards per carry, through eight games (1,463 combined yards), when he takes that horrible hit by Kermit Alexander (the 49ers, ironically). Then he comes back in 1969, less than a year after surgery when there weren't scopes and he's in a cast for eight weeks—and runs for 1,032 yards, in 14 games. He doesn't even tape the knee, either.

Oh, what's the big deal about 1,032? Just that he was the only guy to gain 1,000 that season and he did it for a 1-13 team. That's all.

It all really ended the next year, when Gale hurt the other knee in the third game and missed that season, then carried 13 times in 1971 before he just had to say no more.

Like Butkus, who was the draft choice before him in '65, the knees did what no one ever really could: stop him.

WALTER

Walter's only companion at the top of Backfield Olympus is Jim Brown, who was Walter's equal with the ball, was a linebacker's nightmare swinging out of the backfield to take a Frank Ryan pass in the flat, and was far underrated as a blocker. Just ask Sam Huff sometime.

But the measure of Walter's greatness as a runner is that he did so much of his damage behind offensive linemen eminently forgettable outside of Chicago. Brown had Gene Hickerson, Dick Schafrath, John Wooten, and others out in front of him, plus Gary Collins out wide anytime the defense sold out to stop Brown. Early Walter had Dennis Lick, Revie Sorey, Noah Jackson, Dan Neal, Ted Albrecht, and such in front of him. Decent players, but nowhere what Brown had for getting people out of his way. And nowhere what he would have late in his career with Jimbo Covert, Mark Bortz, Jay Hilgenberg, Tom Thayer, and Keith Van Horne, who added a couple years and a couple thousand yards to his career.

Twelve years after his retirement, Walter still held or shared eight NFL rushing records. When Walter set the NFL record for yards in a single game, it was against the Minnesota Vikings in a contest that ended 10-9 Bears. Walter got 275 yards on November 20, 1977, and afterwards Minnesota cornerback Bobby Bryant spoke for a battered band of Vikings and hundreds of tacklers in the years to follow: "It's similar to trying to rope a calf," Bryant explained. "It's hard enough to get your hands on him, and once you do, you wonder if you should have."

If you got your hands on him it meant you had fought your way through one of the meanest forearms or straight-arms ever to grace a gridiron. Walter was beyond "old school," he was graduate school, with a linebacker's mind-set and an assassin's heart.

Legendary coach and analyst John Madden once counted 18 Payton tackles after interceptions in a season, which also speaks to the level of passing game Walter had diverting attention from him.

Defensive end Clyde Simmons, one of the great pass rushers in NFL history, faced Payton in 1986, Simmons's second season and Walter's next-to-last. Simmons's first NFL tackle was memorable: Walter Payton. Years later the tackle came up in conversation.

"Did you hit me hard?" Payton asked.

"No," Simmons said. "I was just happy to hold on."

So which one is the player you want in your backfield for one play, one game, one season, and one career?

(Hint: For some help here I went to Doug Buffone, the great Bears linebacker who came to the Bears the year after Gale was drafted and retired after four years with Walter. I figured, who knows these two guys better than Dougie?)

49

ONE PLAY

My first thought was that for a single down you had to take Walter; he was tough enough to dive for a yard, versatile enough to swing out of the backfield for a pass, or even take a handoff and throw the ball. That's a lot to defend against for one play.

But Doug shook his head and said it had to be Gale. Why? Because on every snap Gale had the chance to turn a play into a touchdown. The quick-strike capability was his decision point and there haven't been many players with the kind of long-lance threat in the history of the game.

The fact is, the better choice for a first-down conversion is probably Walter. The TD threat is Gale. For one single play…Gale.

ONE GAME

If the game is in the mud, no question: Gale. But if it is a 60-minute event under normal circumstances, Walter gets the edge. How many times did he simply take a Bears team on his back and refuse to let it lose? Bears-Packers II in the '85 season was the epitome of smash-mouth, and it was Walter who battered the Pack into submission.

Walter is the better chance of protecting my quarterback if I need to throw and he's a better grinder. So for a single game…Walter.

ONE SEASON

Year after year after year, Walter piled up seasons of more than 1,200 yards on the ground. In 1977 he had 1,852 rushing yards, 14 TDs, plus 269 receiving yards—in a 14-game season.

But has there ever been a rookie season like Gale's in 1965? He had 2,272 total yards and 22 TDs, including those 6 against the 49ers. He averaged 5.0 yards for his career, including 6.2 in 1968 when his career came to its virtual end.

One unfortunate thing is that he didn't get to play longer under Jim Dooley, one of the underappreciated offensive minds in Bears coaching history. Put him behind the same level of offensive line Walter had once Keith Van Horne and Jim Covert started staffing the tackles, and for one single season...Gale

ONE CAREER

Walter. No one worked harder to overcome an injury than Gale did after that knee nightmare in '68, but no one worked harder to become the consummate football player than Walter. The combination of runner, blocker, receiver, and even passer, with the record of durability, makes Walter the choice. You build franchises around players like that.

If you can find them. And the Bears did. Twice.

CUBS-CARDINALS RIVALRY
Who Cares?

8 The Cubs and St. Louis Cardinals are in the same National League Division and they are talked about as one of sports' greatest rivalries. This is, presumably, a joke.

The teams barely fit any of the criteria for a rivalry, at least rarely in the last 70 years or so, not since the two teams were both very good in the 1930s. But the two cities are nearly 300 miles apart and rarely play games that matter other than to fans and media who inexplicably seem to want to keep this "rivalry" thing going for no apparent reason other than to make the games seem important.

Cardinals fans come to Wrigley Field because it's an excuse to come to a big city. Cubs fans go to Busch Stadium because they're Cub fans...they'll go anywhere.

Ali-Frazier was a rivalry. Red Sox-Yankees is a rivalry. Bears-Packers is a rivalry. Giants-Dodgers was and is a rivalry. Graziano-Zale was a rivalry.

Cubs-Cardinals is not a rivalry. Sosa-McGwire was not and certainly is not a rivalry. When those two engaged the country with their home run duel in 1998, it was a love fest, thanks to Sammy. They didn't dislike each other. It in fact was more a fun home run derby of seeing who could top whom, no "rivalry" with any edge or rancor to it whatsoever.

Managers Dusty Baker and Tony LaRussa don't particularly like each other. This is not a Cubs-Cardinals thing; it's simply two massive egos being placed in repeated proximity (the teams play each other 19 times a season). Eventually something is going to happen. Besides, they started feuding when Baker was managing the Giants, not when he got to Chicago.

Ryne Sandberg hitting game-tying and game-winning home runs off Bruce Sutter on June 23, 1984, does not a rivalry make. That was simply Sandberg winning the National League MVP award in two swings of the bat.

The Cardinals have won more World Series than any team other than the Yankees. The Cubs' biggest World Series discussion point is whether or not there really is a curse. This is a neighborhood disagreement.

Cubs-Cards doesn't qualify on the grounds of proximity. St. Louis is considerably farther from Chicago than, for instance, Green Bay, the latter being a day trip for the so-inclined.

Constant competitiveness by itself isn't necessarily a requirement for a rivalry. The Bears and Packers have rarely been good at the same time, but the roots of that "relationship" are deep in the Halas-Lambeau-Lombardi-Ditka-Gregg soil. Besides, those two teams play each other twice a year in a 16-game schedule, so every game takes on enormous significance simply because each is the mathematical equivalent of a 10-game series in baseball's 162-game schedule.

When Chicagoan Steve Goodman wrote his classic ballad "A Dying Cub Fan's Last Request," the late songwriter mentioned Jack Brickhouse, and some beers—not the Cardinals.

The Lou Brock-Ernie Broglio trade does not fuel a rivalry, just the questions about someone's scouting capabilities.

If simply having an interstate running between two cities (I-55) is the basis for a rivalry, imagine how much Laramie and Cheyenne, Wyoming, must hate each other.

Indiana-Purdue is a rivalry. Michigan-Ohio State is a rivalry. Notre Dame-USC is a rivalry.

Cubs-Cardinals is not.

SAY IT IS SO, JOE

The Black Sox, Including Charlie Comiskey: In or Out?

9 Things are not always what they seem in life, and certainly they aren't in baseball. Nowhere is that more so than with the 1919 White Sox, or, as history has dubbed them, the Black Sox.

Eight men were banned from the game for involvement in fixing the outcome of the World Series, even though their trials resulted in no guilty verdicts. But there is so, so much more to this situation than the usual should-Joe-Jackson-and-Buck-Weaver-be-banned debate. Either Joe Jackson goes into the Hall of Fame or somebody in particular should now be booted out. More on that in a moment.

To begin with, they weren't called the "Black Sox" because of the stain from this scandal. They were called Black Sox because that's what color their socks and everything else were after owner Charles Comiskey cut out their laundry money on the road. The nickname was in place before the fix was.

55

The long-time debate is usually whether or not Jackson and Weaver should have been banned after 1920 by Commissioner Judge Kenesaw Mountain Landis. Weaver knew about the fix but refused to join the conspirators and had a very good Series against the Cincinnati Reds. His "crime" was knowing and not reporting it. Weaver fought for years to have his name cleared, with the logic that what he did was to not rat out the rats. He didn't give up his teammates.

I can go along with that to a point. But by not putting the word out, even quietly, Weaver was screwing Eddie Collins and his teammates who weren't part of the scam. He, and Jackson, cheated their "clean" teammates out of a chance to win the World Series. But Weaver shouldn't have been banned for that. He kept his mouth shut, tried to over-play the cheaters, and did what probably most of us would have done. Like it or not, there are social codes and customs and Weaver was abiding by one.

The same goes for Jackson, who accepted the money but then went to Comiskey and wanted to be benched. Comiskey refused not once, but twice. When Jackson went the second time, he took the $5,000 and wanted to give it to Comiskey. The story is that Harry Grabiner, Comiskey's secretary, wouldn't let him in to talk to Comiskey.

The only conclusion: Comiskey knew! He acknowledged on the stand in the "Eight Men Out" trial that he'd heard rumors of a fix. But he didn't offer a reward for information until after the Series, and when people did come forward, Comiskey stiffed them on any reward money. And why would a legendary skinflint, who cut meal and laundry money and salaries, suddenly pony up the fees for some of the most expensive defense lawyers available for the players? And yet he was allowed to be voted into the Hall of Fame in 1939, despite being a disgrace to the game and in fact being a more reprehensible figure in this episode than two of the victims who at least tried to do the right thing on the field (Jackson hit .375 in the Series and did not make a single error; neither did Weaver).

Comiskey was one of the founders of the American League. He'd been a player-manager and was the first first-baseman to play off the bag when no one was on base. He owned the Sox from 1900–31.

That apparently is good enough to get you not only into the Hall of Fame but also absolved from the exact "crime" that led to two of your players being banned. Why? Because money matters and Landis was not about to penalize one of what was an owners' cabal.

Back to Jackson and Weaver: if you are going to ban them for knowing, then baseball needs to ban even current players who knew a teammate was doing something outside the laws of the game. If steroids are banned, and you see a teammate juicing and you don't bring it up, you're out, at least based on the precedent of Jackson and Weaver. Somebody doing some marijuana in the hotel room before a game, maybe a little coke? If you don't report him, join Jackson and Weaver over in the Waiting Room.

Weaver is not a Hall of Fame candidate. He was a decent player, not plaque-worthy. But if the doors of the Hall are closed to Jackson, then they should at least swing outward when Comiskey, whose dealings with players contributed to the scandal in the first place and then did nothing despite knowing, is thrown out on his can.

SOCCER AND CHICAGO? NEVER

10 There's no point in endlessly debating whether or not soccer is boring (it is) or whether it is a game of skill (it isn't). What is worth a hard look is whether or not the game will ever take in Chicago.

The answer: not a chance.

The best chance the game has is in loosened U.S. immigration policies that'll allow more folks from soccer lands to become Americans, in particular Chicagoans. Because without that, the soccer seed falls on barren ground the way it always has.

It's not that soccer doesn't arouse passion. Type "I Hate Soccer" into your Google and you'll find out. All you need to know is that soccer has been around since the nineteenth century in Chicago and it still draws less than the Blackhawks. The average attendance for the Chicago Fire in the Major League Soccer (MLS) was 17,887 when the team was formed in 1998. Its average attendance for the 2005 regular season was 17,238. This is not growth.

This is for a team that won the MLS Cup and U.S. Open Cup in 1998, 2000, and 2003. And this is after Chicago was a venue for the Women's World Cup in 1999, when games did draw 65,000. But that is like measuring White Sox fan appeal by World Series attendance. The initial MLS Chicago franchise was withdrawn in 1994 for lack of investors even though the U.S. National Team had played three games here in 1992–93.

Soccer is popular with kids because their parents make them play it. U.S. kids don't grab a soccer ball and head out to the park to get into a sandlot game; for that matter, they don't pick up a mitt and a bat and go to a ball field either.

Part of the problem in Chicago is that people are used to following and appreciating sports with skill sets other than running and kicking a ball.

In soccer, anything more than incidental contact between players is a penalty. This is not Chicago, or even America. Americans love a good collision.

One amusing point about soccer is the arrogant attitude that Americans are somehow mental defectives for not understanding and appreciating the sport. Fans of NASCAR don't denigrate soccer types because they don't understand racing, but race fans not being big on soccer brands them as incompetents. Soccer fans in Europe are goons and hooligans but soccer non-fans in Chicago are dullards apparently.

As for soccer being a world game, soccer fans boo each other's national anthems. And it doesn't wash to say that's just being competitive. No, that's just being classless. NASCAR fans wouldn't do it.

Just give soccer some time? How about a century? Soccer was organized in Chicago back in 1899 with a lot of immigrant population driving the game. It still never caught baseball, which was popular enough for the city to have two professional teams within the city limits by that time.

It isn't that soccer is a bad game. It's just uninteresting. It has mass appeal around the world precisely because it doesn't require much to get. Marvel at the dribbling and footwork of David Beckham? Allen Iverson does more with a ball and has to shoot into a net a fraction of the size of Beckham's. The intricate positioning, breaks, and passes? Get a Gretzky tape sometime.

Enough people do follow it in Chicago and everywhere else that there isn't any real question about it being a significant sport. Just not ever in Chicago.

And yes, I know it's really called "football," not soccer. By any other name, it still doesn't make it in Chicago.

DREAMIN' BULLS

The Five Best Bulls Ever

The current local cagers have only been around since 1966 but they followed in the stumbling footsteps of the Chicago Packers/Zephyrs, who lasted all of two miserable seasons and headed off to Baltimore to become the Bullets/Wizards. Any team with "Packers" in its roots had no place in Chicago anyway.

Part of the deal here is to standardize rules and other elements, like conditioning, strength work, and officiating. Some played in physical times, others when the game had been changed to favor offense, one-on-one basketball. Maybe John Mengelt rewrites the Bulls record books if he's playing in Jordan's game. Hey, it could happen.

Almost every Bulls team has had at least one stand-out player. But if I'm picking my five to get and hold the play-ground court, these are my Fab Five:

11 GUARD: MICHAEL JORDAN

What about: The gambling stuff? The clearly bogus claim that he was leaving the game to spend more time with his family? The arrogance? The turning on the Bulls?

Yeah but: Forget about it. MJ, like him or not, Wizard or not, phony or not, is the greatest single player in the history of the game, or at least co-title-holder with a young Wilt. A soaring highlight film when he came to the Bulls from North Carolina, he made himself from a really, really good player into a great one. He built himself a jump shot the same way that Tiger Woods took an already exquisite game, broke it down, reshaped it and refined it, and came back even better than the original.

Jordan built himself a defensive game that was, along with Scottie Pippen's, as much a part of the Bulls' core as any offensive force they were. Everybody in the NBA can score. Not everybody is willing or good enough to stop somebody from doing it. Every single night. Every single possession.

Did the NBA look the other way at the carries and extra steps? Absolutely. The Doctor got the same preferential treatment. So did George Gervin. So what? Two of his most epic game winners—the jumper over poor Craig Ehlo, and that final shot in '98, hand in finish position—were outside shots, not high-wire acts.

12 GUARD: JERRY SLOAN

What about: Norm Van Lier? The Storm was the hood ornament, perhaps the face, of the best Bulls team never to win anything. He was a high school football player who took the toughness to the court, took no crap, and just played, baby.

It's hard not to put Stormin' Norman on the team. He came from Cincinnati in the 1972 season and immediately made the Bulls better. He was an All-Star three times, first- or second-team All-NBA defensive team from 1971–78, led the NBA in steals in 1974, and was top five in assists from 1971–78. And he was a winner.

Trouble is, there are only a couple slots on this Dream Team and a few too many applicants.

What about: Reggie Theus? He averaged more points per game than Pippen without the benefit of anyone else commanding more than token defensive attention, was as big and as fast, and dammit, was better looking than just about any other Bull.

Yeah but: Sloan was a leader, a near-champion as both player and coach, a player whose toughness overshadowed the fact that he was a tremendous pure basketball player. He has an NBA championship ring if Dick Motta is smart enough not to overplay his veterans against Al Attles and the San Francisco Warriors in '75 in both Game 6 and Game 7.

Sloan's number 4 was the first number the Bulls retired. The Bulls got him in the expansion draft and he averaged

17.4 points and 9.1 rebounds per game in 1966–67. He was picked to only two All-Star teams but was voted to the All-NBA defensive first-team four times, second-team twice. Not bad in the era of Walt Frazier, Jerry West, and Stormin' Norman.

Injuries took him down for 29 games in 1969–70 but he averaged 18.3 and 8.8 in 1970–71 when the Bulls started a run of four straight 50-win seasons.

He was done in by a knee injury that required surgery and he played in barely more games (22) than times he had his knee drained (20). He's fourth all-time in Bulls points and rebounds, and ninth in steals.

And besides, "In my prime I could have handled Michael Jordan," he said. "Of course, Michael would have been only 12 years old."

13 FORWARD: CHET WALKER

What about: Scottie Pippen? No. Did he merit a spot on the NBA's Top 50 of the half-century? Oh, please. He didn't ride in on Jordan's coattails; he came along on a full-fledged bridal train.

He'll always have those magical 1.8 seconds. And those awful migraines.

The first problem with Pippen is that he's a tweener. Bob Love was better than Pippen was at posting up and creating anywhere. Having seen Walker from college, in his prime and through the Bulls years, Chet the Jet was Pippen's equal in the open court. Sloan was a better pure guard, as tough a rebounder, and as tenacious as a defender.

The bigger wart, though, is guts. Pippen shot better than 48 percent from the field even if he was a bricklayer at the line. He was one of the great defensive players the Bulls ever sent onto a court. He's potentially one of the great matchup problems for any Bulls opponent of any era.

But Love, Sloan, Walker, and certainly Dennis Rodman would have gutted him and left him whining about Krause or whatever. When Doug Collins or Phil Jackson took Jordan and made him switch teams in scrimmages, the team trailing always won. If they did that to Pippen, game over.

Yeah but: Walker was a warrior. He was a phenomenal team player, fitting in with Wilt, Billy Cunningham, Luke Jackson, and the rest on that incredible '76ers team. Then he came to the Bulls in a trade and quietly averaged almost 21 per game on a team when the focus seemed always to be on Bob Love and the rest. He was a banger inside with the athleticism to run the floor and shot 85 percent from the line to go with his 48 percent from the field.

The trouble for Walker is that he's so linked to that Philadelphia team. Too bad. He is one of the two best forwards ever to play for the Bulls and played as many years in Chicago (six) as he did in Philly. He ranks fifth in all-time Bulls scoring, put up 56 one night for them, and they went to the playoffs every year he was a Bull.

You take Scottie. I'll take Chet. Let's play.

14 FORWARD: DENNIS RODMAN

What about: Horace Grant? Nice player, never shot worse than 50 percent from the field, was good for about 9 boards a game and played tremendous defense as one of the Dobermans. But he only once averaged as many as 15 a game for a season. A great Jerry Krause draft choice but down the list of great Bulls forwards.

What about: Bob Love? Butterbean is the toughest one to leave off the first unit. He was at the core of that early '70s group and he was a scorer who was good enough to make all-defensive teams even while he was averaging 20-plus for six straight seasons. And from 1973–76 he never averaged fewer than 6 rebounds a game while being a three-time member of the All-NBA defensive second-team.

But a career shooting percentage of .432 is a problem for me. That tells me that the big scoring average came with a lot of shooting. But if the right defensive forward is on him, that accuracy rate dips even lower.

And I have the guy I want to put on him:

Yeah but: Dennis Rodman. A complete eight-ball who was a Bull for only three seasons, normally not enough to make my all-time team. But all three of those seasons in Chicago were championships and he was a linchpin on a Detroit team that won two championships with less pure basketball talent than teams they were beating.

66

Rodman is, pure and simple, one of the greatest pure rebounders in NBA history. He was a student of the craft like no one else, knowing shooters' tendencies and how balls tended to come off rims from them. I have Rodman in that elite rebounding class with Wilt, Jerry Lucas, and Bill Russell. Wilt was just way above everybody else physically. But Lucas and Russell were positioning geniuses, good-but-not-great leapers, and just way above their league for smarts.

Same with Rodman. Plus, you have to love that he'd not only get the rebound but also completely antagonize whomever he elbowed or kneed out of the way. The guy won seven straight rebounding championships. Only Wilt, with 11 championships in 14 years, won more. Rodman and Wilt were the only ones ever to win rebounding titles for three different teams.

But the Rodman pick is about defense. So what if he averaged about 5 points a game? Whoever he guarded was at least 5 points below their average before the night was over. He was defensive player of the year twice and made seven All-NBA defensive first-teams. The guy could and, more important, would play some D. He took Karl Malone to the shed when it mattered in the '98 Finals.

The 72-win season was a Rodman year. So were the 69 W's the next year. For one game or one year, he's my power forward.

15 CENTER: ARTIS GILMORE

What about: Tom Boerwinkle? He was the consummate role player, the perfect complement to the swirling Type-A hoops personalities of Love, Sloan, Van Lier, and Walker. He played against some of the greatest pivotmen in NBA history night after night: Kareem, Willis Reed, Wilt, Thurmond. More important, Boerwinkle made everybody else better by being the passer, the picker. Trouble is, he wasn't a scorer, dominating rebounder, or intimidating defender. Not enough points awarded here for just being a facilitator.

What about: Nate Thurmond? Robert Parish? Both Hall of Fame players. Both wore Bulls uniforms. Both are on the NBA's Top 50 for the first half-century. But Babe Ruth was a Boston Red Sox and a Brave. That doesn't put him on an all-time Boston roster. These guys were way, way past their primes when they were Bulls. Just stopping by on the way out the NBA door doesn't count.

What about: Bill Cartwright. Definitely an integral part of legendary Bulls teams and arguably the player who got them over the top because of giving them some presence in the middle. But Cartwright was never a dominant rebounder and even if he sacrificed a solid scoring game when he left the Knicks for the Bulls, he scored progressively fewer points every season he was with the Bulls and never more than the 12.4 his first year. Even Luc Longley was more of a scorer.

What about: Walt Bellamy? The big Bell Ringer? Just not a Bull long enough, but if he were…

Bellamy is in the Hall of Fame and averaged 31.6 points and 19 rebounds a game in his rookie season. Only Wilt's 50.4 per game were better on the scoreboard and only Wilt and Russell averaged more boards. The next year he pops for almost 28 and 16. Then the team is in Baltimore and he's a Bullet. If the team stays in Chicago, he's the man in the middle. But the Bulls didn't win championships in his short Chicago run the way they did with Rodman.

Yeah but: Gilmore played 12 years in the NBA and those seasons after five in the American Basketball Association. He was an All-Star 11 times in 17 years and was All-ABA all five seasons in the ABA. He was an NBA All-Star when he was 36.

Gilmore was an all-time great with the Kentucky Colonels of the ABA, really helped that league become a factor, and was playing with Rick Barry, Julius Erving, George Gervin, Dan Issel, and others who took the money and still ran when they hit the NBA. Gilmore averaged 22.3 points per game and 17.1 rebounds with Kentucky.

But is he the all-time Bulls center?

Definitely. He averaged at least 17.8 points in all six of his Chicago seasons. Gilmore got to town as the first pick in the ABA dispersal draft, going to a really bad Bulls team that unfortunately started the 1976 season with 13 straight losses. It was an unfortunately bad start for someone the city looked upon as a franchise savior and the one who would take the

69

Bulls back to where they'd been just two years earlier.

The Gilmore Bulls still came back to reach the playoffs by winning 20 of their last 24 games but lost in the first round to Portland. Only once more during Gilmore's six years in Chicago did they make the playoffs, in 1981.

Finally the guy just had enough and asked to be traded, and he was, to San Antonio in 1982 for Dave Corzine, Mark Olberding, and cash. He ended up back with the Bulls in 1986–87 for 24 games but was cut.

A-Train put up 17.1 points per NBA game and 10.1 rebounds plus nearly 2 blocks per game even after coming into the league late. In fact, the joke is that he is not in the NBA's half-century Top 50 while Thurmond and, more to the point, Bill Walton are. Thurmond averaged 15–15 for his career. Walton was 13.3 scoring and 10.5 rebounding, although his numbers with Portland (17.1 ppg., 13.5 rpg., 2.6 bpg.) were better when he was a starter and before he went on to finish his career in Boston and self-promotion.

Gilmore's problem was that he was too nice, and maybe just too good. He never looked like he was playing hard, which is absurd. You don't slop your way to 10 rebounds a game in the NBA, especially when you're on a team with no visible means of support for you. One Chicago writer had the rich insight to declare that Gilmore had a 6'2" heart inside a 7'2" body. Right. The guy played 250 straight games before he injured a knee, then came back to run up another long string of consecutive games.

If there's a regret it's the A-Train took as long as it did to reach Chicago. But when it did, just try to stop it. A class guy, a Hall of Fame player. Easy choice as my center.

HEARING VOICES

"Hey Hey"? "Holy Cow"? Who Is the Best Announcer Chicago Ever Heard?

16 Announcers in Chicago become part of not just the team, but almost of the family and your life. Vince and Lou, Kup, Harry, Brick—they were on a first-name basis with all of us.

But which were the absolute best in a sports city with many of the absolute best?

The reason why most of Chicago's great voices don't have the cachet of Mel Allen, Johnny Most, or Chick Hearn is simply that Chicago's teams don't win a lot, the way the Yankees, Celtics, and Lakers have. But in their own way, they are Chicago's own private Vin Scullys, the sound of baseball on a sunny summer afternoon or a Bears game on a wintry December Sunday. Nothing like 'em.

This is another of those cases where you hate to leave anyone out of the elite ranks. Like Jim Durham on the Bulls. Durham had that unique ability to drop a touch of insight and even commentary into the flow of his call without coming across as pontificating. And a shot didn't miss; it was "Rimming...no!" Durham left after the first Bulls championship when he and the Bulls couldn't agree on money, so now he's doing NBA games for ESPN radio. But what a treat to have him for Jordan's first seven seasons in Chicago.

Pat Foley has the misfortune of being the Blackhawks' announcer during their nadir, which means he's a borderline cult figure; unless you made the effort to tune in to a wretched team in a sport with a death wish, you missed how electric Foley is. Shame on the Hawks for letting him go the way they did. Typical Hawks.

Bears play-by-play guy Jeff Joniak doesn't have the classic pipes that some of the greats have been blessed with, but what Joniak brings to the mike is arguably the best background reporting for his job. Joniak is a news hound and it makes for some real insight in his broadcasts, which is rare.

Vince Lloyd (Skaff) hooked up with Lou Boudreau for 23 years on the Cubs and managed to make it a pleasant transition from Jack Quinlan, not always easy. It wasn't always about the baseball; it was about the fun, and that's really the point, isn't it?

But five legends stand out above the rest:

5. PHIL GEORGEFF, ARLINGTON PARK

One of the classy, fun people in a colorful business.

Phil called (not "announced") 96,131 races over a span of 34 years before he retired in 1992. He was the voice of racing for Arlington and Washington Park who went into the Guinness Book of Records in 1988 when he called his 85,000th race.

I used to marvel at how Phil could possibly call correctly every horse in nine full races on a day's program, with the races coming only a matter of minutes apart. I was lucky enough to cover the newly reopened track in 1989 and Phil was always up for company in his booth atop the grandstand, and one day he showed me how he did it.

He "called" the horses going to the post, as they were walked out to the starting gate. He had a program in his hand and was doing a speed-study of the colors, not the numbers, as I'd figured. His reason: sometimes things got muddy and a number could be obscured. But between the helmet, the silks, and the rest of the package, chances were pretty good that something with the color would always be visible.

Every race started with that "Aannndd they're off!" and ended with the best part: "Heeere they come, spinning out of the turn."

I know, "spinning" was more harness than thoroughbred. I don't care. It was Phil.

4. LLOYD PETTIT, CHICAGO BLACKHAWKS

"A shot...AND A GOAL!"

Maybe that's really all you need to know about Lloyd, if you've never had a chance to listen to a broadcast or tape of one. Just as Wayne Larrivee was part of what made the great Bears teams such rich listening, Lloyd was really the sound of his team. Lloyd was the action and not Howard Cosell or Don Dunphy on their best days could call a fight as well as Pettit. You simply could feel the action building from Lloyd's voice; he knew the game, he knew the players, and it showed. And heard.

It is no accident whatsoever that the era of the Blackhawks' road games on TV and Pettit on the broadcasts was the zenith of Hawks presence in Chicago. Pettit called Hawks games for eighteen years and was enshrined in the Hockey Hall of Fame. Easy choice.

Pettit doing the Hawks' away games TV did more to sell the Blackhawks than anyone ever other than Bobby Hull. In the mid-'60s he was doing maybe ten to 12 road games a year and he was part of the glory of the game, when it wasn't yet so diluted.

Lloyd Pettit died in November 2003 in Milwaukee. I wasn't a hockey fan for the most part but I listened to Lloyd Pettit and savored every minute of him.

3. HARRY CARAY.

Without a doubt the most colorful play-by-play figure in Chicago. Just not the best. Not even the Cubs' best.

No mistake; Harry was tremendous. He was named baseball broadcaster of the year seven times. He had an energy that turned the ballpark into a sports bar. He was a baseball nut (he did play semi-pro baseball) and nothing says how universally good he was more than the fact that he was an institution with three different teams.

How many announcers would set up a shower in the centerfield bleachers? Or have the stones to lean out of the broadcasting booth and bellow "Take Me Out to the Ballgame"? Harry did. Giving you how names would sound if they were pronounced backwards: perfect.

And you have to love the irreverence, the willingness to blast away with Jimmy Piersall at things that weren't going right on the field. Harry didn't hesitate to fire on Lee Stern for putting the White Sox on pay TV, for instance, when the two were part of a symposium together.

How many Harry quotes do you have time for? "Aw, how could [Jorge Orta] lose a ball in the sun? He's from Mexico." Or "Broads, booze, and bullshit. If you've got all that, what else do you need?" "It might be...it could be...it IS! A home run!"

But he doesn't get number one, or even number 2, for a couple reasons. For one, his name. Harry Caray was a cute morphing of Harry Carabino; better for marketing. You don't get No. 1 in Chicago if you do a vanity name change.

75

And Harry was ultimately selling Harry, whether in the form of Falstaff, Bud, or something else. Harry gave you a feel of the ballpark. And more than a few observers thought some of the apparent malaprops were as carefully scripted as any David Mamet drama.

So with all that, Harry gets number three to go with his statue outside of Wrigley Field.

2. WAYNE LARRIVEE.

The best pure play-by-play man ever to grace a microphone in Chicago sports. Period.

Wayne's first year in Chicago was the 1985 Bears season and WGN could have not picked a better voice to succeed Joe McConnell, a tremendous announcer in his own right. Wayne broadcast Bears games for 14 seasons, with sidemen like Hub Arkush and Dick Butkus. You will need to go long, long way to find someone with whom Wayne didn't work seamlessly.

The genius of Wayne was in sorting out and making sense for the listener of a game in which 22 people are all doing something significant on every play. He called formations as the players came to the line but did it without being geeky or losing the casual football listener.

Wayne was so good that he could bring that kind of clarity and energy to NBA broadcasts. He's done Cubs broadcasts. College basketball. And his "Back Page" radio features were treats and had that personal, I'm-just-talking-it-over-with-you feel.

When he left to take the Packers job, Wayne had to follow Jim Irwin, who retired after 30 years. And to his credit, Wayne and color man Larry McCarran never tried to be Irwin and Max McGee, legends in Packerland. Wayne didn't need to be anybody; he is as good as it gets himself.

Chicago lost Wayne in 1999 when he took his dream job, that of doing Green Bay Packers games for WTMJ. A tough loss for any Bears fan, but for all the great calls and great times, Wayne gets a pass here.

1. JACK BRICKHOUSE

"Back, back, back, back…HEY HEY!!"

The only difficult part of this call was being sure that the choice of Jack as the best of all time in Chicago was for quality of work and not personal. This was one of the truly nice people in a business of not-always-nice people, who passed my real test for someone being a "nice" person: they were pleasant and warm toward people they didn't know.

Jack was summer in Chicago, the Cubs broadcasts, and the one who made it fun to listen. He had those homey Brick-isms like "Whew boy" and "Wheeeee" but that was part of why you listened. He was a kid broadcasting kids games to kids at heart.

And he had his memorables:

"Any team can have a bad century."

"There was never any question about [Enos Slaughter's] courage. He proved it by getting married four times."

Jack's was the voice on Willie Mays' catch on the Vic Wertz drive in the '54 World Series, doing the broadcast for NBC. He called more than 5,000 baseball games and was an unabashed fan right along with his listeners.

He was the youngest broadcaster in the country, at 18 years old in 1934 with WBMD in Peoria. In 1940 he got to WGN and did Cubs, White Sox, and Bears games. He did the Bears for 24 years with Irv Kupcinet, including the 1963 championship season.

Jack broadcast Chicago Bulls, Packers, and Zephyrs. He did Chicago Cardinals broadcasts in 1947 when they won the NFL championship. He did Golden Gloves boxing and did heavyweight fights between Joe Louis and Ezzard Charles and between Charles and Jersey Joe Walcott. He did wrestling for nine years.

There were occasions when Brick did commercials in the morning, a Cubs game in early afternoon, The Jack Brickhouse Show on radio, then something else that night. Jack covered political conventions for WGN. Jack filling on a rain delay was classic.

But he was more than an announcer. In the 1950s he was getting hate mail from bigots for his touting of Ernie Banks, Gene Baker, Chico Carresquel, blacks and Latinos, as "our guys." Jack didn't blink. They were Cubs and Sox and that was that.

He is the greatest announcer, sports or otherwise, that Chicago ever turned out.

CUDDLY CUBBIES

Who Makes—and Misses— the Cubs' Dream Team?

With no team even making it to a World Series, you could debate whether or not the Cubs even deserve an all-time or Dream Team. But they've sent enough players to the Hall of Fame, several at some positions, and eight position players and three pitchers are—debatedly—the best the Cubs ever fielded.

17 RIGHT-HANDED PITCHER: MORDECAI BROWN

A fun pick would be John Clarkson, into the Hall of Fame in 1963 and with a 53-16 record pitching 623 innings, 68 complete games in the 70 he started. But that was the 1880s so there is reason to marvel at the numbers but not enough to make him The Right-Hand Man. Forget about Charlie Root too. Besides, he gave up the homer that the Babe called, and at home.

What about: Greg Maddux? He's a Brave. Unfortunately.

What about: Ferguson Jenkins? For 300 innings a year,

nobody touches Ferguson Jenkins. He finished more than half of his starts as a Cub and had six straight of his own 20-win seasons. His career 3.34 ERA was higher than Brown's but he was below the N.L.'s average every one of his Cubs seasons before the mop-up years at the end.

The trouble clincher for me was that Fergie was ultimately 167-132 as a Cub with a 3.20 ERA. Good, but there's better.

Yeah but: "Three Fingers" Brown was the franchise when the Cubs were great in the early part of the century. He put up eight straight seasons with 20 complete games, a 188-86 Cubs record and six straight with 20 wins. He had no ERA above 2.80 in nine Chicago seasons, 1.80 for his Cub years and a 5-4 World Series record, and that included going twice against the Detroit Tigers with Ty Cobb and Sam Crawford.

Fergie was a better hitter, but Brown was also finishing games when he wasn't starting them and could make a reasonable closer. That gets him the nod.

18 LEFT-HANDED PITCHER: HIPPO VAUGHN

Not much to choose from, which is probably a significant part of why this franchise has been so bad for so long. Lots of good Cubs in the 1800s but MLB has them in a separate group and it's hard to go that direction.

What about: Kenny Holtzman? Holtzman was superb with the Oakland A's, but 80-81, and a 3.76 ERA with the Cubs.

Yeah but: Vaughn was 151-105 with a 2.33 ERA throwing from 1913–21, and the guy completed 177 of his 270 starts. He was 6'4", 215 pounds, sometimes up to 300, hence the nickname, and had by far the most interesting losses by any Chicago lefty. Hippo was on the losing end of the double no-hitter with Cincinnati in 1917 when the Reds scored in the tenth and he lost 1-0 to Babe Ruth in game one of the 1918 Series.

What you had to like about the guy was that he liked to go after batters by beating them at their strength. Management didn't like it, and his going AWOL after he was pulled from his last game in 1921 probably didn't help that. But he was the best lefty the Cubs ever had and one of less than a half-dozen players to win 400 games combined for major, minor, and semi-pro careers.

19 CLOSER: BRUCE SUTTER

What about: Randy Myers? Myers is the best lefty closer ever in Chicago but with a 3.52 ERA.

What about: Lee Smith? This is the hard one to pass on. Smittie had 180 Cubs saves and a 2.92 ERA. But what puts him number two are the walks (one every 2.6 innings pitched) and strikeouts (slightly less than one per inning), the latter really more important than ERA since what you're looking for from a closer are outs where nobody moves.

Yeah but: Besides a winning record (32-20), Sutter had a 2.39 combined ERA. And he struck out more than one batter per inning pitched while giving up a walk every 3.3 innings. He was N.L. Fireman of the Year four times and the Cy Young winner in 1979. If I'm in trouble, he's coming in.

20 CATCHER: GABBY HARTNETT

What about: Jody Davis? Davis was part of the '84 fun when he was putting up one of his six straight years with double-digit homers, and he had his best year in '83 with 24 homers and a .271 average.

Yeah but: Hartnett was the N.L. MVP in 1935, an All-Star six times, and anytime you have a home run commemorated by a special ID ("Homer in the Gloamin") to help win a pennant, you're way up on any list. Hartnett caught more than 100 games twelve times and hit .297 for his career, including seasons at .339, .344, and .354. Easy choice.

21 FIRST BASE: CAP ANSON

I know Anson was an 1800s guy. But he hit .329 for the Cubs and drove in 1,879 with a ball that had all the pop of a balled-up sock. Bill Buckner was a .300 hitter in Chicago and Mark Grace was a .308 man for his career. I never saw Anson play; but he had 124 triples, so he could at least run, which is a whole lot more than Buckner or Grace can say.

SECOND BASE: RYNE SANDBERG

One thing Chicago has had is second basemen; five Hall of Famers, including Nellie Fox and Eddie Collins over on the other side of town, and that's not even including Glenn Beckert.

What about: Johnny Evers? The Cubs had Evers defining the double play with Joe Tinker and Frank Chance when the Cubs were the power of the National League. It was Evers who had the smarts to stand on second and scream for the ball on September 23, 1908, when the Giants' Fred Merkle left the basepaths to beat the crowd after an apparent game-winning single, the play that branded Merkle "Bonehead" through baseball history.

What about: Billy Herman? He hit .309 for the 1930s he spent in Chicago, including three trips to the World Series. Herman led the N.L. in putouts by a second baseman seven times and still holds the record for putouts in a season.

Yeah but: Ryno brought some power to the position, besides a glove that Joe Morgan may not have liked but was as good as there was in the National League; just look at the consecutive games (123) without an error. And he went four years without a throwing error.

Sandberg was the N.L. MVP in 1984, a vote that was pretty well decided when he hit those two homers, in the ninth to tie and the tenth to win, off Sutter on June 23. He had 282 homers for his career and when he hit 40 in 1990, it was the first time for that many by a second baseman since Rogers Hornsby in 1922.

Pencil him in and bat him anywhere in the lineup.

23 SHORTSTOP: ERNIE BANKS

What about: Joe Tinker? If there was anybody other than Ernie, it'd be Tinker, who was the shortstop on pennant winners in 1907–08 and 1910. But he never hit .300 for the Cubs or drove in more than 75 runs in a season.

Yeah but: Two MVP awards. 512 home runs. Fifteen All-Star games. "Mr. Cub." Next category.

24 THIRD BASE: RON SANTO

What about: Stan Hack? This was a career .300 hitter who hit .348 in 18 World Series games. A completely different type of third baseman than Santo, Hack scored 100 runs seven times, led the league in stolen bases in 1938–39, and led the N.L. in hits in 1940–41.

What about: Bill Madlock? He has the highest Chicago-career average of any Cub (.336) and won a couple batting titles before the Cubs wanted him gone after only three seasons.

Yeah but: Ronnie was a .277 hitter who struck out too many times but still whacked 337 Cubs homers and also won five Gold Gloves. He hit 30 homers four straight years and had eight straight seasons with 90-plus RBI besides 13 years of 135 or more hits.

The only real debate with Santo is whether or not he should be in the Hall of Fame. As a dominant player in his era, yes, he should be. But it's hard to have another Hall of Famer (Banks, Williams, Jenkins) from a team that never won a pennant.

25 LEFT FIELD: BILLY WILLIAMS

What about: Hank Sauer? Sauer was the N.L. MVP in 1952. But he was a .269 hitter as a Cub and struck out almost once every seven times he batted. That's a whole lot better than a lot of power hitters the Cubs have had.

Year but: There's only one left fielder's number retired and flying from a flag pole at Wrigley for a lot of reasons. Williams hit 392 Cubs homers and had 13 straight seasons with no fewer than 84 RBI. He may not have been the fastest pair of legs out near Waveland Avenue but he didn't strike out much and his 1,117 consecutive games were the N.L. record until Steve Garvey broke it. Hall of Fame.

26 CENTER FIELD: HACK WILSON

What about: Andy Pafko was a bright spot in a position that's given the Cubs almost as much trouble filling as third base. Jim Hickman had some good years; Bobby Dernier, Adolpho Phillips, and Jerome Walton flashed.

Yeah but: Wilson was the greatest right-handed hitter ever in Chicago, North or South sides. He'd be the best Cub in center if only based on his 1930 season: 56 homers, a National League record that stood 68 years, until Sammy and McGwire broke it; 191 RBI, still the Major League record; and a .356 average.

Six years as a Cub. What would he have been without so many nights with John Barleycorn?

27 RIGHT FIELD: ANDRE DAWSON

What about: Kiki Cuyler? He brought the highest average to the Sheffield side of Wrigley. Sammy? He brought the biggest bat to the spot.

Yeah but: One guy brought it all. Hawk was the most complete outfielder ever to patrol the Friendly Confines, any field, the prototype right fielder. He had one of the great arms of his era and even after his knees were destroyed on the artificial turf in Montreal, he was still able to cover ground and make plays.

He was a teammate who made people around him better, not something you could say about some others out there. Hawk beat it out of Montreal in 1986 by signing a blank contract with the Cubs, and they filled in $500,000, which became the all-time Chicago bargain when he became the first player on a last-place team to win MVP: 49 homers, 137 RBI, .287 average.

Dawson played six seasons in Chicago and hit .285 as a Cub, about the same as Sammy. He hit a home run every 18.7 Cubs at-bats, significantly off Sammy's pace of one every 12.8. His RBI rate was also slightly below Sammy's. But his strikeout rate was about half of Sammy's rate of once every 3.8 Chicago at bats.

But for defense and a throwing arm in the outfield position where they matter, Hawk is the whole package.

THE NO-GOODNIKS

Who Does Chicago Most Love to Hate?

28 Chicago has its favorites: anybody who gives it everything they have, talented or not, success optional. If you're a Bear, Cub, Bull, Sox or Hawk, you're a hero until you act like you take the crowd for granted.

But beyond the passing, minor annoyances that plague every sport and every sports town, Chicago has its own special collection of Darth Vaders and Freddie Kruegers, forces that touch the very heart of its sports darkness. They are more than the occasional Leon Durham letting a grounder escape or the odd Steve Garvey who ends playoff dreams. They are the ones whose very names spark immediate hostility.

Some are teams. Some are individuals from those teams who deserve their own private honor above and beyond.

The sad thing is that so many of the sports evildoers did their business right in town. Think Ted Turner is hated in Atlanta? Or George Steinbrenner in New York? Or Ralph Wilson in Buffalo, where his team lost four straight Super Bowls? No. Only in Chicago is the list full of so many of the very ones responsible for giving fans something to care and cheer about.

Some were close calls but earned their ways off the list.

The St. Louis Cardinals certainly have some bad history with the Cubs, but to me it's not as currently rancid as the Sox–Minnesota Twins. John Starks should have hired someone to start his car for him when he was mugging Bulls as a New York Knick in the mid-1990s; but ultimately he was a small fish.

Gordie Howe coming in from Detroit was a problem for Blackhawk Nation, but not as much as the latest Mr. Blackhawk. Bill Wirtz took Hawk road games off free TV. He virtually killed hockey in Chicago by himself. He was an aggressive leader in management's hard-lining in the lockout that cost hockey a season, and from which it may never recover. His stated reason for refusing to broadcast home games on free TV has been that it would cut deeply into attendance; why would people pay to come when they could stay home and watch for free, went his line.

Well, the sport died in Chicago. Fans couldn't see the game, they never took to certain players, and they had precious few chances to actually see the team they were being asked to back with their allegiance. The Blackhawks had to pay a radio station, WSCR-AM, to carry their games. Isn't it supposed to be the other way around?

Author Matt Weinberg probably said it best in the title of his book on Wirtz, *Career Misconduct*. In it, Weinberg chronicles what he says are antitrust violations, bribery of public officials, misappropriating money from his niece's trust fund, collusion against players, lying, and general no-goodness. Someone with too much time on his hands created Wirtzsucks.com for those in need of bad Wirtzing.

"Dollar Bill" Wirtz has been listed among the world's wealthiest men, by virtue of his ownership of the Blackhawks, half-ownership of the United Center, and liquor distributorships that court filings in 1999 showed had annual sales of about three-quarters of a billion dollars.

A rich guy who has his own private sports fiefdom—perfect villain.

But only these five make that exclusive "enemies" list:

5. MICHAEL MCCASKEY

His players considered him a spoiled kid who was born on third base and acted like he'd hit a triple. He threatened to move the Bears to Indiana. He hired Dave Wannstedt. He pushed for the drafting of Stan Thomas. He flirted with the possibility of taking the Bears to Los Angeles and Indiana.

He turned the NFL's charter franchise into a laughingstock when, after firing Wannstedt in January 1999, he brought in

Dave McGinnis to be the head coach. McGinnis was the first finalist McCaskey chose from a list he'd had Personnel Vice President Mark Hatley put together after a tedious search process. But the mishandling of the McGinnis negotiations destroyed McCaskey's time atop the franchise.

Papa Bear George Halas supposedly said "Anybody but Michael" to run the Bears as he was nearing death in 1983. Whether or not that actually happened has become almost superfluous; those were the sentiments of millions of Bears fans, if not precisely the founder's.

McCaskey did, in 1994, agree to retire the numbers 40 and 51 of Sayers and Butkus, at a time when he was unquestionably the most disliked figure in Chicago sports and desperately needed some favorable PR. He had by then earned the distinction of being the man who fired Ditka. Which he had done after allowing Da Coach to first ask for the chance to keep his job for one more year to try turning it around after his 5-11 record in 1992 (only the second losing season, only the second in which he'd failed to win at least ten games, since 1984).

He'd either jettisoned or allowed to leave: Wilber Marshall, Otis Wilson, Willie Gault, and Jim McMahon, effectively dismantling the team that had won for him the NFL Executive of the Year award for the accomplishments of the '85 team. McCaskey had stiffed the '85 Bears with a smaller allotment of Super Bowl tickets than the New England Patriots and wouldn't open the postgame party to former players. This after nixing the acupuncturist for McMahon, Gault, and others being brought to New Orleans on the team plane.

When McCaskey fired Ditka and brought in Wannstedt, McCaskey effectively took over as the GM, to the point of watching game film on Monday mornings. He tried to make over the Chicago Bears in his image and likeness, which wasn't at all popular with former players. Many felt unwelcome in what was the Dallas-ization of the Bears.

Sad but true—the head of Chicago's Team is more disliked than nearly anyone who ever played against his team.

4. JERRY KRAUSE

He was the one who brought Scottie Pippen, Dennis Rodman, Horace Grant, Bill Cartwright, and more here in the first place. He pushed for Jackson to succeed Doug Collins. People disliked Krause because of how he was with, and was portrayed by, the media, and some of the personal ridicule heaped on him was disgusting. He earns the improbable honor of being one of the top Chicago sports villains and also being one of the top team-builders in Chicago sports history.

But he will be remembered as the single most divisive reason that the great Bulls run closed out of town, with Jordan in Washington, Jackson in Los Angeles, and Pippen in Houston and Portland before coming back. Krause is not a welcome individual around the United Center, at least among fans.

3. CHARLES MARTIN

The Green Bay Packers defensive lineman died in 2005, but his infamy survives him. Not once, but twice he took out Jim McMahon with cheap shots that evoke anger and might-have-beens to this day.

On September 16, 1984, barely a month after Forrest Gregg and Mike Ditka began their blood feud, the Bears faced the Packers. McMahon was taking pain shots for hand and back problems. But the shot he took from Martin was far more painful. McMahon slid at the end of a play and was drilled by Martin anyway, causing his back to stiffen and forcing him to leave the game.

That was only a foreshadowing.

With the Bears intent on returning to the Super Bowl for a second straight year, they hosted Green Bay on November 23. McMahon threw an interception and was standing away from the play when Martin picked him up and drove him shoulder-first into the Soldier Field turf, which at that time was still artificial. It was changed to grass in 1988, in part because of this incident.

McMahon's season and the Bears' dreams of a Super Bowl repeat came crashing down. He needed shoulder surgery and was done for the season, which meant an opportunity for Doug Flutie, if it can be called that. Without McMahon, the Bears were soundly beaten by the Washington Redskins and never again reached the Super Bowl.

In 2005, while doing my book *The Rise and Self-Destruction of the Greatest Football Team in History: The Chicago Bears and Super Bowl XX*, a gentleman told me of sitting next to a man on a plane many years after the Martin incident. That individual told my source that he had been paid to give Martin a plain brown envelope containing money for the purpose of taking out McMahon. True or not, Chicago fans will always wonder, and have a special place in their Hall of Hate for Charles Martin.

2. THE BAD BOY PISTONS

Poor sports. Jerks. Mean guys. Bill Laimbeer. Isiah Thomas. Dennis Rodman. Rick Mahorn. I mean, what's not to hate? They were punks, thugs, and just plain not-nice guys. They were lucky enough to have a couple of NBA championship seasons in the gap between the passing of the Bird-Magic 1980s, beating the Lakers for one title when Magic and Byron Scott were both out with injuries, and the Jordan Bulls 1990s. They were the origin of the NBA's flagrant-foul rule.

Thomas was the captain and a sort of angelic assassin, a tough kid who had come out of the Chicago area, survived Bobby Knight at Indiana with a national championship, and became one of the NBA's elite guards. And he was a phony. He was the one behind the freeze-out of Michael Jordan in the 1985 NBA All-Star game because he didn't like Jordan getting all that attention in his first All-

Star game. Jordan let it be known that if Thomas was part of the 1992 Olympic Dream Team, he wouldn't be.

Thomas and Laimbeer led the smirking Pistons pointedly off the court after being finally beaten by Jordan and the Bulls in the 1991 playoffs. Thomas, Laimbeer, and Joe Dumars walked off the court before the game was completely over. Petty doesn't even begin to describe it. Afterwards, Laimbeer kept giving the answer of "They won" to every media question. Class acts.

Laimbeer was a smarmy goon with an arrogance born of family wealth and a Notre Dame education. He came to the Pistons from Cleveland in a 1982 trade. He was a dirty player, pure and simple, and half the time hid behind massive tough guy Mahorn, nicknamed "McFilthy" from his days with "McNasty" Jeff Ruland and the Baltimore Bullets, and who hurled Bulls coach Doug Collins over the scorer's table in one memorable dustup. Mahorn's style was to administer a hard foul to an opponent after that player had already been fouled, Mahorn reasoning that the second foul was a freebie.

Rodman made a career out of being a freak, playing with a work ethic above reproach but then needlessly insulting peers, like Bird in the 1987 playoffs by saying that if Bird weren't white, he'd be just another guy. Thomas naturally agreed with him. In December 1993, Rodman pulled a $7,500 fine for head-butting Stacey King of the Bulls.

The problem with the Pistons was the same one that the Philadelphia Flyers "Broad Street Bullies" posed: They were good. They won two championships and even with qualifiers, that's an accomplishment. Even for punks.

1. FORREST GREGG

He is, quite simply, the Prince of Darkness to all things Chicago. He was a Packer. He was a mean Packer. He coached mean Packers, made them be mean with his will of evil. Worst of all, he made mean Packers try to hurt Walter.

The Bears-Packers rivalry was always great. Gregg made it mean and ugly. Gregg was Charles Martin's coach.

The roots run deep. It was the Bears who ended the coaching tenure of Bart Starr, Gregg's teammate on the great Lombardi Packers teams, with a 23-21 win at Soldier Field to conclude the 1983 season. In the second week of the 1984 preseason, the Bears and Packers played at Milwaukee's County Stadium, where the benches for the two teams were next to each other on the same sideline, and things changed forever.

Gregg wanted to change the loser mindset that by this time had become endemic with the Packers. So he had his players taking runs at Bears kickers and other nastiness not usually part of preseason games. Then with the Packers up 14-3 nearing halftime, Gregg called a time-out with 1:12 left in the first half, trying to get in for another score instead of the customary letting time run out.

Ditka erupted. "Why the hell are you calling a time-out?" he bellowed. Gregg said he needed to work on his passing game. Ditka called him a sorry sonofabitch, Gregg responded in kind. Game on. A month later Martin did his first number on McMahon.

So it was probably no accident that Ditka saved the real unveiling of William "The Refrigerator" Perry for the Green Bay game in 1985, Monday Night Football, when he could most humiliate Gregg and his bunch.

The next time the teams met, a month later, was Gregg's low point: Safety Ken Stills smashed McMahon after the whistle on the second play of the game. On the ninth play Mark Lee drove Walter over the Packers bench. Finally, at the end of the first quarter, Stills came from well away from a concluded play to level Matt Suhey long after the whistle had blown.

During Super Bowl week, Suhey had to be restrained from going after Gregg when the two happened to be at the same New Orleans restaurant. The next year was Martin's shoulder-dump of McMahon and effectively the end of the Bears' run to glory that season as well.

Players in the '86 Charles Martin game wore towels from their belts with the numbers of various Bears. Martin had McMahon's and Payton's. Those towels could only have appeared with Gregg's blessing.

All on Gregg's watch. In Chicago sports, there is no greater single villain.

HOW ABOUT A TRUE NATIONAL NCAA BASKETBALL CHAMPIONSHIP?

29 Eddie Einhorn, the Sox semi-owner and pay-TV maven, had a lot to do with taking the NCAA tournament from having its 1963 Loyola-Cincinnati championship game on tape delay to having "March Madness" become part of America's speech. The tournament needs him almost as much now.

College basketball life has caught up and passed the NCAA postseason tournament. For all of the great action and stories like George Mason University's trip to the 2006 Final Four, the NCAA tournament is missing out, and so are fans, players, and schools. All the acrimony, uncertainty, unfairness, and silliness need to end. The way to do it:

Every single NCAA Division I school is entered in the tournament and has a chance to win the national championship.

Instead of expanding the tournament from 48 to 64 teams the way it was, or to 65 teams so two can vie for the

64th berth, or even to 128 or whatever, establish the format that has worked so marvelously for high school basketball for so long and which has produced the Hebrons and Milans (Indiana).

Every March, one of the great stories can be one of those who'd-a-thunk-it schools, like George Mason University reaching the Final Four in 2006. I say there should be George Masons every year.

The NCAA knows that the more teams in the Big Dance, the better; that's why they expanded the field in 2001 with a play-in game where two teams play for the 64th team in the field. They just didn't go far enough. Open the whole thing up the way every state holds its high school championships after the season, with a giant play-in that leaves nobody out.

The point of the whole thing anyway, let's be honest, is money. That's the fuel rod that gets lowered into college sports every fall and starts the reactor running from football on into basketball. So what about the money: what do a lot of schools lose? The powers lose some meaningless preconference games against opponents who are more than happy to travel to those powers' houses.

Instead, reverse the schedule. After a couple of exhibitions, play the conference tournaments, which should be stripped of the ultimate unfairness of an automatic berth to the winner, at the outset of the season. The attendance and television payoffs will be there because of the rivalries. So a lot of meaningless early season games against nobodies will be replaced by games with some built-in passion. Those tournaments should have nothing to do with post-season bids anyway, except for wins and losses in the overall schedule.

And in the conference tournaments, no matter when they're played, seed only the top four teams in a field of ten to 12 teams. Do it like a tennis tournament; you never seed an entire field, you seed the top players and then you have a draw. Same in the conference tournament, and do it in the national tournament too, when that finally arrives.

Northwestern, for instance, played teams like Florida Atlantic, Delaware State, and DePauw in the 2005–2006 season. How much more interesting would it be if the Wildcats were in a true national championship and those games were replaced by tournament games?

The bigger the school, the less interested it will probably be in an expanded tournament. It gives them less control over their schedules and potentially fewer games on their home courts. North Carolina played Gardner-Webb and Cleveland State in its 2005 preconference schedule. The Tarheels drew 19,781 for G-W and 16,422 for Cleveland State. Those were in the Dean Dome. They drew almost 13,000 against Murray State playing in Dayton, Ohio, in round one of the NCAA tournament.

But what the NCAA gives up in a few tournament games under the present format, it more than makes up in volume.

Instead of 65 teams playing, you have more than 330. Very convenient, actually.

That is basically four 128-team brackets, not just 16 teams the way it is now. Perfect, on two counts. One, you need to win seven games to win your regional, then two more for the true national championship, so you play nine games for the title. Now it's just a short stack of six games, with some good ones shut out.

Two, a handful of teams don't qualify based on not winning a game that season (no need to be ridiculous about this, after all). Like a Wimbledon or U.S. Open draw, it plays down neatly to four regional winners going into a Final Four. Again, there are seeds of a fixed number of seeds per draw, usually 16, and they're placed throughout the draw.

Then an actual draw is held (regionally would be nice), and some teams get a tough draw, some get what looks good but could be a minefield—just like now, except that instead of some committee doing all sorts of schedule gymnastics and still leaving out a legit prospect, they're all in somewhere. If you're a top team, you should be able to get through a tough draw, so no whining allowed.

This is America, land of opportunity. Let's go play.

WHAT WERE THEY THINKING?

The Worst Trades Chicago

30 The worst Chicago deals that ever went down sometimes took their teams down with them.

"Worst" deals are definitely ones where you took it in the shorts. You had an idea you thought was good when you went into it but when you came out, everybody's laughing except you. You probably had your reasons, but when it's all over, they don't count for much and nobody can remember them very well.

The Bears haven't made many deals worse than giving up their first-round pick in the 1997 draft for quarterback Rick Mirer, who lasted one miserable season and then was gone. The Bears gave away the 11th pick of the draft; when that pick came, the players available included running back Warrick Dunn, tackle Tarik Glenn, defensive end Trevor Pryce, and tight end Tony Gonzalez, all eventual Pro-Bowl stars. The Bears were still trying to find their Gonzalez a decade later.

Sending Trace Armstrong to Miami for draft choices that turned into Todd Sauerbrun and Evan Pilgrim was a case of giving away a guy who would go to Pro Bowls and a Super Bowl and getting nothing in return. They gave Jim McMahon to the San Diego Chargers in 1989 for a second-round pick; a franchise quarterback, albeit injury plagued, for a draft choice. McMahon was such a part of what made the '80s Bears who they were.

The Cubs trading Jamie Moyer and Rafael Palmeiro to the Rangers for Mitch Williams and a cluster of other players ranks among the worst deals, but getting Palmeiro out of Wrigley was partly for reasons having nothing to do with baseball. Williams may have been fun as "Wild Thing" but his time here was a waste of years and players.

The Black Hawks (their name at the time) deserve honorable mention for dealing away Phil Esposito. Espo, who wound up in the Hall of Fame and won two Stanley Cups, was traded to the Boston Bruins along with Ken Hodge, who became a tremendous player in his own right, and Fred Stanfield. What keeps this from being an all-time no-no is that in return the Hawks at least got Pit Martin, a solid player for a long time. But giving away Esposito...

When you have the kind of losing history that the Cubs, Sox, Bears, Bulls, and Blackhawks have had, you were making plenty of mistakes. These are the absolute worst ones:

4. ELTON BRAND FROM THE BULLS TO SAN DIEGO FOR A DRAFT PICK, 2001

Jerry Krause finally recovers some of the sparkle he had when he drafted Scottie Pippen and Horace Grant, and he takes Duke star Elton Brand with the first-overall pick of the 1999 draft. Great pick. On a team of mostly stiffs (which is part of how you qualify for No. 1 picks), Brand averaged 20 points and 10 rebounds a game for two years.

Whereupon Krause sends the Bulls' best player to San Diego for the rights to a select a high school kid, Tyson Chandler, who is averaging 5 points and 9 rebounds a game five years later while Brand is now up to 25 and 10. The defense of the trade is that the Bulls were a dismal 32-132 with him, so where's the loss? Try playing those 164 games without him and find out.

David Falk, agent for Brand, Michael, and others, said it perfectly: "Anybody who says Jerry Krause can't build a team, I take issue with. He's done an unbelievable job building the Clippers."

3. LOU BROCK FROM THE CUBS TO ST. LOUIS FOR ERNIE BROGLIO, 1964

The reason this legendary giveaway isn't in the top two is because at least the Cubs thought they were getting a good player and giving up one that wasn't particularly good. The hard part of the Broglio deal was that it actually looked like a beauty. The amazing part is that it was the Cards who thought they'd given up too much at the time. Broglio was coming off an 18-8 season, preceded by a 12-9 and 21-9 in two of the three previous years. He had 38 complete games in the four pre-trade seasons out of 115 starts and was a 200-inning man with an ERA in the 3.00 range. But he had only 33 more career starts, a 7-19 combined record, and was out of baseball after 1966 with a sore arm.

The Cubs also added aged veteran Bobby Shantz, who was something special ten years earlier but had only forty-three more innings left when he came to Chicago.

Brock was hitting about .260 through his two years but had a very average 50 stolen bases the previous two seasons, wasn't really a very good baserunner, and was a complete liability in right field. But with the Cardinals he exploded, hit .348, and stole 33 bases, then was a big part of the Cards beating the Yankees in the World Series.

Maybe the villain in the deal was on the Cubs' medical staff for not recognizing that Broglio was finished and so was Schantz.

2. BOBBY LAYNE FROM THE BEARS TO THE NEW YORK BULLDOGS FOR $50,000 AND TWO PICKS, 1948

On pure personnel grounds, this is really the worst. George Halas called this "the worst deal I ever made," and that puts it pretty high on any list just for that assessment. The Bears gave up a Hall of Fame quarterback, one of the greats of the next decade, and did it basically because Papa Bear wanted some cash. What makes it so jaw-dropping is that Halas gave away a guy he knew was going to be good, just for a little scratch and crapshoot picks.

Layne was the Bears' first-round pick in the '48 draft. Not only that, he came in already indoctrinated in their T-formation. New Texas coach Blair Cherry wanted to run that offense and spent time in the 1947 training camps of the Bears and Chicago Cardinals studying the new offense. Layne went from a single-wing tailback to quarterback in his senior season.

Ironically, the trade had two parts and could have been one of the best in Chicago history. The Bears had traded to acquire the rights to the Pittsburgh Steelers' number one pick, chose Layne, and then staved off a $77,000 offer from the Baltimore Colts of the old All-American Football Conference.

Layne rode the bench in '48 behind an aging Sid Luckman and Johnny Lujack. But he flashed what he was going to become when he came off the bench to lead the

Bears to a win over the Packers. The next week he led a rout of New York/Boston.

The problem was that Halas owed Cardinals owner Charlie Bidwill $50,000. After Bidwill died, Bidwill's widow went to Halas and said she would forego the debt if he'd let the Cardinals have Layne. Halas wasn't going to let the budding superstar loose in Chicago, so he sent Layne to New York for two draft picks and that amount of cash.

Layne eventually wound up in Detroit, where he led the Lions to NFL championships in 1952, 1953, and 1957, plus the title game in 1954. The Bears? A couple second places in 1954 and 1955 and a title-game annihilation by the Giants in 1956. The draft choices? Chuck Hunsiger and Billy Stone never made it to a single Pro Bowl.

1. THE "WHITE FLAG TRADE," JULY 31, 1997

It wasn't just that the White Sox gave up three veteran pitchers—Wilson Alvarez, Danny Darwin, and Roberto Hernandez—to the San Francisco Giants for six young players, all minor leaguers. It was Sox owner Jerry Reinsdorf declaring that anyone who thought the Sox, then trailing Cleveland by 3 1/2 games, could catch Cleveland was "crazy." The *Chicago Tribune* headline said it perfectly: "Surrender: Sox Deliver a San Francisco treat."

The fact that Keith Foulke and Bobby Howry turned out to be decent major-league relievers doesn't matter.

Neither does whatever Alvarez or any of the others went on to do. There were still two months to go before the end of the season and yet management quit on the season to start building for the future. And if any player did that, started taking days and games off, getting thrown out just so he could work on his baserunning and sliding, he would be in Double-A so fast he'd think he was a battery.

Robin Ventura had his gruesome broken ankle earlier in the year, rehabbed, and fought to get back. Then this deal went down. "I didn't know the season ended in August," was his observation.

The Giants went on to win their division in '97, but lost to the Florida Marlins in the NLCS. They lost to the Cubs in a one-game playoff in '98. The Sox had losing records in '98 and '99. Alvarez said that he thought Sox management gave up and that's all anyone would remember about the deal. And that's why it's the worst trade ever made by a Chicago team.

THE HEAD OF THE CLASS

Chicago's Greatest College Basketball Team: '63 Ramblers or '05 Illini?

31 The list of contenders for the honor of "best" is alarmingly short. Northwestern has never sent a team to the NCAA tournament, so the Wildcats do not even have a qualifier. Chicago State, Illinois State, Northern Illinois, even Southern Illinois with Walt Frazier—none of them come remotely close to making the elite ranks.

There are really only three true possibilities:

DePaul under Ray Meyer in 1979 reached the Final Four with Mark Aguirre averaging 24 points a game as a freshman. The Blue Demons were number six in the country and upset UCLA in Pauley Pavilion to win the West regional before falling just short at 76-74 to Larry Bird, Carl Nicks, and Indiana State in the semifinal game.

That particular team finished 26-6 and helped DePaul onto the dubious list of greatest teams never to win a championship. They added people like Terry Cummings and other talent, which moved them higher in the national rankings but only set them up for some of the most painful upsets in Chicago sports history. DePaul went 132-15 from 1977–82.

But the Demons didn't win anything, not even a round in the Final Four. Whether they were out-coached or out-played, something was missing. They weren't always beaten by teams with more talent, including the Bird team.

So the Blue Demons fall short of the elite on the list.

Those are the 1963 Loyola Ramblers and the 2005 Illinois Fighting Illini.

Illinois was good. It was a guard-based team built around Dee Brown, Luther Head, and Deron Williams, with James Augustine and Roger Powell underneath. Their comeback in the OT win over Arizona was the greatest comeback I have ever covered in any sport.

But they lost to North Carolina in the NCAA Finals 75-70 after Head missed a three that could have tied the game.

The Ramblers were part of more than just Chicago history. In 1961 the line was that you played two blacks at home, three on the road, and five if you had to win. Ireland became the first Division I team to field five black players, five years before Don Haskins made history with Texas Western.

In the second round in '63, the Ramblers were supposed to play Mississippi State, the segregation bastion of the nation. Since Mississippi teams were prohibited from playing integrated teams, Governor Ross Barnett banned

State from traveling to the tournament to play the predominantly black Ramblers. State sent a decoy team to divert state police, then snuck out of state to play Loyola.

Loyola beat Illinois in its regional final, defeated Duke in the semifinals, and then finished with the overtime victory over Cincinnati that rivals the Illinois rally versus Arizona, and was doubly remarkable because it was in the final.

The '63 Ramblers out-comebacked the '05 Illini. Loyola trailed by 15 points with less than 14 minutes remaining. Jerry Harkness tied the game with a jumper in the final four seconds. At 58-58 Harkness got a pass to Les Hunter, who missed a shot from the line, but Vic Rouse tipped it in as time expired.

So Loyola gets the edge in results; they were champions. Illinois was the No. 1-ranked team and lost. Loyola played the No. 1 team and won.

Both teams were actually guard teams, if you consider Harkness a guard, which he really was. Jack Egan and Ron Miller match up well against Dee Brown and Deron Williams. Harkness, who played far bigger than his 6' 2" height, gets a big edge over Head, certainly on the basis of clutch; Harkness hit his tying shot, Head didn't.

Les Hunter and Vic Rouse were 6'7", so no height advantage to James Augustine (6'10") and Roger Powell (6'5").

The difference: Illinois needed some bench to do what they did. Loyola's starters played all 45 minutes of the national championship and still had spring to win with a tip-in at the buzzer. No question: Ramblers.

NOT IN MY (WHITE) HOUSE

To Go or Not to Go, and How to Behave, on White House Visits

32 So there you are, a national champion in whatever—baseball, lacrosse, basketball—and the President of the United States extends the invitation to come visit him in the White House. A photo op with America's reigning First Citizen. Should you go?

If you want to, sure. If you don't, no. And it's nobody's business but yours whether or why you do or don't.

Not everybody sees it that way. And for whatever reason, Chicago sports figures seem to bring out the debate in fans over whether failure to make the trip is OK or an act that ranks somewhere between disrespect and civil disobedience.

Mayor Richard Daley was "disappointed" when Ozzie Guillen didn't come with his White Sox in Februrary 2006. Guillen, who had only recently been accorded his U.S. citizenship, was in the middle of a family vacation in the Dominican Republic and sent his regrets. But Daley didn't express his disappointment that left fielder Scott Posednik didn't cut into his honeymoon for the trip, nor that Tadahito Iguchi chose to be in his hometown in Japan for an honor.

Sox chairman Jerry Reinsdorf determined that only the regular traveling staff of players, coaches, front office staff, and trainers were permitted to attend. So no family members were included, and Guillen said that a little time with the President wasn't worth losing some with his family. Besides, Guillen had been there with the Florida Marlins after their win in the 2003 World Series, and that visit included family members and even batboys.

Northwestern's women's lacrosse team, which brought the Wildcats their first national championship in any sport, was among 15 teams that were hosted on July 12, 2005. It was July in Washington, D.C., which can be the dictionary definition of hot and humid, and a lot of the girls wore flip-flops, which went well with the summer casual dresses that were appropriate. But the footwear became an incident of debate all its own.

If that's the way the young women chose to dress, that is absolutely fine. They were not sloppy, just casual, and if you can't be casual and comfortable in your own house, where can you?

After the Bulls won their first NBA title in 1991, none other than Michael Jordan skipped the visit. He didn't have a vacation or anything else, just said, "I don't care who the President [George Bush I] is. It's none of your [reporters] business. If you want to ask me what I did [instead], I don't have to tell you. I have to live my life the way I want to."

Exactly. Most people probably would go. Most would probably dress up for the occasion. But the White House is our house and the occupant works for us. We own the place and I don't know too many people outside of Ward and June Cleaver who dress up around the house anyway.

And this is America. You don't have to justify what you don't feel like doing.

THINKING RIGHT

Who Is the Greatest Right-Handed Hitter Ever in Chicago?

33 Frank Thomas or Sammy Sosa? Or is there somebody else?

Luke Appling had a .310 lifetime average. Ryne Sandberg is in the Hall of Fame. Bill Madlock had a .336 Chicago Cubs average for the three seasons, and was a two-time batting champ, once MVP.

But first the first two bigger-than-life names to consider: Sammy and Frank. Let's try to put these two guys in baseball perspective.

Frank was twice the American League MVP, in 1993 and again in 1994. He was the A.L. batting champion in 1997. The marvel is that he was selected to only five All-Star teams, but part of that had to do with being a DH.

The guy was, pure and simple, one of the greatest right-handed hitters the game has ever seen, and you can throw in Rogers Hornsby, Willie Mays, Frank Robinson, the righty half of The Mick, or anyone else you want. He was the first player in baseball history to hit at least .300, hit at least 20 home runs, and have more than 100 walks, RBI, and runs scored. Not in one season; in seven straight seasons. Hornsby didn't do it. Banks didn't do it.

The Big Hurt was a victim of his own stature. He was 6'5", 270 pounds, and as Wilt Chamberlain so aptly said, nobody likes Goliath. He hit more than 40 home runs in five different seasons. In 2005, when he was out for most of the season with an ankle injury, he had 105 official at-bats and hit 12 home runs. Think about that: an off year, rusty, and he steps in with a home run every 8.6 times at bat.

Sammy is the only player in baseball history to hit 60 or more home runs in a season three times. Aaron didn't. Ruth didn't. Maris certainly didn't. Mantle didn't. Mays, Jackson, Killebrew—nope. If you want to cry "'Roids!" go ahead. Bonds didn't either.

If there's an amusing note to his homer binge from 1998–2001, it was that the only season he won the HR crown was in 2000, the only year he didn't hit 60 (he hit 50).

He won it again in 2002, with 49. Bill Clinton invited him as a guest at Clinton's 1999 State of the Union address.

Love him or hate him, he was one of the dominant players of his era, which will probably be enough to get him into the Hall of Fame. But was he the equal of Thomas?

If you're only looking at Sosa's HR numbers, you're missing the overall. He was a 30-30 man (homers and stolen bases) twice, in 1993 and 1995. He also hit .300 four times: .300 in 1994, .308 in 1998, .320 in 2000, and .328 in 2001.

If you want to disqualify the home run totals because of chemistry, fine. But Sammy was getting 30 steals in seasons before he muscled up and had those tremendous batting-average years both with and without the juice. Sammy simply could hit once he put his mind to it.

One notable curiosity is that both Sosa and Thomas were brought to Chicago in the same year by Larry Himes. He was the Sox general manager who grabbed Thomas with the seventh-overall pick in the 1989 draft. And he was the one who traded Harold Baines and Fred Manrique to the Texas Rangers for Wilson Alvarez, Scott Fletcher, and Sosa on July 29, 1989. And it was Himes, as head of Cubs baseball operations, who brought Sosa to the North Side in 1992.

Sammy hit for more power; Frank hit for better average. They both drove in prodigious amounts of runs. But one point made this debate easy to settle: runners in scoring position.

When it counted, Thomas was the man. Sammy had a .274 career batting average, but it dipped a couple points when runners were in scoring position and it really dropped, to .251, with runners in scoring position with two outs. Instead of tightening down when it was most important, Sammy became less of a hitter.

Frank had a career average of .307 through 2005, the end of his White Sox years. With no one on, he hit a respectable .298. But with runners in scoring position, he batted .318. He got it. And with a man on third with two outs, Frank hit a stunning .387. He hit .354 with the bases loaded.

The Big Hurt was a better pure hitter than Sammy and he was a better clutch hitter. Sammy has a slight edge in home runs, hitting one every 14.2 at bats to Frank's one every 15.5 trips to the plate. But those are just glamor hits. Frank averaged one run batted in every 4.75 at bats for his Chicago career. Sammy was one for every 4.94 at bats, besides being on base less and striking out more.

So the greatest right-handed hitter ever? Not so fast. Frank's an easy pick over Sammy. But neither of them top the list. The best ever:

6. ROGERS HORNSBY

The Rajah is certainly the best hitter ever to wear a Chicago uniform, Sox or Cubs. But he only rates number six because he had only 1929 as a full season here, although "full" doesn't begin to describe it: batted .380, hit 39 homers and drove in 149, and he wasn't even the only monster in that lineup. But other than the .331 he hit in 100 games in 1931, he was really only a part-time player after that so not enough to qualify. Besides, he's a Cardinal, not a Cub.

5. ANDRE DAWSON

The Hawk had six phenomenal years in Chicago, capped by the MVP year he had in 1987, hitting 49 homers for a last-place team. He hit .284, averaged an RBI every 5.55 at bats, and homered once every 18.7 trips to the plate.

4. SAMMY

A lot of production for a lot of years.

3. ERNIE

Banks was a back-to-back MVP in 1958–59 (the only full seasons he hit .300), which says something about how he was viewed in an era when white players were still getting the nod in close calls. Ernie hit a prodigious home run total when shortstops did nothing of the sort. He had virtually no one in the lineup around him to force pitchers to throw

117

to him. He hit for virtually the same career average (.274) as Sammy, but struck out half as often; only once in his career did he have 100 whiffs.

2. FRANK

Power, average, contact, and a batting eye that rivals Hornsby's.

1. HACK WILSON

He only played in Chicago for six seasons but Wilson had the same career average as Thomas (.307) and topped Frank in key areas. He drove in a run every 4.48 at bats; for the years in Chicago he drove one in every 4.1 at bats, which translates into one every game, and he hit a homer every 16.6 at bats.

Wilson was a legendary substance abuser and it destroyed him and his career; he fared well enough against the aces of his era but couldn't beat John Barleycorn.

But for the time in Chicago, no one was better.

FLYING HIGHEST

The Best Blackhawks Ever

The unfortunate thing about the lost year of hockey, with the lockout and all the rest of the hard feelings, was that it effectively killed hockey in Chicago. Too bad. Because once upon a time, the hottest ticket in town wasn't Michael and the Bulls or Sammy and the Cubs, but Bobby Hull and the Hawks.

They are one of the charter six franchises in the NHL and they have had a long list of greats passing through the Chicago Stadium and the United Center. What makes picking the all-time all-timers a little sticky is that two of the positions, goalie and center, are spots where the Hawks themselves thought so much of two players that they retired numbers of both: Tony Esposito and Glenn Hall in goal and Stan Mikita and Denis Savard at center.

But even within the best of the Hawks, an elite core stands above all:

GOALIE: GLENN HALL

What about: Tony Esposito? He was the face of the Hawks from when he was Rookie of the Year in 1969, clearly the true heir to Hall's throne, until he retired 15 years later, all seasons ending with the Hawks in the playoffs. Tony-O won three Vezina Trophies as the league's best goaltender. Good enough for the Hall of Fame.

What about: Eddie Belfour? Eight years with the Hawks and part of the team that got to the Stanley Cup Finals in 1992. For his career he allowed only 2.65 goals per game and at 201-138-56, he had the best record of the three finalists.

Yeah but: Hall played before masks, which meant standing in against shots from Frank Mahovolich and the Richards without a shield. And Hall still managed a career goals-against average of 2.62, better than either of his two chief rivals for the top spot between the pipes.

All three were goaltenders you win because of. But Hall, who like Belfour won two Vezinas, gets the No.1 spot because he did what neither of the others could achieve: win a Stanley Cup (1961).

DEFENSEMEN: CHRIS CHELIOS AND DOUG WILSON

What about: Keith Magnuson? Maggie was my favorite defenseman because of the way he played with flair and never shrank from the dirty work of dealing with even the ultra-goons, even if he didn't always do as well as his nose and jaw would have liked. But Pat Stapleton and Bill White were better at breaking up offensive charges and playing classic NHL defense.

What about: Pierre Pilote? Tough call on Pilote, who was the centerpiece of the defense in the early '60s and for his 13 years with the Hawks. He played 821 games and won an amazing three straight Norris Trophies in 1963, '64, and '65, stamping him as the best overall defenseman of the decade. And Pilote had 400 assists, meaning that while he was turning back opposing forwards and centermen, he was finding time at a rate of nearly once every other game to have a hand in a Blackhawk goal besides the 77 he scored himself.

Yeah but: Chelie is a Chicago guy, even if he did wind up in Detroit with the Red Wings and open a couple of restaurants over there. He and Wilson were genuine offensive threats besides being superior disruptors on defense.

Chelie, who spent his first seven NHL seasons in Montreal and the last six in Detroit, scored 92 goals in nine Chicago seasons and he was a triple-figure PIM guy; he had that nice badass gene that great defensemen need and he had seven straight "plus-differential" seasons with the Hawks, all double-digit positives.

Wilson was the best two-way defenseman in Hawks history. He could control the blue line and was a must on the power play. He set the franchise record for goals by a defenseman with 225 over a 14-year run in town. In 1981–82 Wilson had 39 goals and 85 points; that's more goals than Bobby Orr in all but one of his prime years with Boston.

36 CENTERMAN: STAN MIKITA

What about: Jeremy Roenick? Like every one of the elite, JR was more than a player; he was an enormous part of the personality of the franchise. Roenick was in town for eight years and averaged more than a goal every other game through his 524 played. He and Mikita were tough guys as well as talented and there is something wrong with the sport of hockey or the business of the Black Hawks when a guy like Roenick doesn't finish his career in Chicago.

What about: Denis Savard? Savvie was the greatest pure stickhandler the Hawks have had on their ice, everything from his legendary Spin-O-Rama move to just pure speed hockey in an era and sport that too often degenerated into mucking and grinding. Savvie, who like Chelie also came from Montreal, is third all-time in Hawks scoring. He had 61 goals in 131 playoff games for the Hawks.

Even when Savvie was through in Chicago he was helping out. Besides joining the team as a coach, he was traded to Montreal after his ten Black Hawk seasons in return for Chelios.

Yeah but: What nudges Savard into second place at the position is simply that Mikita, in a lot of folks' minds, is the greatest single hockey player the team has ever had the good fortune to put in a sweater, Hull included. Mikita holds the franchise record for assists, games, and points and is second all-time in goals. Four times he led the NHL in scoring and still was a two-time winner of the Lady Byng Trophy for sportsmanship; he did it all and did it with class.

Twice he was the NHL's MVP. That helps make him the best of the best in this spot.

37 RIGHT WING: MUSH MARSH

What about: Tony Amonte? Definitely a finalist and played the nine seasons of his prime in Chicago. But he wasn't a truly dominating player and never totaled 90 points in a season despite being a major part of the Hawks' offense from 1993–2002.

What about: Steve Larmer? Larms not only was an iron-man with 884 consecutive games played for the Hawks; he also was a pure hockey player who was willing to check as well as score. His line with Savard and Al Secord ranks as one of the best trios the Hawks have assembled.

If there is a "disappointment" with Larmer, it's that he won a Stanley Cup—after the Hawks had traded him to the New York Rangers.

Yeah but: Marsh, nicknamed after a popular cartoon character of similar diminutive stature, played one year of junior hockey and then jumped to the NHL, where he had a 17-year career with the Hawks beginning in 1928. He scored the first-ever goal in Toronto's Maple Leaf Garden.

What cinches his spot on my team is history. His biggest moment was bringing the Hawks their first Stanley Cup when he scored a goal in the second overtime period of Game 4 in the 1931 Cup Finals. Mush was the oldest living NHL player for years before dying in 2002.

38 LEFT WING: BOBBY HULL

No argument. The Michael Jordan of the Hawks: seven goal-scoring titles, three overall scoring championships, and two Most Valuable Player awards in the NHL in the 1960s. The first man to score 50 goals in a season. The greatest offensive threat the Black Hawks ever sent against an opponent's goalie. With Murray Balfour and Bill Hay, the "Million Dollar Line."

The Winnipeg Jets and World Hockey Association backed up the "Million" label with cash that the Hawks didn't think he was worth, so the Golden Jet went to the new league and helped pry open the coffers for future generations of players by helping the baby league gain credibility and a start.

He was one of the toughest in a truly tough sport and yet staged a one-game strike in the 1977–78 season to protest violence in hockey.

The best ever in Chicago.

PAINT ME A PICTURE

Who's Done the Best Color Analysis of Chicago Sports?

 Whether or not players, managers, coaches or anyone else in a sport want to acknowledge it, a lot of fans know something about the sport they love to follow. Because of that, many listeners have a special place in their hearts—and ears—for the experts who provide the color commentary for their teams' broadcasts.

Chicago has had far more great color analysts than great teams.

The best hockey color man was Dale Tallon, whose 17 seasons with Pat Foley were high points for Black Hawks fans who couldn't afford tickets and had no TV option. He had an obvious chemistry with Foley, himself one of the greats behind a mike, and he had more than just hockey color: "I wouldn't say it's cold," Tallon once declared, "but every year Winnipeg's athlete of the year is an ice fisherman." He was blunt, funny, and good enough to merit his own bobble-head doll with Foley.

Irv Kupcinet may have been the most amusing Bears commentator for his time as Jack Brickhouse's sideman ("Dat's right, Jack"). Dick Butkus was exponentially better, beginning in 1985 when he was hired along with Jim Hart in the booth with Wayne Larrivee. Butkus was the gruff voice of Bears football who laughed right along with the world when the Refrigerator began his run. No one played the game any better and no one ever called its nuances and shadings better either.

Butkus would get the nod as the No. 1 Bears color man were it not for the job Tom Thayer does alongside Jeff Joniak in WBBM-AM's two-man booth. Thayer has learned how to bring an edge to his calls without tilting to either curmudgeon or homer, and with his cachet as an '85 Bear, intensity, and sense of humor, he is a fan favorite.

Jimmy Piersall was the love-or-hate booth man with Harry Caray on the South Side and no one will ever accuse him of taking a pass on a tough subject. Jimmy just made a few too many subjects unnecessarily tough and when he took a dislike to a player, for whatever reason, it came across in his calls and sometimes didn't make complete sense.

The "honorable mention" in the category goes to John Paxson, who won three championships as a player, including the 1993 championship which finished with his game-winning 3-pointer in Game 6 against Phoenix, and one as an assistant coach.

Paxson also spent seven seasons as the color man working with Neil Funk and did both radio and TV with a dry wit, as well as the kind of game grasp that was behind Michael Jordan asking him to consider becoming Wizards head coach when Jordan went to Washington.

3. JOHNNY "RED" KERR, BULLS

The Redhead has been everything for the Bulls—player, coach and voice—working through the Jordan years with a self-deprecating sense of humor and a grasp of the game befitting a Hall of Famer.

Johnny gets the number three spot for, if nothing else, his reaction to Michael's immortal jumper over Craig Ehlo and for all the chalk he endured from Michael's pregame "dusting" ritual. But few broadcasters ever painted a better picture for a listener.

2. STEVE STONE, CUBS

Stonie was and still is one of the most uncompromising and insightful baseball voices ever in a booth on either side of town. For 21 years he paired with Harry and then Chip Caray on Cubs broadcasts. By the time he resigned after the 2004 season because of a deteriorated relationship with manager Dusty Baker and management, Stone had achieved near cult-figure status among Cubs listeners. He got along with Harry and was a counterweight to that legendary broadcaster's idiosyncrasies.

127

Fittingly perhaps, his departure came after a 2004 season in which the Cubs ranked as one of the disappointments in all of baseball. Stone's "mistake" was calling it exactly the way he and legions of Cubs fans were seeing it. He proved prescient in being the first to point strongly to the mechanical problems in the delivery of Kerry Wood that would contribute to the promising righthander's seemingly endless run of physical and pitching problems.

Stone put managerial strategy under a magnifying glass, usually with a sense of humor or irony. His criticisms of players' roles, in and excuses, for the 2004 collapse eventually moved reliever Kent Mercker to call the booth to complain from the clubhouse—during a game. Listeners ask just that color men deliver accurate insights and many were the days that fans were talking about a Stonie comment or thought almost as intensely as they were about the game.

1. LOU BOUDREAU, CUBS

Lou was a Hall of Fame shortstop, an MVP, and his number 5 was retired by the Cleveland Indians. But Chicagoans would argue that they, not Cleveland, got the true best from "The Good Kid."

Lou broadcast Cubs games on radio for nearly 30 years, with Jack Quinlan and then Vince Lloyd, and he was part of a broadcasting team that, with Jack Brickhouse, was the voice of Chicago baseball for millions of fans. Doug Rader might become "Doug Radar" and Chris Cannizzaro might be "Chris Can-za-narrow" but few color analysts ever brought more to the game for listeners. And none to my knowledge ever brought a cowbell to it for each Cub win and home run.

Lou's insights were almost understated and he never belabored who he was in the game, despite the reality that he truly had forgotten more about the game than most of the players he described would ever know.

In the 1960s Lou and Jack Quinlan read commercial spots between innings, often with hilarious missteps.

"The Good Kid" died in 2001 and somehow the game was just a little less colorful for his passing.

DOME MADE
What Is It About Notre Dame?

40 To some, South Bend was where God went to rest on the seventh day, which really was Saturday, and hung out to watch his favorite team play. To others, South Bend is where the Almighty banished Lucifer when he cast the Devil out of Heaven, and Satan is alive and well over there under the Golden Dome.

If the Internet has done nothing else, it has loosed the Notre Dame lovers and haters to bash and counter-bash to epic levels.

What is it, though, that makes people either love or hate Notre Dame? Few Chicago sports fans are without at least some attitude on what is really the town's adopted college football team.

I say football, because basketball was an afterthought in South Bend for so long that it is far below football as an elicitor of emotion. The smarminess and self-righteousness of Digger Phelps during a time when Notre Dame was a force on the national stage notwithstanding, doesn't compare to the football program as a rage-inducer.

But why, exactly?

Some of it is rooted in hatred of the Catholic Church, going back a bit into the Rockne years and after. The fact is, not until John Kennedy got through a presidential race successfully did the anti-Church thing lose some, but not all, of its edge. Catholics had a smug our-way-or-the-hot-place attitude (I know this from my years of catechism) and there was a lot not to like. And right there, overlooking the Notre Dame stadium, is none other than "Touchdown Jesus," in case anyone thinks this is other than Catholic-based.

But the nub of the real antipathy isn't theological. It's basic America.

Two things that Americans, and Chicagoans in particular, despise are elitism and hypocrisy. You can be the absolute best at something, but you'll lose Chicago if you've got a case of attitude, that yours is somehow a little better than everybody else's. When that's connected to a core reality that there has too often been a rancid interior, now you have the basis for some real hatred.

It's important, though, to grasp how really superb the Notre Dame program has been. The Irish helped elevate college football to its national prominence with the games against Army during the 1920s. Grantland Rice creating the "Four Horsemen" mystique was a huge part of this.

The Rockne era was as good as it gets anywhere. The graduation rate for Notre Dame athletes is a gold standard, and not many quality athletic programs even come close. How can you quibble with that? You can't.

But Notre Dame firmly established its elitist image when it made the 1991 deal with NBC to broadcast their games, and to hell with the rest of the NCAA if they didn't like it.

The problem with being elitist, or being perceived as elitist, is that you'd better not ultimately have a sewer running through the middle of everything. In 1993, "Under the Tarnished Dome: How Notre Damed Betrayed Its Ideals for Football Glory" laid open some of the charade that had been the Lou Holtz regime, including supposed steroid use, brutal coaching tactics, and questionable academic standards for the institution that had held itself up as one of the academic elite.

Ara Parseghian's decision to settle for a tie in the '66 Michigan State game can be explained but it can't be justified, except on the grounds of cowardice. You're ultimately afraid to lose. "Fighting" Irish? Nope. Think Joe Montana takes the air out of the ball that way against Houston in that Cotton Bowl? Hardly.

In 1998, assistant coach Joe Moore successfully makes the case against coach Bob Davie for dumping him because of age. Things like the Kim Dunbar scandal made the hypocrisy of sanctimoniousness ring even louder. And when the university dumped coach Ty Willingham with time still on his contract, no amount of rationalizing, or winning, makes it right. When you talk about the sanctity of contracts and then do that to an apparently classy individual, you've proven all your haters right.

"Wake up the echoes...shake down the thunder." Indeed.

MR. EXCITEMENT

The One You Hated Most to Miss

41 Chicago has seen enough greats in every sport, but a handful above all others were the best to watch, the must-see's, the get-back-from-the-kitchen-in-a-hurry, pure-charisma sports figures.

The elite ones all not only changed the faces of their franchises and became the signature figures of their teams. They also became part of the personality of the city, part of the swagger of Chicago.

Ernie Banks is a contender, as magnificent as he was in the 1950s and on into the 1960s. The 512 home runs were definitely the best things the Cubs had going for them in the years when the Billy Goat Curse was taking root. But Ernie was quiet-great. He just went out in the sunshine every day and played the game the way it was supposed to be played. Not flashy, not look-at-me, just good baseball.

Ernie is a guy I would pay to see. But he's not the one I would drop everything to watch every time he came up to the plate.

Dee Brown was the igniter for the Illini national runners-up and was the best point guard in the country in 2006. He didn't do anything at reasonable basketball speed and when he broke containment and crossed midcourt going faster with the ball than his pursuers could without it, it was special. The headband and image helped. But he wasn't the show by himself, and that's part of the deal for holding the title of Mr. Electric.

Mark Aguirre is in the hunt as a college guy. When you average 27 points a game, you're the show. But I don't think I felt like I was watching greatness or anything more than a really, really good college player. Besides, the way his DePaul teams couldn't finish made it more like watching to see when the bottom would fall out.

The most charismatic group ever was the '85 Bears, individually and collectively a must-watch event every Sunday. But the most charismatic single performers ever in Chicago:

3. TIE: WALTER PAYTON AND GALE SAYERS.

Gale was the greatest pure runner Chicago, and maybe all of football outside of Detroit, has ever witnessed. The human body simply cannot do some of the things that Gale did.

Walter, like Gale, had me leaning forward every time he got the football. Every run with Walter was a potential classic and that's one of the main criteria for the award. Dan Hampton said the greatest run he ever saw in his career was a run by Walter that ended up a one-yard loss.

2. BOBBY HULL

Was there ever anything that brought the Chicago Stadium to a full boil than the Golden Jet getting the puck on the left wing with a head of steam, curved stick in one hand, the other one holding off a defenseman, and then coming free to loose one of the great slapshots in hockey history?

It wasn't that he was the first player to score 50 goals in a season. It was how he scored so many of those goals. One of the fastest skaters of his era and one of the strongest—and with that golden mane flowing...

1. MICHAEL JORDAN

The problem with watching the games of the Jordan Bulls is that there was no down time, except on the rare occasions when he sat. Between defensive stops and the possibility that every possession could be something for SportsCenter's highlight reels, it was absolute must-see.

Every night.

At the turn of the century, ESPN did a survey to rank the greatest athletes of the twentieth century. The top three were "greatest" for far more than simply their accomplishments: The Babe, Muhammad Ali, and No.1, Michael.

GALE SAYERS VS. BRIAN URLACHER

Speed vs. Speed

 The greatest pure runner in the history of the Bears (and football itself) against the linebacker who owned the entire football field. Who'd win?

THE CASE: Gale Sayers

The Kansas Comet was crazy-good. He was indeed a comet, streaking across the football heavens for a brief 68 games that were still so memorable that he was, at age 34, the youngest NFL player ever elected to the Pro Football Hall of Fame.

Nobody ran like Gale. Not Barry Sanders, who defied physiology and physics with his cuts and darts but could not have matched Sayers for poetry in full gallop. Not O. J., who was so spectacular when he turned a corner and ran by a defense while it was still trying to untangle itself, but had Pro Bowl guards to help. He was nothing like the Gale from

Kansas, who had anything but Pro Bowl guards. Not Walter or Jim Brown; they're just different runners altogether

No, it was Gale Sayers, about whom Green Bay's Herb Adderley said, "He's the only guy I think who could be running full speed, stop on a dime, tell you whether it's heads or tails, and not even break stride." The Bears made him the number four pick of the 1965 draft—same round as Walter a decade later—and got him in spite of the Kansas City Chiefs picking him No. 1 with their territorial rights in the AFL draft. Sayers just wanted to play in the NFL, period.

One debate is whether or not Gale is better that Walter Payton. That's for another time. Right now the question is how he would do against the fastest, most mobile linebacker the Bears ever had.

THE CASE: Brian Urlacher

For pure mobile horror, no one was the equal of Butkus. But for pure mobile, there was never a Bear like Urlacher. The only one in that debate would be Wilber Marshall, nicknamed "Pit Bull" by his '85 Bears teammates, a certified carnivore and one of the great speed hitters ever.

One deciding difference: Marshall was 240 pounds. Urlacher is 260. He is, simply, a freak.

Urlacher was a free safety at New Mexico. Urlacher was a wide receiver at New Mexico. Urlacher returned kickoffs and punts at New Mexico. Urlacher was the defensive MVP of the Senior Bowl at middle linebacker, a position he had

137

never played before. He ran a 4.5 second time in the 40-yard dash, which would have made him just so-so as a running back or receiver in the NFL, if anyone 260 pounds at 4.5 could be thought of as so-so. The Bears were considering using him at safety when they drafted him.

Urlacher is one of only five players in Bears history to be selected to Pro Bowls in his first four seasons. One of the others: Gale Sayers. Urlacher was the NFC's starting middle linebacker in 2000, his rookie season, the year the Bears put him at strong-side linebacker at first, an admitted mistake. When he got his first start, it was at middle linebacker. He had a sack that first game. And the next. And the next. For the first five games in fact, the third-longest rookie streak of games with at least 1 sack.

The fifth of those games was against the Minnesota Vikings, when he had two. The thing was, the quarterback he was taking down, and running down, was Daunte Culpepper, also 260 pounds and emerging as a truly scary mobile quarterback. The Bears knew what they had with Urlacher. They assigned him not so much to blitz the Vikings giant but to "spy" him—sit around the line of scrimmage, do some short pass coverage, but most importantly, mirror Culpepper's moves. Where Culpepper went, Urlacher went, only faster. It was an ominous foreshadowing if you were a quarterback.

Urlacher got positively ridiculous the next year. Against the Atlanta Falcons and speed-blur quarterback Michael

Vick, Urlacher had eight tackles, one for a loss, plus a sack, a forced fumble, an interception, and finally a 90-yard return of a Vick fumble for a touchdown.

It wasn't all a speed thing either. Three weeks later, against the San Francisco 49ers, Terrell Owens came across the middle on the first play of overtime. Owens heard Urlacher coming. Owens retracted his arms, let the pass go off his hands, and Mike Brown returned it for a touchdown.

Just to flesh out the resume, Urlacher won the NFC Special Teams Player of the Week honor when he caught a 27-yard touchdown pass for the winning points against the Washington Redskins.

But the highlights aren't the real perspective. Think about this:

In 2001, when Urlacher truly burst upon the NFL, skeptics charged that it was all happening behind the Twin Titans of Ted Washington and Keith Traylor, two-gappers who, along with 290-pound ends Phillip Daniels and Bryan Robinson, tied up entire offensive lines. Urlacher could roam sideline to sideline, grab a dog and a brew at a concession stand, and still run back to make a tackle just east of Des Moines. He finished with 148 tackles. Six sacks. Three interceptions.

In 2002, Washington was hurt most of the year. Urlacher lost his prime protector. The result: 214 tackles. Four and a half sacks. Seven passes broken up.

Jump to 2005. Bears in a totally different scheme, defensive linemen shooting one gap instead of keeping blockers off linebackers. A pair of 260-pound ends, Tommie Harris barely 290 pounds most of the year, and none of the D-linemen tasked with keeping blockers off Urlacher. Totals: 171 tackles. Six sacks. Five passes broken up.

In a word: Freak.

He needs a challenge. He spied Vick into frustration and quitting, Culpepper got hurt, Favre got old. How 'bout…

Gale Sayers.

One on one. Out in the open.

THE MATCHUP: 1965 Sayers vs. 2001 Urlacher

They both got savvier with a couple more years, but ultimately it's about raw athleticism. The runner versus the tracker. Urlacher is in his scheme, but for him there is only one scheme today: Spy Sayers.

And so it happens: First and 10, ball at the Sayers 42. Pitch to Sayers and he is breaking outside his right tackle, blockers stringing out the defense. All except Urlacher, who is picking through the chaff, not only without losing speed, but building it as he tracks Sayers through the bric-a-brac. Suddenly Gale has his tiniest crease and makes that loose-legged, 90-degree cut to his left and he is through the first wave, with a cornerback whiffing completely on a tackle and Mike Brown barely getting a hand on him.

And there is Urlacher, closing like a Great White on a bleeding fish, accelerating at impact. But this is Sayers. He plants his left foot and starts a flash-cut to his right. Urlacher reads it and has him now.

Anyone else, maybe. Not Sayers. With legs that seem to be operating independently, he now plants the right foot with his next step and comes to a near complete stop, side-slipping back to his left. Urlacher's reaction: an "OH S**T!" that half the stadium hears. Sayers is gone. Through Lance Briggs, through Alex Brown pursuing from the back side, 58 of the most unforgettable yards in NFL history.

Vintage Sayers.

The Appeal

But wait. Urlacher is fuming. Nobody does that. Not Vick. Not nobody. He circles to his left and sets off after the number 40 angling through his overmatched-if-still-trying teammates. They're not going to catch him.

But Nate Vasher is angling over from his cornerback position, getting off a block, and moving to interdict Sayers. If Sayers cuts back right to outrun Vasher, Urlacher will run him down from behind because in a pure footrace, Urlacher is faster.

The Verdict

Gale had eyes in the back of his head. How else do you explain some of those cuts for no apparent reason other than somebody was closing from behind? Bye, bye, Bri.

THE GREAT MATCHUPS: JORDAN BULLS VS....

43 It's difficult to bridge eras, between the changes in players, style, rules and the whole sporting environment. But if we could, what would you give to see two particular matchups?

One is a series between legends from three elite teams: the Bulls, Boston Celtics and Los Angeles Lakers. The greatest fivesome from each team.

The second is a series between the teams as they actually were.

A BULLS DREAM TEAM OF JORDAN, SLOAN, GILMORE, WALKER, AND RODMAN AGAINST:

Celtics legends: Bob Cousy and John Havlicek at the guards, Bill Russell at center, Larry Bird and Kevin McHale at the forwards. Great matchup, with the wills of Jordan, Havlicek, Rodman, and Russell on the same court. But Russell did not lose championship chances.

Decision: Celtics.

Lakers legends: Magic and Jerry West in the back court, Kareem in the middle, James Worthy and Elgin Baylor along the back line. Rodman will monumentally annoy Worthy and Baylor from time to time but between Magic working the entire floor and Zeke from Cabin Creek sharpshooting from outside, only one outcome.

Decision: Lakers.

But the Celtics and Lakers have far longer histories to draw from, so they have more All-Stars. How about actual teams versus actual teams, in this case the Celtics of Russell's prime, Bird's prime, and Magic's prime versus the Bulls with either Horace Grant or Dennis Rodman?

THE RUSSELL CELTICS

Some point-counterpoint: The Celtics only had to win two playoff series to win a championship, vs. the Bulls' four. But the talent pool was so diluted in the 1990s because of expansion. Then again, the NBA was still wedded to white players if possible in the Russell era. But white players

143

were all but extinct for lack of interest by the 1990s...and so on that stuff goes.

Forget about "athleticism." Standardize the eras and the conditioning and strength training. You think Bill Russell couldn't play now?

Michael never saw anyone who played defense like Russell. Russell was a selective shot-blocker and if he could stand up to Wilt, nothing the Bulls could throw at him was going to be a big problem. The Celtics won eight straight championships and 11 in the 13 years that really were Russell's era. The Bulls couldn't beat the Isiah Pistons for years before they started their run.

Michael would be too much for K. C. or Sam Jones or Satch Sanders. Call Havlicek and Pippen a wash; Hondo was the bionic swingman and found ways to win besides being great. Give the pivot to Russell over Bill Cartwright or Luc Longley. Tommy Heinsohn out-physicals Horace Grant, but Dennis Rodman is worth 10 points a game defensively and matches Russell rebound for rebound.

Decision: Jordan Bulls in seven and two of the games require OT to settle.

THE MAGIC LAKERS

Forget about the Bulls' first championship run over the Lakers. That was with Vlade the Inhaler in the pivot. Make it Jabbar in the middle and a young Magic running

Showtime. The Lakers won five titles in nine years and that was with a pair of wins over the Bird Celtics.

The wild card in this matchup is the Lakers' defense. It was overlooked too often with all the fast-breaking and skyhooks. But between Michael Cooper, James Worthy, and an entire team that grasped the importance of the stop, this was a monster. The Lakers weren't running after "made" baskets by their opponents; it was after steals, blocks, or missed shots, and missed shots don't happen in the NBA without defense.

Jabbar completely dominates the middle. Jordan fouls Cooper out by halftime. Rodman has Worthy struggling to get a rebound and double figures. The hard part for the Bulls is Magic; he had Jordan's will and force of personality and he didn't need to be scoring to dominate a game. Jordan or Pippen has to work so hard on defense that there may not be the legs there for jumpers in the fourth quarter. Magic had too many ways to break you down and whoever he posts up down low, he owns.

Decision: Magic's Lakers in six, with Magic the series MVP.

THE BIRD CELTICS

A front line of Larry Bird, Kevin McHale, and Robert Parish in the Hall of Fame. A sixth man (Bill Walton) in the Hall of Fame (insert joke here). A guard in Dennis Johnson who was arguably the NBA's best defensive guard ever, Jordan included. Danny Ainge wasn't bad either.

But as great as this team was, it couldn't consistently beat the Magic Lakers. Rodman's matchups with Bird in the late 1980s were epic, if rendered with a slight rancidity because of Rodman's obvious racism. The Bulls nearly upset the Celtics in the 1987 playoffs, before they really matured, and with Pippen in his prime, Rodman in his element and Jordan in his, the result is inevitable.

Decision: Jordan Bulls in five. Bird and Rodman are ejected twice for throwing down.

GAG ME
Chokes: Who Had It the Best and Lost It the Worst?

So many choices, so little space.

To be an epic choke you have to have something virtually won, not just a seventh-game problem, unless it's blowing a huge lead. And it has to be something with high stakes, not simply an April baseball game or September NFL game.

Chicago sports are full of chokes. That's how you go most of a century without winning championships in baseball or basketball and don't win that many in the others. Champions win in the pressure moments; losers....

The beauty, the symmetry of Chicago sports is that every one of our teams has not one, not two, but lots of chokes. Most of the all-time Chicago bumbles involved not only specific game chokes, but also choking away more than one contest as part of an even bigger choke.

The Bears gagged in 1995 when they had a 6-2 record and a halftime lead on the Pittsburgh Steelers. Then they lost that game, Pittsburgh went on to the Super Bowl, and the Bears went into a death spiral that cost them the playoffs. They had a 13-7 halftime lead on Washington in the 1986 playoffs and gave that game away.

The Bulls led the Los Angeles Lakers 90-83 with 2:58 remaining in the fourth quarter of Game 7 in the 1973 NBA semifinals. They then locked up in a succession of turnovers, missed shots, and mental gaffes. Norm Van Lier still had a 20-footer that could have won the game at the end, but Wilt Chamberlain came out of nowhere to block it. "Kareem and Wilt kept getting in our way," Van Lier said of the Bulls' early '70s.

But five gags stand out above all the others:

5. 1971 BLACK HAWKS, NHL FINALS

(It was the Black Hawks back then and didn't become "Blackhawks" until 1986.)

The Hawks led Montreal 2-0 in the second period when Bobby Hull clanked one off the top pipe. Then Jacques Lemaire floated a long shot past Tony Esposito, a truly bad miss, Henri Richard scored twice, and the Hawks collapsed to lose the game 3-2 and the series.

What made this one galling was that it was in Chicago. The Stadium. By a team with Hull, Espo, Pat Stapleton, Bill White, and Stan Mikita.

4. 1975 BULLS, NBA SEMIFINALS

When you lead 3-2 in a playoff series, you are supposed to finish the deal, especially when Game 6 is in your house. The Jordan Bulls did. The Motta Bulls...didn't.

The Bulls had double-digit leads in both the sixth and seventh games of their series with the Warriors. But Motta played his starters too much and they wore down, even managing to lose the sixth game by 14 points in one of the biggest points swings ever, anywhere, in a championship situation.

The Bulls were out-coached, out-played and out-every-thing'd. Not once, but twice, virtually two entire second halves. That is roughly about an hour of choking in playing time.

3. 1969 CUBS. REGULAR SEASON

The excuse that came down over time was that the Cubs didn't really choke in '69; the New York Mets just played phenomenally well and won it. Bull.

The Cubs led the Cardinals by 8 [½] and the Mets by 9 [½] games on August 14. They had three Hall of Famers in Ernie Banks, Ferguson Jenkins and Billy Williams, plus third baseman Ron Santo and his 29 homers and 123 RBI. By early September the lead was down to 2 [½].

The Cubs then gagged for eight straight losses, including three in Wrigley Field to the Pirates. Then they lost two to the Mets, and as of September 10 the Cubs were out of first place. Then they sucked it up and really showed what they were made of.

Not exactly. By the end of the season the Cubs were eight games out.

The easy out is to point to the Mets going 23-7 for September. The real point is the Cubs going 8-17. With the lead they had, the Cubs didn't need to play great, just respectable. Too much to ask, apparently.

2. 1984 CUBS. NLCS

The Cubs had the best record in the National League. That would have given them home-field advantage in just about any other playoff arrangement in any other sport, but the Padres got the final three of the five playoff games in Jack Murphy Stadium. So when the Cubs won the first two

149

games and then lost the final three, at least they could say they lost them on the road.

But losing those last three to the Padres wasn't just dropping a three-game series. It was one of the greatest chokes in Chicago sports history because of how they did it. The first team ever to blow a 2-0 lead in a league championship series. And it was a truly elegant choke, one that built in magnitude. The Cubs led in every single game of the series and gagged.

The cracking started in Game 4 when the Cubs led 3-2 after the fourth inning. By the ninth inning it was 5-5. The Cubs loaded the bases in the top of the 9th and didn't score a run. In the bottom of the ninth, Tony Gwynn singled and Steve Garvey homered off Lee Smith and the Cubs had blown a second straight game in which they had a lead.

The Cubs led 3-0 after the top of the sixth inning in Game 5. But Rick Sutcliffe was tiring and apparently everybody except manager Jim Frey could see it. The Padres got two in the bottom of the sixth and then four in the seventh, thanks to first baseman Leon Durham letting a roller from Tim Flannery trickle through his legs to let the game be tied. Maybe the Bull was just giving Bill Buckner something to aspire to two years later.

Maybe it was karma. Harry Caray was the radio play-by-play man and Milo Hamilton, who'd been passed over for the job Harry got and hated Harry, was the color man.

This beauty makes the Cubs the only team to place two

entries in ESPN's list of all-time Top 25 chokes. And it's not even the biggest one.

1. 2003 CUBS, NLCS

Forget Steve Bartman. He just had to endure being the scapegoat for the biggest meltdown ever in Chicago and one of the all-time team classics anywhere. So he doesn't even get mentioned in the rest of this account. At least he caught the ball that came near him. Too bad Alex Rodriguez can't say the same.

The Cubs had a 3-1 lead on the Florida Marlins and three of the best pitchers in baseball ready for their turns: Carlos Zambrano, Mark Prior, and Kerry Wood. All lost.

The Cubs got exactly 2 hits off Josh Beckett to lose game five. Game 6 was a gag for the ages. They led 3-0 going into the 8th inning behind Prior and even got the first Marlins batter out. But Prior walked 3 in his 7 [⅓] innings and put Luis Castillo on after Juan Pierre's double. The Cubs gave up 8 runs and the game; they gave it the fitting end by going three-and-out in both the eighth and ninth.

It got worse. They led 5-3 after 4 innings in Game 7 with Wood pitching. The Wood walked two of the first three in the 5th but Dusty Baker left him in anyway and didn't pull him until he'd put two on in the 6th. The Marlins scored 6 runs and the Cubs managed 1, once again going three-and-out in both the eighth and ninth, and that was it.

History.

WHAT'S IN A NUMBER?

Chicago's True Magic Number

To say it's a numbers game doesn't begin to cover it.

Some numbers in sports are beyond simple numerals. 100 will always be Wilt's number. 3 will always be the Babe. 44 is Hank Aaron. 16 is Joe Montana. 51 is Butkus. 13 will always be Wilt and Dan Marino.

But in Chicago there is really one number that has been mysteriously magical: 23.

It was Pete Maravich's number at LSU. It was Calvin Murphy's number in the NBA. Don Mattingly's in New York. All retired numbers.

But for whatever reason, the number "23" has taken on uniquely mystical properties when it is on the back of a uniform with Chicago on the front. It's just not magical everywhere: only in New York (Mattingly), Detroit (Willie Horton), and Chicago has the number 23 been worn to a level so distinguished that it was retired by its baseball team.

Maybe it's rooted in numerology, that the number itself or the combination of the two digits has some cosmic connection to Water Tower Place or somewhere. It is a prime number, one of those that are divisible only by themselves and 1. It is also the first number beyond the highest number (22) used in the construction of numerology charts. What this means should be obvious. (Should be; if you understand it, please call me.)

Maybe 23 is the waist size of Orion's Belt.

Is it the greatest number in Chicago sports history? A reasonable point of debate. Walter's number 34 is as historic as it gets. Ernie's number 14? Right there as well. Say those numbers anywhere in Chicago and it's instant recognition.

But whatever the real story is, putting a 23 on the backs of a disproportionate number of Chicago athletes is better than putting an "S" on their chests. Every Chicago team has had a memorable 23 and two of them have retired the number.

BEARS

The 23s that have passed through Wrigley and Soldier Fields have not been on their ways to the Hall of Fame, but after a decidedly pedestrian beginning, the number has taken on some steady luster and gotten two of its last three wearers to Hawaii for Pro Bowls.

It was a smooch of death in the Bears' early years when only one player between 1920–38 wore it for more than three seasons, although occasionally to championships. Davie Whitsell wore 23 in to the '63 championship during his six-year stint in the number that was its Bears breakthrough.

Shaun Gayle brought real shine to it in his 11 years, Super Bowl, and Pro Bowl. Marty Carter then had four good years as 23 before Jerry Azumah wore it through his seven-year career that ended in 2005 with one trip to the Pro Bowl.

BLACKHAWKS

The Hawks haven't had what you would call true impact number 23s. Then again...

Stu Grimson earned the moniker "Grim Reaper" for his fistic prowess and he ranks among the all-time great enforcers in Blackhawk annals, even though he was just in Chicago for three seasons. Grimson was 6'5", 239 pounds, and a pure bad-ass. He fought the toughest; his five go's with Bob Probert were the second-most of any Reaper opponent.

The Reaper had 2,113 penalty minutes and 17 goals in 16 NHL seasons. The boy could and would fight.

BULLS

The world knows the number 23 because of Michael. If there ever was an incongruity in sport it was seeing him in number 45 in his comeback. Of course, things didn't really turn back around for the Bulls and him until he went back to 23 where he belonged.

Michael had the number at North Carolina and it worked pretty well for him there. So it made some sense for him to wear it and immortalize it in Chicago as well.

CUBS

The right-away 23 that jumps up is Ryne Sandberg, a Hall of Fame second baseman and obviously one of the truly great players in the long, disappointing history of this organization. He came to the Cubs in one of the team's and Chicago's greatest trades and stayed a Cub all the way through his career, which also helps inscribe the number in Chicago lore.

But even before Ryno, the number had some superb cachet on the right side of the North Side infield. Phil Cavarretta was an All-Star from 1944–47 and was the National League's MVP in 1945, the last time the Cubs got to a World Series. He batted .293 over twenty-two seasons in Chicago, the last two with the White Sox, and led the league in hitting with .355 in '45.

Cavarretta's number? 23.

Of course he did get to three World Series with the Cubs and lose all three. Details, details.

WHITE SOX

Pitcher Virgil Trucks wore 23 for three outstanding seasons in the mid-'50s, going 47-26 in what was the best three-year stretch of his career. But Trucks was really a Detroit Tiger most of his career. Still, he did experience some of the 23 magic.

The guy who really installed some serious 23-ness on the South Side was Robin Ventura. For 10 years, from 1989–98 he was a fixture at the Comiskey Parks. He played in fewer than 100 games just once after his call-up rookie season, and that was after his gruesome broken ankle suffered in spring training. Ventura was the Sox's Ryne Sandberg, just quiet and a baseball player who won six Gold Gloves at third base— five with the Sox and one with the Mets. Only Brooks Robinson and Mike Schmidt won more.

He was sometimes too nice a guy. When Nolan Ryan, one of baseball's most over-hyped shams, buzzed him, Ventura charged the mound but didn't close the deal and Ryan got him in a headlock and started thumping his noggin. But a better legacy is Bill James, who named Ventura as the best third baseman of the 1990s in his *Historical Baseball Abstract.*

SMART THINKING

If Duke and Stanford, Why Not Northwestern?

46 Duke wins national championships in basketball. Stanford wins them in everything. So what is Northwestern's problem? And don't say "academics," because those other two disqualify that excuse.

Guess what: Northwestern doesn't need an excuse. If you have a problem with the athletic success of the Purple Rascals, the problem isn't with them.

The fact is, the Kitty Snarlers have gone to Bowl games, under their last two head coaches, Gary Barnett and the late Randy Walker, the first coach to take them to three. They won the national lacrosse championship in 2005, their first national crown in 64 years of sports in Evanston, and repeated in 2006. The Kitties had several representatives reach the final sixteen in NCAA tournaments and had Matt Grevers win a national championship in men's swimming. Women's softball; another top finish nationally.

The Cats ultimately finished 29th in standings for last year's Directors' Cup, which is a system that awards points for performances of as many as ten men's and ten women's teams. Stanford finished No. 1. Duke finished fifth. The Cats finished sixth among Big Ten teams, behind Michigan, Ohio State, Wisconsin, Penn State, and Minnesota.

That wouldn't be necessarily all that great except that Stanford has 35 NCAA teams. Ohio State and the others from the Big Ten have 25 to 33. The Fighting Furballs have 19, not even enough to fill in the dance card of 20 total that could be used for their ranking.

On a level playing field, the Cats do well enough, even with their numbers disadvantage. If you factor in the so-called minor sports—the lacrosses, the tennises, and such—Northwestern is in the league with the true bastions where "student-athlete" isn't an oxymoron. The hazing "scandal" was a smudge but was overblown by coverage and was dealt with swiftly and correctly by AD Mark Murphy, one of the bright bulbs in college athletics.

The crux of the NU perception question is men's basketball. That is a sport where size of the institution makes little or no difference; just ask George Mason University. But Northwestern has never earned a bid into the NCAA tournament while Duke and Stanford are powers with near-annual chances to win national titles.

The problem is critical mass, and Northwestern has never been able to reach it in hoops. That is where the school lands the "aircraft carrier" of Al McGuire, the program ticks significantly up, and then begins to draw more top prep talent who want to be part of something good happening.

Don't blame the academics. Don't blame the coaching. Don't blame the size of the arena, unless it's part of explaining why the studs coming out of high school don't take as serious a look at Northwestern as they do at the Rupp Arenas of Kentucky, the Dean Dome at North Carolina, and the Pauley Pavilions of UCLA.

Duke has the advantage of being right across the way from North Carolina and North Carolina State, so kids who don't make the short list at the others can get in on some of the great rivalries in college sport just by going to the other school.

Northwestern has a beautiful lakefront campus—at least it's beautiful in the months of the year when the wind chill isn't in the minus-degrees. Duke and Stanford don't have to worry about how their campuses will look during a January athlete visit.

Leave the Kitty Snarlers alone. They're doing just fine.

MANAGING SOMEHOW

Managers: In the Past 50 Years, These Few Did It Best

47 Neither the Cubs nor the Sox have had excess success over the last half-century, a time span I picked in order to eliminate the teams and work of Joe McCarthy and Frank Chance and even Kid Gleason. Those Cubs and Sox teams were so talent-heavy and also in a different era, so the more recent managers had a tougher job working with less and therefore a better test by which to judge.

He may have blown the most chances in the shortest time of any of his predecessors and Sox counterparts, but Dusty Baker goes in on the plus side of the line. He makes questionable remarks, is evasive and shaky on matters like Barry Bonds, failed to keep his team focused in 2005, was part of the 2003 collapse, didn't manage Sammy Sosa whatsoever, and may be the worst handler of pitchers Chicago has ever seen.

But Baker put a rope around the Cubs and started pulling them in the right direction, and the overall carries more weight than the specifics. Baker created for the city, not just the fans, the expectation of winning instead of the hope. Sure, he's got a full dose of snake oil and has manipulated everyone from the media to the fans to his players.

But I'll take someone you either love or hate over somebody who's gently vanilla. He's been good for Chicago baseball, if not good enough to rate a ranking with the elite because of what his teams failed to do.

Tony LaRussa won a division with the 1983 "Winning Ugly" Sox and went on to far greater success in Oakland and St. Louis. But he was no better than a .500 manager in his Chicago tenure.

Leo Durocher took over the Cubs in 1966 and had no losing seasons after his 103-loss start in '66. But The Lip was part of the problem, not the solution, in '69 and not being able to win even one pennant with the team he had does not a top manager make.

Jim Frey and Don Zimmer won divisional pennants but the inconsistent play of those teams, especially the '84 collapse under Frey, compromises the overall.

3. JERRY MANUEL, WHITE SOX 1998–2003

Mild-mannered Manuel may go down as the most underrated baseball man to pass through, considering that he managed the Sox for six seasons and only once finished lower than second place in the division. His 2000 team won the division and earned him A.L. Manager of the Year and if the 2003 team had been able to close out the division race, he might still be running the Sox.

2. AL LOPEZ, WHITE SOX 1957–65

El Señor never had a losing season in Chicago, had five second-places behind the Yankees, and reached the 1959 World Series. His 1954 Cleveland Indians and 1959 Sox were the only American League teams other than the Yankees to win a pennant from 1949–64. His 840 wins are second in Sox history behind only Jimmy Dykes (899), who needed 13 seasons to do achieve what Lopez did in nine.

Lopez died in 2005, four days after the Sox won the World Series. A nice farewell gift.

1. OZZIE GUILLEN, WHITE SOX 2004–2005

Too soon to pick a first-time manager as a "best"? Not in Guillen's case. The obvious is the World Series championship that unlocked a baseball door in Chicago that most thought was welded permanently shut. But there's more to establish Guillen already as the best field general a Chicago ball diamond has seen.

Guillen changed the entire persona of a team in one year and set it permanently in place the year after. Guillen has become the most refreshingly honest face a local team has had, with his ready-fire-aim personality that may self-destruct someday (but I somehow doubt it).

Guillen didn't check his emotions outside the stadium, so when he thinks someone like Magglio Ordóñez is taking a shot at him or his team, he fires back whether it's required or not. He "explains" decisions by pointing out "because I'm the manager, that's why."

Guillen was suspended for calling an umpire a liar. He said one of his players was faking an injury. He unnecessarily abused some of his players, specifically young pitchers. And when the club started a September slide, he didn't panic, just bluntly said, "We flat out stink." He told the Washington Post, "I don't know if I'm a leader but I have the biggest mouth."

No other manager or coach won a championship so soon after taking over a Chicago team, and he finished second and first in his first two seasons in charge.

But his most impressive accomplishment: He is taking Chicago away from the Cubs. And it's more than the baseball, it's him. He is a true player's manager, far more than his counterpart on the North Side, because he can separate the nonsense from the important stuff and no player is going to run the clubhouse. I'd have bought a ticket to see Guillen deal with the Sammy Thing if it had showed up in a Sox clubhouse.

THE JERK FACTOR

Who Have Been the Most Dislikeable Mopes of All?

48 Not everybody is nice to the media. That's OK; the media aren't particularly nice to each other. Why should athletes be any different?

But there is an elite group of Chicago athletes who have gone above and beyond the level of normal repugnance and treated not only media shabbily but also, more important, verbally or otherwise abused fans—the real reasons they (and the media) have jobs.

Notably perhaps, jerkism does not play well or long in Chicago. Most of the true dirtbags were in Chicago uniforms for a very brief time, usually three years or fewer. On the other hand, maybe you give some of them real credit for building up a body of jerk in so short a time.

Sammy Sosa and Frank Thomas got into funks from time to time but were not consistently repugnant to deal with for fans or media. Both were more than capable of saying wrong things or of ego spasms or of media boycotts. But more often than not they were OK with chatting casually in spite of propensities for sports diva-ism. Frank in particular belongs in a different area altogether (see "Give 'Em a Break").

Albert Belle, however, was a truly nasty person to deal with, both for media and the public. Besides routinely issuing hostile utterances to scribes and broadcasters, Belle stiffed the fans for autographs even on assigned signing days set up by the team. He also missed few opportunities to be surly with all on a near-daily basis in his three ornery seasons in Chicago, sandwiched between similar runs in Cleveland and Baltimore.

To be fair, Belle, like Bryan Cox in Miami, was confronted by some disgusting fan behavior over his career. He just had a way of one-upping even the most obnoxious.

Dennis Rodman earned consideration for his self-promotional phoniness and selective indulgence of fans and media. That so much of his act was calculated and choreographed makes it worse, not better.

Cade McNown is on the list somewhere but is edged out only because he was a small-time problem, although his teammates would probably put him near the top of their rankings of repulsive.

Management figures challenge for places somewhere in the rankings. Some would rate Bears president Michael McCaskey and Black Hawks owner Bill Wirtz as complete jerks; my feeling is that those are villains as far as the fans are concerned, more than pure jerks. They may have issues, but not near the pedigree repulsiveness of the others. Michael McCaskey and others in the family privately do charitable works that few outside a select circle know of and they want it that way.

White Sox manager Terry Bevington's name appears on most ballots for his boorish two and a half years on the South Side. At one point *Chicago Tribune* beat reporter Paul Sullivan simply printed a transcript of a Bevington press conference rather than try to capture the smarmy, inane utterances of a manager who once signaled to the bullpen to send in a left-hander even though none was warming up.

3. LEE ELIA, CUBS MANAGER

Actually, Elia is difficult to rule on because his whole meltdown and tirade against fans and some of the media after a one-run loss in April 1983 was recorded by legendary sports radioman Les Grobstein and lives today as one of the all-time...somethings in Chicago. The short version:

"The motherfuckers don't even work. That's why they're out at the fuckin' game. They oughta go out and get a fuckin' job and find out what it's like to go out and earn a fuckin' living. 85 percent of the fuckin' world is working. The other 15 percent come out here [Wrigley Field]. A fuckin' playground for the cocksuckers. Rip them mother-fuckers. Rip them fuckin' cocksuckers like the fuckin' players. We got guys bustin' their fuckin' ass, and them fuckin' people boo."

The reason why Elia doesn't rate a spot in the top two is that he was defending his players, not simply being repulsive for repulsive's sake. Elia was a curmudgeon to deal with for just about anyone other than GM Dallas Green, who eventually had to fire the man he'd brought in from Philadelphia to manage the Cubs.

2. DAVE KINGMAN, CUBS OUTFIELDER

Kingman, hitter of some of Chicago's most prodigious home runs, was also one of its classic hostiles, disliked among not only the media members he treated with rudeness and contempt, but also his teammates, one of whom described him as having "the personality of a tree stump."

Kingman's high point may have been in April 1980 when he dumped a bucket of water over the head of Daily Herald sportswriter Don Friske. He was particularly anti-social with female sportswriters, making professional life just a little more difficult for a group that had it hard enough gaining respect even among peers. While with the A's, he sent a rat to one of the women covering the team.

167

1. JOHN ROPER, BEARS LINEBACKER

Nicknamed "Ravage," Roper would have nothing to do with any local media, however amiable, but he would talk to anyone from Houston, his hometown. More despicable was his treatment of fans, in particular children. When one youngster held up a program and a pen and asked for an autograph one afternoon at Halas Hall in Lake Forest, Roper snarled, "Get the fuck outta my face!"

Typical. He was intensely disliked within the locker room and eventually traded to the Dallas Cowboys in 1993 by Dave Wannstedt. Roper's career effectively ended when he dozed off in a Jimmy Johnson team meeting. A fitting end.

DREAM SOX

No Holes in These Sox

There haven't been a lot of championships on the South Side, but there have been some superior talents that have gone through the Comiskey clubhouses. These are the all-time All-Stars at 35th and Shields:

49 **RIGHT-HANDED PITCHER: Red Faber**
Had he not gone for the money in 1919, Eddie Cicotte likely would have been the greatest Sox right-hander. He pitched nine seasons for the Sox, fin-

ished 71 percent of the games he started, and won 156 while losing 101. "Knuckles" threw 35 shutouts, and since his hitting the Cincinnati leadoff hitter was the sign that the fix was in for the '19 World Series, we know he had mighty good control.

What about: Ted Lyons? Lyons went into the Hall of Fame in 1955, certainly a great right-hander, who completed an incredible 356 of the 484 games he started. Unfortunately, he only won 260 and lost 230 with a career ERA of 3.67. Not special.

What about: Early Wynn? Gus was a 300-game winner and a dominant figure with his 22-10 mark in the World Series year of '59. But he was only in Chicago for five seasons and that was the only really good one. Gus's legend was made back in Cleveland with Bob Feller, Mike Garcia, Bob Lemon, and, for too brief a moment, Herb Score.

Yeah but: The linchpin of the Sox staff for 20 years was Faber. He was a spitballer but didn't throw more than a handful each game, just to keep hitters guessing. He led the league in ERA in 1921–22 when he won 25 and 21 games. Give him the ball.

50 LEFT-HANDED PITCHER: Billy Pierce

What about: Mark Buerhle? Buehrle may turn out to be the best Sox leftie ever, a throwback who works fast, throws basic strikes. It's a rare night that he doesn't take the game right into the innings of the closer, if he needs one at all.

Yeah but: The southpaw standard on the South Side is Billy Pierce. How many times was it Pierce versus Whitey Ford, one of the great matchups of the 1950s? Pierce pitched for 18 seasons and topped 200 innings nine times in one 10-year stretch. In that run he completed more than half (162) of the games he started (306). He won 211 games and put up a career ERA of 3.27. That makes him the best White Sox leftie.

51 CLOSER: Hoyt Wilhelm

What about: Rich Gossage? Goose got his "start" in Chicago, arguably one of the stupider moves in town. Gossage was a decent man out of the pen but in '76, after he put up a 1.84 ERA, the Sox made him a starter, naturally. When he went 9-17 with a 3.94 ERA, off he went to Pittsburgh for Richie Zisk.

What about: Bobby Thigpen? Thiggie was a monster for seven years, putting up 201 saves out of 348 games finished in Chicago. At his peak he was putting up ERAs no higher than 3.76 until his last season and he fit the power-closer model.

Yeah but: No one was more of a final word out of the bullpen than Wilhelm, whose six years in Chicago were the longest stretch with any team in his Hall of Fame career. He was the genesis of the concept of "relief ace," followed by Pittsburgh's Elroy Face, and actually had a significant winning record (41-33) for the Sox. His ERAs that started at 2.64 and dropped into the 1.00s for the next five years set the standard for what relievers are expected to do.

Wilhelm was a cold-blooded finisher. After a Purple Heart in the Battle of the Bulge, you think he's worrying about Tony Oliva or Harmon Killebrew or Carl Yaztrezemski?

 ## CATCHER: Carlton Fisk

What about: Ray Schalk? Schalk is in the Hall of Fame with a .253 career batting average. He was consistent and part of a run of superb Sox teams, hitting .304 in the '19 World Series.

Yeah but: Fisk spent 13 seasons in Chicago, eleven in Boston. He helped make the White Sox perennial challengers and brought out the best in pitching staffs. He never hit .300 and had only one Chicago season with more than 26 homers. And his .176 average contributed to the debacle in the '83 ALCS against Baltimore. But somehow the specific numbers didn't matter as much as the leadership factor.

It's too bad his relations with the Sox were so acrimonious that he chose to be enshrined in Cooperstown in a Red Sox cap. He's the best catcher the White Sox ever had.

FIRST BASE: Paul Konerko

What about: Ted Kluszewski? Big Klu helped the Sox get to the '59 World Series when he came over from the Pittsburgh Pirates for the latter part of the season. His back was ruined but he was still a dominant hitter in the Series with 10 RBI and 3 homers.

What about: Dick Allen? Don't-call-me-Richie didn't really fit in anywhere but was magic for three seasons here: .308, .316, and .301. He was MVP in '72 with the .308 average going with 37 homers and 113 RBI. Chuck Tanner had some success handling an unmanageable player but the Sox still traded him after 1974 when he "retired" with a month left in the season.

Yeah but: Forget about it. Paulie has hit between .277-.304 in six of his seven Chicago seasons, averages more than 90 RBI, and hits for power. After his MVP show in the '05 ALCS, you'd take anybody else?

SECOND BASE: Eddie Collins

The hardest call. Take your pick between Hall of Famers. Nellie Fox hit .288 for his career, was MVP in '59, and led the league eight times in singles.

Collins played 25 seasons, had a career average of .330 that included eight straight at .319 or higher. He was the 1914 MVP and six times was a top-five finisher for that honor.

I have to take the higher average: .330? Are you kidding? And he was above the stink of '19 too. Good, and honest. Nice combo.

 ## SHORTSTOP: Luis Aparicio

What about: Luke Appling? The Sox have probably had more A-listers at shortstop than any other position. Appling was there for 20 years and hit .310, won the batting title twice, and even hit a home run off Warren Spahn in an Old Timers Game.

On average alone Appling would be the choice. But Little Looie broke many of Appling's records, even if he only hit .300 once in his career, and he was seventh all-time in stolen bases when he retired. You win in baseball by being strong up the middle and there was never a defensive shortstop close to Aparicio.

 ## THIRD BASE: Buck Weaver

When Kenesaw Mountain Landis banned Buck Weaver for life, it opened the career door for Willie Kamm, who hit a very respectable .281 for his career and had more than 130 hits in all but one of eight Chicago seasons.

We know that Buck Weaver doesn't rat out his team-mates, which is another issue altogether. We also know that he is the best third baseman the Sox ever put on the field, and reputedly the only man Ty Cobb would not try bunting against.

Buck was a .272 lifetime hitter who actually played more of his career at short than at third. But he hit .327 in the '19 Series.

Joe Crede has a shot to be the South Siders' greatest third baseman if he settles into anything approaching a consistent level of play. But until then, it's Buck.

57 LEFT FIELD: Minnie Minoso

What about: Ron Kittle? Al Smith? If Kitty had maintained anything close to the pace of his rookie season (35 HRs, 100 RBI), he would have been the fixture in left. As it was, Kittle hit 93 out in his three full seasons with the Sox but he could barely hit his weight (220) and that's not good enough. Smith came to Chicago from Cleveland in the deal that took Minnie to Cleveland and played five seasons for the Sox and is a solid second to Minoso in left.

Yeah but: It's fitting that he was the first black player to wear a Sox uniform. Because of race, Minnie didn't get to play regularly until he was 28 and he still hit for a .298 lifetime average and made All-Star teams seven times. He led the A.L. three times in stolen bases. He was a three-time Gold Glove winner.

And you gotta love that he was given the honor of presenting the Sox lineup card at the final game in Comiskey on September 30, 1990.

CENTER FIELD: Joe Jackson

What about: Jim Landis? This was one of the best defensive centerfielders of his time. But he only hit better than .280 once in 11 seasons.

What about: Chet Lemon? He tops Landis not just because of his near-.300 consistent hitting, but also because he put some flair into those South Side Hitmen pajamas that Mary Frances Veeck made the team wear.

Yeah but: There has been only one truly great centerfielder in Chicago, North Side or South Side: Shoeless Joe. He didn't get to Chicago until 1915 and he never had a full season, Cleveland or Chicago, when he hit lower than .300. He could throw a baseball 400 feet on the fly.

Jackson is not in the Hall of Fame because of the obvious little problem with 1919, also a matter for another discussion. But Jackson's career average is .356. Only Ty Cobb's and Rogers Hornsby's are higher. Enough said.

RIGHT FIELD: Harold Baines

What about: Jim Rivera? Jungle Jim was a legend for his belly-flop slides long before Pete Rose copied them. Rivera's catch off Charlie Neal to save Game 1 of the '59 Series was every bit the equal of Willie Mays's grab against Vic Wertz; Rivera just didn't happen to do it in New York, so how good can it really be, right?

Yeah but: Baines ranks ahead of Hall of Famers like George Brett and Mike Schmidt in career RBI. He was a perennial All-Star who should never have been let out of Chicago.

Baines was a .300 hitter even when he was brought back late in his career. Before his knees wore out, he was a solid defensive player. His biggest fault may have been viewed as not being media-friendly, which will probably hurt him at Hall of Fame voting time. But not here.

60 DESIGNATED HITTER: Frank Thomas

Because it's the American League, they get a DH. And there's no one to even put in the competition. He may not have liked the job (if there were no DH, I'd probably rank Frank ahead of Konerko at 1B just for the bat) but the Big Hurt is the best right-handed hitter the Sox ever had and second only to Hack Wilson as Chicago's best.

BEARS ULTIMATE D

From a Franchise Built on Defenses, Which Are the 11 Best?

The Bears have defined, and been defined by, defense through much of their history. And Bears defense has been defined by eleven above all the rest.

61 END: Doug Atkins

What about: Ed Sprinkle? The Hook, his clothesline tackle. Maybe the meanest, most vicious hitter other than Butkus who has ever put on a helmet with a "C." *Colliers Magazine* even did a 1950 article on him: "The Meanest Man in Football." He played in the first three Pro Bowls, which didn't start until he'd been in the NFL seven years. And he still draws boos when he's introduced at charity golf events in Green Bay.

Yeah but: Don't waste time. Atkins was 6'8", somewhere between 265–280 pounds, and one of pro football's all-time greats. There are so many Atkins stories, but my own best one was watching a 1950s Bears-Giants game and seeing him hurdle Hall of Fame left tackle Roosevelt Brown who was standing upright. Plus, anybody with the stones to drink Halas's private halftime bottles of spiked pop has to be the best ever.

TACKLE: Dan Hampton

What about: Wally Chambers? For a while Chambers was the best, a Pro Bowl defensive lineman from teams that were 3-11, 4-10 and 7-7. But he was injured in 1977 and was traded to Tampa Bay in 1978 for the first-round draft choice that turned into Hampton, who turned out better.

Yeah but: The only problem with Hampton is whether he is a tackle or end on the all-time team. He went to two Pro Bowls at each spot. He was the left end on the '85 team but he'd been the NFL defensive player in '82 at tackle.

Hampton had 25 sacks in his first three seasons, started his 48 games consecutively and was on the NFL Team of the '80s, which was really the Golden Age of the NFC.

Doug Plank is the name associated with the '46 defense because of his uniform number. But Hampton was the true key to what this thing was. It was Hampton that Buddy Ryan sent inside head-up on the center, and with the guards already busy, "Danimal" was leading the destruction by the greatest defense in football history.

63 TACKLE: George Musso

What about: Some of the old guys? Like Ed Healy, who Halas called "the most versatile tackle I ever saw"? Like Link Lyman, who pioneered stunting, slanting, and shifting defensive line play, who went from no football in high school (his school had seven boys) to playing at Nebraska?

Those guys could play and frankly, put them in today's game, with the same strength and conditioning programs, the schemes, all the rest, and they would be more than tough enough and fast enough and all the rest. But there's just a couple of guys who are better.

What about: Steve McMichael? Never in the Hall of Fame, just one of the toughest guys ever to play for the Bears or anyone else. He was an every-down tackle when that job was starting to be specialized. Led the Bears in sacks twice. McMichael is true "old school." The reason he's not one of the top two is that there's somebody who was that old school.

Yeah but: Musso is in the Hall of Fame after playing guard, tackle, and defensive tackle, and you gotta love a guy who signed with the Old Man for $90 a game and squeezed him for $5 in expense money.

END: Richard Dent

What about: Ed O'Bradovich? An absolute terror and anchor on the left side of that '63 team. Pure mean. Chased Giants running back Phil King all over and off the field and when the Giants kept him from getting King then, he went to King's hotel looking for him.

Yeah but: The Colonel is the only Bear in franchise history that compares with Atkins as a pass rusher and belongs in the Hall of Fame, period. He went to the Pro Bowl four times, including 1993 when the team lost the last four straight to take gas all the way out of the playoffs.

The Colonel almost missed the '85 season because of a contract impasse with the Bears and nearly went the way of Todd Bell and Al Harris. He got into camp and became the MVP of the Super Bowl. Nobody was more of a student of rush techniques and nobody set Ditka off more for his practice habits. But he was there every Sunday when it mattered, turned in the greatest sack, "The Flying Sack" of Joe Montana, ever photographed. The Colonel should have ended his career in Chicago, without those out-of-place stops in San Francisco and Indianapolis.

WLB: Brian Urlacher

What about: Wilbur Marshall? The Pit Bull. Next to Hampton, the best pure football player on that '80s monster defense. Mean as a rattlesnake and as fast; just ask Eric Hipple. He wasn't fast enough to stay with Nat Moore that Monday night in Miami, but he was a true source of terror in the handful of seasons he spent here.

Yeah but: The reason why Marshall isn't the fantasy "Will" 'backer is simply that I'm moving somebody even better out there. Urlacher was a safety at New Mexico and the Bears considered putting him there while they were drafting him. Coaches admit they erred when they handed him the strong-side job on draft day, someplace he'd never played.

Where they should have put him, instead of over the tight end, was where Marshall was so unblockable. What Urlacher did when he had Ted Washington and Keith Traylor keeping blockers off him in 2001 gives me an idea what he would have been like out in space, covering backs and blitzing without a wall of blockers in front of him.

Take Marshall's speed, add 20 pounds and pass coverage, and you have the ultimate weak-side 'backer. L. T. who?

66 MLB: Dick Butkus

What about: Bill George? Certainly had the savage streak and he was the guy who really created the position in its true form, and he was a linchpin of that '63 team, the only guy Johnny Morris said he was ever genuinely afraid of on his own team. But Butkus took his job so that takes him out.

What about: Mike Singletary? Ten straight Pro Bowls.

181

The Eyes. Samurai. The cerebral madman who was Buddy Ryan's mind on the field.

Yeah but: Samurai had some of the greatest players of his era in front of and around him, which even he admits were keys to his getting to the Hall of Fame. And he wasn't as good in coverage or at pure physical mayhem as the ultimate linebacker and maybe the greatest defensive football player ever: Butkus.

Butkus never got to a playoff game. But he played every game like it was one. I'm not sure there ever was a Bear who commanded more attention from the other side than Butkus. Easy choice.

SLB: George Connor

What about: Otis Wilson. I'm not sure anybody in any era was any better. This was the guy who helped create "woofing" and was as ferocious a blitzer as ever came off the edge of a Bears defense. He worked his tail off to learn Buddy's scheme and way of doing things and was so much a part of the personality as well as the play of that '85 bunch.

Yeah but: Otis, like Wilbur Marshall, just wasn't at the pinnacle long enough. And once you factor in the era equalizers, I think the guy I send out alongside Butkus and Urlacher is Connor, the first of the big, fast mobile outside linebackers. The guy was All-NFL five times and in both 1951 and 1952 was chosen for both offense and defense.

The NFL created this thing called a Pro Bowl in 1952 and Connor was voted to the first four before injuries forced him to retire in 1955. What would he have been playing just defense? I don't know, but I got a spot all picked out for him.

CB: Allan Ellis

What about: Donnell Woolford? Nate Vasher? Very good. Pro-Bowl good.

Yeah but: Ellis was perhaps the best true cover corner the Bears ever lined up against a wideout in single coverage. He was voted to the Pro Bowl for his 1977 season that had 6 interceptions and 47 solo tackles.

The knee injury that he suffered four days before the first game of the '78 season ended a stellar career behind defensive lines that were anything but.

CB: J. C. Caroline

What about: Rosie Taylor? Rosie had as good a year as Petitbon had in '63 with those 8 INTs. Petitbon didn't lead the NFL; Taylor did. Three times to the Pro Bowl.

What about: George McAfee? Very difficult to go leave him out of my starting defensive 11. He's still top 10 on the Bears' all-time list with 25 picks, and this from one of those eras when the pass was a distant second to the run.

Yeah but: Caroline still shares the franchise record with

2 TD returns in a season. And this by someone who spent time early in his career on offense. Caroline went to the Pro Bowl as a rookie after he had 6 interceptions as a DB and averaged more than 4 yards on 34 carries as a halfback and scored twice on runs.

Caroline also was a six-footer who could hit and also could run; he ran punts and kickoffs back in his early years besides playing offense and defense.

70 S: Richie Petitbon

What about: Mike Brown? Definitely one of the great impact players from the deep secondary who put his name in Bears lore with those touchdown returns to win consecutive overtime games in 2001. One of the better combos of hitter and coverage safeties in the middle and was in charge of things behind Urlacher.

What about: Todd Bell? May have been the most-feared hitter the Bears ever had in the deep middle, and his annihilation of Joe Washington in the '84 playoff win over Washington was franchise-altering. That he missed the '85 season because of the contract problem is a sad legacy, especially after he'd made the Pro Bowl and was such a centerpiece in everything Buddy wanted from that defense.

Bell was good enough to be back as the starting strong safety in '87. And he's almost good enough to be in my fantasy secondary.

Yeah but: Petitbon intercepted 5 passes in 1961, 6 in 1962, and 8 in 1963. He averaged 35 yards per return in '62 and 20 in '63. Gary Fencik is the only Bear with more career interceptions than Petitbon's 37 picks and he played in the era when run support was more important than pass coverage and he still had all those INTs.

He went to four Pro Bowls, more than any other Bears safety. And his 3 picks against the Packers in '67 are still tied for the franchise one-game record. He has the franchise records for return yards in a career, season, and game, as well as the longest single return at 101 yards. He was great with the '63 defense. Can you imagine him in the '46 with that front seven? I can, which is why he's my top safety.

 ## S: Gary Fencik

What about: Red Grange? Made himself into a good DB after a knee injury ended his days as a running back. Dave Duerson? If Buddy didn't think he could tie Bell's cleats, he doesn't make my all-time team. Mark Carrier? Those 10 INTs as a rookie were more like fielding punts forced by what was still a scary front with Dent, Hampton, and McMichael, plus Trace Armstrong. Three Pro Bowls, but just not that elite player down deep.

What about: Shaun Gayle? Very difficult to leave him off. Best pure tackler I ever saw, smart and a hitter from the Doug Plank-Todd Bell tradition at Ohio State. Gayle understood schemes and was a flat-out assassin with a brain.

Yeah but: Fencik gets a tough nod with a pair of Pro Bowls early in his Bears career and just all-around great play game in and game out all the way through his years. Letting him go was what Don Shula said was the biggest personnel mistake he ever made.

Fencik also holds the franchise record for interceptions. He knew where balls were going, knew what to do when he got near them, and knew what to do to receivers who got to them first.

72 K: Kevin Butler

What about: Jeff Jaeger? He was the most accurate kicker ever for the Bears, just under 76 percent for about four years in Soldier Field, and he popped 21 straight FGs from November 1996 through November 1997, when he was about the only bright spot in the Bears' offense. Paul Edinger? Second to Jaeger in accuracy and hit FGs in 10 straight games in 2000. His 83.9 percent in 2001 is the best single season ever for a Bears kicker.

Yeah but: Butler kicked here for 11 years, and kicker years are like dog years; one is equal to probably three for a regular player, because of the fickleness of the job.

Butthead converted 24 straight field goals from October 1988 to December 1989, a record. Twice he hit field goals in thirteen straight games, also a record. He was one of the closers for the '85 offense; when a drive stalled, the Bears were going to get points, and Butler's 144 points that '85 rookie year are still an NFL record for a first season.

Butler's career numbers stack up favorably alongside some of the kickers already in the Hall of Fame. He probably won't get a lot of serious consideration for the Hall so he'll have to be satisfied being the kicker for the Bears Dream Team.

73 P: Bobby Joe Green

What about: Brad Maynard? The guy who was the team MVP in some really pedestrian years in the 2000s has one of the best gross averages for a career of any Bears punter. He was within 6 punts of the franchise record in 2004 with his 108 boots and he'll be a solid third all-time in punting yards when his career in Chicago is finishd.

Maynard will be first or second in punts inside the 20 for a career; he's already got the top two single-season totals for that measure of accuracy and control, including 6 in a game, which is the Bears' best ever.

What about: Bob Parsons? Most punts for a career and for a season, second-most yards for a career and season, and all by a guy who was a tight end on offense.

187

What about: Maury Buford? The foot for the '85 Bears and teams of the '80s. Put up single-game averages of 54.6 and 54 yards in two 1985 games.

Yeah but: Green was pure money for more than a decade, kicking in Wrigley Field and helping a great defense with field position the way Buford did with the '80s teams.

Green gets the edge based on consistent power. Two of the top three single-season averages belong to Green and he was good enough to kick 12 years for Halas, an accomplishment by itself.

If you had your pick of greatest single defense in Bears franchise history, is it '85 with the cachet? '86 with the points mark? Even '01 or '05 with league leaders? Or were the tough guys of another era just as good or better?

The 2005 defense had statistical high (or would they be "low"?) points, but because they were beaten by virtually every top quarterback they faced, they don't make the elite; all those comparisons with the '85 defense were silly anyhow. The 1965 defense, with some of the '63 greats still solid plus a rookie Dick Butkus, was strong but you don't make the all-time list giving up 275 points.

The one that is most difficult to leave off is the 1940 team, which was at the center of a run for three NFL titles in four years, although I discount the '43 crown a little only because the league, including the Bears, was weakened by the war. But this was most of the group that blasted the Washington Redskins and Sammy Baugh 73-0 in the 1940 championship.

Bonus!

The fact is, you could win an NFL title with any of the three best single-season Bears defenses:

3. 2001 BEARS

The bad loss to Donovan McNabb and the Philadelphia Eagles in the playoff is a severe blight on the record and a case of a lot of still-developing players being outplayed, essentially by one player they couldn't contain. The group lost twice to Green Bay and Brett Favre. And the team unquestionably had its share of lucky bounces, two going to safety Mike Brown for overtime TDs.

But it was a perfectly matched unit, with a massive defensive line in front of the best set of Bears linebackers outside of Wilbur Marshall-Mike Singletary-Otis Wilson. The defensive line had Ted Washington, who belongs in the Hall of Fame when he retires, and Phillip Daniels getting nine sacks. Behind that was a second-year Brian Urlacher flanked by Warrick Holdman and Roosevelt Colvin, who had 10.5 sacks and is a player the Bears are still trying to replace.

It was only for a season, but the 203 points allowed to the likes of Favre, Randy Moss, Terrell Owens, and Michael Vick speak volumes.

2. 1963 BEARS

The 10.4 points per game allowed during the 14-game regular season are better even than the '80s teams, and the '63 champions gave up 10 points in the NFL title game, same as the '85ers—and the '63 game was against Y. A. Tittle, Frank Gifford, Roosevelt Brown—all Hall of Fame offensive players.

Four Bears from this team went to the Pro Bowl and Doug Atkins, Bill George, and Stan Jones went to the Hall of Fame. DBs Richie Petitbon and Roosevelt Taylor went to multiple Pro Bowls. Add in Joe Fortunato, Ed O'Bradovich, and a few others, and you have the number two defense in franchise history.

1. 1985 BEARS

The '85 unit stands as the standard bearer for an era. This bunch gave up a total of 27 points to a stretch of six opponents; they scored 27 points on defense over the same six games. It was the most dominant defense of all time for one season and was No. 1 or two in yards allowed for a run of five seasons, including 1986 when it set an NFL record for fewest points allowed in a sixteen-game season.

Most of the players felt they lost something when Buddy Ryan left to coach the Philadelphia Eagles, but they were still good enough to remain dominant for most of the decade afterwards with members of the team still around. And in 1984, with 72 sacks, it was the defense that established what was to come in the season that followed.

DOWN FOR THE COUNT

Who Killed Boxing in Chicago?

74 Once upon a time, in a squared circle not so far away, the pugilistic arts were practiced in Chicago by some of history's greats. Now there is the Golden Gloves competition, which once rated page one coverage in sports sections, and that's about it. What happened? And who made it happen?

Nothing happened, and that's part of the problem. Chicago, in fact, was a victim of the times and the people who took advantage of those times. Chicago had a hand in its demise as a big-time sports venue for other than its local teams. Unfortunately there is no coming back.

The sad thing is that Chicago used to matter to boxing, and vice versa. It was nearly done in when lightweight legend Joe Gans admitted taking a dive in a 1900 fight, nicknamed "The Big Fix," against Terry McGovern—the state banned prizefighting for the next 26 years. The first year it was reinstated saw the Jack Dempsey-Gene Tunney "Long

Count" bout before a crowd of 104,943 in Soldier Field in the first $2 million gate in history.

Joe Louis ended the heavyweight championship reign of "Cinderella Man" James Braddock in May 1937 in Chicago, and Ezzard Charles decisioned Jersey Joe Walcott for the heavyweight title in May 1949. Floyd Patterson knocked out Archie Moore in November 1956 for the championship and was himself KO'd by Sonny Liston in September 1962.

But that was nearing the end of Chicago's time in any sort of boxing world. The Patterson-Liston fight was in town only because New York denied Liston a license over suspicions about his mob ties. Call Chicago the City of Second Chances. The last heavyweight fight of note was Ernie Terrell defeating Eddie Machen in 1965 for the title of the World Boxing Association, a meaningless championship.

It wasn't Bob Arum, Don King, or any of the other legendary fight promoters that were killing boxing in Chicago by that time. It was a declining interest in boxing in general, along with a rise in efforts by Las Vegas and Atlantic City in particular to build their images as entertainment titans, not just gambling centers.

And what is one thing that Chicago doesn't have? Casinos near the downtown, so when the world's glitterati would come to town for Mike Tyson-Evander Holyfield or whomever, the entertainment options are decidedly fewer than some other spots. The boxing world is not coming for Second City theatre or to see the Water Tower.

The age of the jet plane began in 1958 and that made it easier and faster to travel, so the well-heeled could jet themselves to glitzy rather than blue-collar venues. Since the last heavyweight title in Chicago in 1965, Las Vegas has hosted 28.

King was a small part of accelerating the shift away from Chicago by setting up Muhammad Ali's "Rumble in the Jungle" against George Foreman in Zaire, not Chicago. There was more money overseas, and boxing was nothing if not about following the money.

It didn't help that Chicago couldn't produce a true champion since the old days. The closest was a 1983 middleweight bout between two Chicagoans, John Collins and Lenny "The Rage" LaPaglia, that was NBC's centerpiece event on a March Saturday afternoon. But Collins upset LaPaglia, who'd won his first 18 fights, seventeen by knockout, and Collins himself was defeated subsequently.

Big-time boxing in Chicago was done.

IT WAS A VERY GOOD YEAR

What Were the Best One-Year Performances?

 Call it the ultimate Fantasy League year by someone in any Chicago sport. A handful of elite players on the town's teams put up individual single seasons for the local ages.

Frank Thomas's back-to-back MVP seasons of 1993–94 were monuments to classic hitting: averages of .317 and .353, 41 and 38 home runs, 128 and 101 RBI. The most awesome stat, however, may be that he struck out 54 and 61 times in those seasons.

Gale Sayers's 1965 season was epic: 22 touchdowns, including those 6 against the San Francisco 49ers, 1,374 yards from scrimmage in a 14-game season, a 31.4-yard average returning kickoffs, 14.9 yards per punt return. The only reason it does not make the legendary three is because of the way the Bears spread the ball around among Sayers, Jon Arnett, Ronnie Bull, and Andy Livingston. Gale accounted for a modest 867 rushing yards, 40 percent of the Bears' total on the ground.

Bobby Hull's 58 goals in the 1968–69 season were his high with the Black Hawks, but his 54 and 97 points in 1965–66 were good enough to win him the league's Hart Trophy, a pretty good indication of how the NHL viewed his seasons (he lost out to Boston's Phil Esposito for the Hart in '68–69). At the time, Hull's 50-goal seasons were spectacular by any standard but none reached the level of a best-ever for one year in Chicago.

3. SAMMY SOSA, 1998 CUBS

Sosa's 66 home runs were the real story of a season that ended with the Cubs reaching the playoffs for the first time since 1989. He was the N.L. MVP on every ballot except two by St. Louis writers who picked Mark McGwire. He shared the *Sports Illustrated* "Sportsman of the Year" award with McGwire, had a ticker tape parade in his honor in New York City, and was Bill Clinton's guest at the 1999 State of the Union address.

Sosa's 416 total bases were more than anyone in fifty years, since Stan Musial's 429 in 1948. He drove in 158 runs, one short of averaging one per game played, hit .308, and had a slugging percentage of .647. He even stole 18 bases.

Other issues or not, it was the second-greatest single baseball season in Chicago.

2. HACK WILSON, 1930 CUBS

As good as Sosa's 1998 was, it included only marginally more home runs than Wilson's 56, a record that stood for 68 years—until Sosa and McGwire broke it. But the .356 average and 191 RBI are simply beyond belief from a power hitter, and for one year Hack Wilson put up a year that arguably eclipsed all but a scant few of Babe Ruth's best.

Wilson struck out only 84 times and did not miss a single game for the only time in his career. For one year, he was the best.

1. MICHAEL JORDAN, 1995–96 BULLS

With Michael the problem is deciding on one "greatest" year when there were so many. But this one stands above all of them because of not only what Jordan did individually, but also what he did with the Bulls, whose 72-10 record is a mark that may never be broken.

Michael put up 30.4 points per game to break Wilt Chamberlain's record with an eighth NBA scoring title. He shot 49.5 percent, had more than 2 steals a game, and took down 6.6 rebounds each night, all the more remarkable not only because he was a guard but also because Dennis Rodman by that time was showing why Jerry Krause had traded Will Perdue for him.

One other measure of excellence: Jordan was the MVP of the All-Star game, the regular season, and the Finals.

STOCK IN TRADE

The Best Deals Chicago Ever Made

76 Sometimes you have to give to get in life. Sometimes the "gives" in Chicago sports were unfortunately a lot better than the "gets." Every once in awhile, though, the locals did it right.

Most "best" deals, at least in the real world, leave both sides feeling pretty good because they each got something. Or they're the deals that both sides finish feeling a little grumpy, but not fleeced. You probably gave a little more than you planned or didn't quite get the whole enchilada you wanted, but neither did the other side so it's probably a decent swap.

One criterion in the list of best trades was that the deal had to be for the players involved at the time. So the Bears' trading a fading Wally Chambers to Tampa Bay for the draft pick that turned into Dan Hampton doesn't qualify. It was a beauty, but only because the Bears hit on the draft choice, the epitome of the player to be named later.

A couple of Sammy Sosa deals could qualify. The Sox

getting him from the Texas Rangers, along with Wilson Alvarez for Fred Manrique and Harold Baines, in 1989 was a steal. Former president George Bush, then the Rangers' managing general partner, called it the biggest mistake he ever made. From the guy neck-deep in Iran-Contra, that's saying something.

The Cubs getting Sosa from the Sox in 1992 for George Bell and Ken Patterson was another bargain. Getting Sammy out of town to Baltimore in 2004 for Jerry Hairston was a decent addition-by-subtraction deal too.

Getting Rick Sutcliffe from the Indians in June 1984 for Mel Hall and Joe Carter? A Cy Young Award winner who'd go 16-1 and anchor the division winners' staff defines "excellent deal."

Will Perdue to San Antonio for Dennis Rodman makes up for some of Jerry Krause's other Bulls doings.

And where would the deal of three worthless players for Joe Jackson rank if Jackson hadn't become one of the Eight Men Out?

Frank "Trader" Lane netted the Sox Billy Pierce for Aaron Robinson, Nellie Fox for Joe Tipton. Those and other deals ended with a pennant in '59.

But none of these quite make my Fab Four best of all the deals in Chicago sports history.

4. JIM WASHINGTON FROM THE BULLS TO PHILADELPHIA FOR SHALER HALIMON AND CHET WALKER, 1969

Chet the Jet, an All-American at Bradley, averaged 19.3 points and 8 rebounds per game for the 76ers' 1967 team, ranked among the greatest in NBA history with its 68-13 record. But the Sixers traded him to the Bulls for backup center Washington and another player. Walker was so upset he considered retirement.

Walker didn't retire and the Bulls started winning. Bob Love was the marquee forward in Dick Motta's offense but adding Walker and then Norm Van Lier made the Bulls of the '70s. It all happened because one Bulls scout saw that the only problem with Walker in Philadelphia was him not getting along with egomaniacal coach Jack Ramsay. The scout? Jerry Krause.

3. IVAN DEJESUS TO PHILADELPHIA FOR LARRY BOWA AND RYNE SANDBERG, 1982

The irony of the deal was that Sandberg was a throw-in. The Cubs really wanted Bowa, a Gold Glove shortstop who still had enough to be part of the 1984 division championship team. Sandberg became a Hall of Fame second baseman, with 2,385 hits and 282 home runs as a Cub. He was a ten-time All-Star, won an MVP award, drove in 1,061 runs, and even stole 344 bases. Bowa didn't do quite that well.

DeJesus was traded three more times before his career ended in 1988. Bowa, one of the all-time baseball annoyers and egos, eventually became the Cubs' manager

2. LARRY JACKSON AND BOB BUHL TO PHILADELPHIA FOR FERGUSON JENKINS, 1966

The Cubs got rid of Buhl, the absolute worst hitting pitcher in the history of history, and Jackson, who had a 24-win season for them in '64 but like Buhl was clearly over the hill and heading down the other side. The North Siders also picked up Adolpho Phillips, who was their center fielder in '69. Well, it was still a good deal.

No, it was a great deal. Fergie became a Hall of Fame pitcher, 20-game winner for six straight seasons and the epitome of what a staff ace should be. He is the only major leaguer with 3,000 or more strikeouts (3,192) also with fewer than 1,000 walks (997).

After a 14-16 run in 1973, the Cubs dealt him to Texas where he promptly went 25–12. But that was the last time he'd win 20 and the Cubs did get Bill Madlock in the deal. Because they added a two-time batting champ in Madlock gets the Cubs a pass from another entry into the "worst trades" category.

1. JACK TAYLOR TO THE ST. LOUIS CARDINALS FOR MORDECAI "THREE FINGERS" BROWN, 1903

Best of all for some Cubsters, this involved the Cardinals. Each side threw in another ballplayer but pitchers Brown and Taylor, a decent hurler for his career, were the crux of the deal.

When Brown was seven he got his right hand caught in a corn shredder on his uncle's farm, lost part of his index finger, and had his thumb and pinkie permanently impaired. He broke the remaining two when he was chasing a hog a couple of weeks later. The injuries forced him to grip the ball differently and the result was a Hall of Fame career for the ace of the Cubs staff on N.L. champs in 1906, 1907, 1908, and 1910.

Brown pitched a shutout in the deciding game of the 1907 Cubs World Series win. He then threw 11 consecutive scoreless innings and beat the Tigers twice in the 1908 Series win after being the Cubs' pitcher in the famous "Bonehead Merkle" contest. He pitched four straight shutouts in 1908, his 2.06 career ERA is third-best in MLB history, and he had a winning record in career matchups against Christie Mathewson.

The Cardinals dumped him after a 9-13 rookie season because they thought his mutilated right hand was too much of a handicap.

SAMMY AND THE HALL

History's Call?

Sammy Sosa's candidacy for baseball's Hall of Fame will arrive in several years. What will be history's verdict?

First of all, let's not put the Hall on too high a pedestal. From 1967–76, while Frankie Frisch and Bill Terry were involved with the Hall of Fame's Veterans Committee, eight players who were former teammates of Frisch and Terry were voted in. Frisch and Terry certainly played on good Cardinals and Giants teams but hey, c'mon....

Back in June 2003 Sammy donated 11 artifacts to Cooperstown, including five bats. The bats were the ones he used to hit some of the more memorable homers in late 1998, including the one he used for number 500 and numbers 64–66 in his race with Mark McGwire. Of course, fittingly, New York Mayor Rudolph Giuliani claimed Sammy presented him with the 66 bat as well. Bats and Sammy didn't always get things straight.

The Hall of Fame Museum was dutifully grateful—and immediately ordered the bats X-rayed. The question now is whether or not it will X-ray Sammy's head when it finally is rendered to a bust when he is enshrined with the greats.

Because he will be voted in, and probably on the first ballot. And like it or not, he should be.

Legendary NFL writer Ira Miller applied an interesting private standard for whether or not a player should be counted among the elite of the greats: If you wrote the history of the sport, would this player command inclusion? If you wrote the history of baseball, you could not leave out Sammy Sosa, for better and worse.

There's enough not to like about him. He was a selfish player and a selfish teammate. Dusty Baker was afraid to handle him properly when Baker got to Chicago, and this was a manager who'd dealt with Barry Bonds in his previous job. (Then again, he dealt with Bonds how…?)

Sammy played his boom box so loud that it was nearly impossible to have a conversation anywhere near it in the locker room. Did anybody have a problem with it? The mysterious clubbing of the offensive sound machine by person or persons unknown after Sosa was gone speaks volumes about players' feelings about the boom box and whether or not they felt they could challenge Sosa.

He swung for the ivy when swinging for base hits might have stood his team in far, far better shape. Worst of all, when he found out he wasn't playing on the final day of the 2004 season, he left the clubhouse before the game. Probably a fitting epitaph, come to think of it.

The crux of any opposition to Sosa isn't his play or his personality, of course. It's whether or not he cheated. The corked bat did come out, but clear (or was it "the cream"?) proof that he used banned or unbanned substances may never come to light. While unprescribed steroids weren't legal during the time that he, McGwire, and others supposedly used them, baseball didn't say you couldn't use them.

Of course, in front of a congressional inquiry, Sammy couldn't say either. But that was just a curious loss-of-English that occurred in front of interrogators.

Peter Gammons, the superb baseball writer for *Sports Illustrated* and then for ESPN, noted that he had voted in favor of Hall admission for several pitchers who he strongly suspected had doctored baseballs during their careers. Loading up the pill was and is illegal. Still, there are Gaylord Perrys in the Hall of Fame.

If you want to build a "no" on Sosa for the Hall, you'd be better advised to point to his batting average or strikeout rate. But charter HOFer Babe Ruth established long, long ago that K's don't keep hitters out of baseball's Parthenon. And think Ruth ever partook of banned substances in the Roaring '20s? What, illegal alcohol didn't improve baseball performance? Are you sure in the Babe's case it didn't? Maybe that was his relax-drug of choice. Voters won't have second thoughts about putting Brett Favre into the Pro Football Hall of Fame even though he had Vicodin issues.

No player hit more home runs in the 10-year run from 1995–2004, when Sosa popped 476. He was one of the dominant players of his era. Put him in, first ballot.

The wonderful thing about life is that sometimes, not always, the scales balance themselves. Ford Frick was absolutely out of line for declaring the Roger Maris's 61-homer mark in 1961 would go in the books with an asterisk. Shame on him; Frick didn't asterisk other accomplishments, like pitcher's records accomplished on a higher mound or shorter distance to home plate.

The beauty of the Sosa numbers is that no one has to print an asterisk next to any of them. Unless you have only recently emigrated from the Antares nebulae, you will always "see" the asterisk next to every one of them.

Hall of Fame or not.

THE ULTIMATE BEARS COACH

Papa Bear or Da Coach?

78 George Halas and Mike Ditka are in the Pro Football Hall of Fame, if for different reasons. Ditka is there as a player and for his part in creating a position, tight end. Halas is there as a coach, with 324 wins, and for his part in creating professional football, the NFL.

The trophy awarded to Super Bowl winners should carry his name, not Vince Lombardi's. Lombardi just happened to die sooner and at a time when the NFL was looking for a way to honor him. Lombardi won the first two Super Bowls; that's nice. Without Halas, Lombardi is just a really good offensive lineman from Fordham.

But was Ditka or Halas truly the greater Bears head coach?

They bear lots of similarities, some eerie.

Both won NFL championships: Ditka just one, Halas ones in four different decades. Ditka won one in 11 seasons, Halas coached for 40 years and won six, or about one for every 6.7 years coaching the Bears.

Both had roles in defining the sport. Halas as a founder, Ditka as a position player. Both had issues with Michael McCaskey; Halas from above, Ditka from below.

Both were arguably left behind by the game they so influenced.

Both had great quarterbacks, but really only one, which was a negative definer in both of their legacies. Ditka had McMahon, never for a full season, and lost him for the stretch runs of 1984 and 1986. Flutie, Tomczak, Fuller, Harbaugh—not enough. Halas had Sid Luckman for more than a decade. George Blanda, Ed Brown, and Zeke Bratkowski were serviceable but Halas's era ended with Rudy Bukich and Bill Wade in a quarterback controversy that did not serve the Bears well at all.

Both had legendary running backs. Ditka had Walter Payton. Halas had Beattie Feathers, George McAfee, and Gale Sayers.

Both had epic, Hall of Fame middle linebackers. Halas had Bill George, who created the position, and then Dick Butkus. Ditka had Mike Singletary.

Both had some of the greatest defensive assistants in the history of the game. Ditka had Buddy Ryan running his defense the first four years, culminating in the legendary '85 season. Halas had George Allen, who positioned George as that first middle linebacker, running his defense in the '63 championship season. Both had irreparable problems with those defensive assistants.

Halas ended up suing Allen. Ditka ended up trading punches with Ryan.

Halas gets an edge in strategic coaching issues if only because he was savvy enough to turn Clark Shaugnessy loose to install the T-formation with Luckman. Ditka believed in a less-is-more offensive philosophy and tolerated the "46" only as long as Buddy was in town. Ditka would have installed the "Flex" defense from Dallas if he could have.

They were joined forever, for better or worse, with the Bears because Halas made Ditka a No.1 draft choice in 1961. He traded Ditka to Philadelphia for Jack Concannon in 1967 (see "Worst Trades"). Then he hired Ditka in 1982 to restore the kingdom.

Both had unfortunate episodes in player relations. Halas was the genesis of Ditka's comment that Halas "throws nickels around like manhole covers." Far too many players tell tales of Papa Bear's tight-fistedness than should be the case for a great franchise.

Ditka had the misfortune of strikes cutting into two of his first six seasons, and exacerbated the problems in the '87 strike when, facing severe pressure from team president Michael McCaskey who wanted to be rid of him anyway, he threw his support behind the Spare Bears, a slight his Real Bears never forgot.

And yet both did more for charity than anyone was fully aware. Halas took care of many old players; Ditka's work on behalf of Miseracordia Home has meant so much to so many.

But none of that is football. Game day, getting a team ready, one was better than the other. But which one?

Neither is acclaimed as an exceptional in-game coach. But both were superb at preparing their teams. Both were physical taskmasters who whipped their teams into physical shape even if they weren't always the most talented. Win or lose, few wanted to play the Bears, good team or bad.

Halas brought the Bears, and the NFL, through many lean years. Some were of his own doing; he was responsible for talent far more than Ditka was.

But in the days leading up to a game, and in the hours and minutes right before it, I doubt if there has ever been a more driven motivator than Ditka. He had one of the greatest assemblages of stars one team has ever had, for the 1984 and 1985 seasons, and weekly brought them to a frothing pitch.

Ditka even managed to have them believe even late in the '85 season that everyone doubted them and that they had so much to prove.

Halas brought the Monsters of the Midway to a boil. Ditka took the '85 bunch where no team has ever gone before. So the greatest coach in Bears history:

Da Coach.

BULL SITTER
The Ultimate Bulls Coach

79 Phil Jackson has six rings to show for his time on the Bulls' bench. Doug Collins endured the Bad Boys from Detroit and got the Bulls to the brink of greatness that Jackson enjoyed. Dick Motta had never seen an NBA game before the first one he coached, yet brought the Bullies to a run of 50-win seasons and to the brink of a championship with less-than-championship talent.

So who is the greatest coach in Bulls history? And who rates after him on the all-time list? It's not who you might think.

5. DICK MOTTA

Hey, the guy won 50 games four different times with Tom Boerwinkle as his center. Not that Boerwinkle was so bad; it was just that this was in the era of a young Jabbar, a young Wes Unseld, and others.

But there was just something missing with Motta even as he was getting the Bulls to the playoffs six straight years. Motta coached defense to a level that Jordan, Pippen, and the Dobermans would have approved, but he botched the 1975 conference finals and for that joins the list of epic Chicago chokers. Others in that spot wouldn't have blown that chance. He overplayed his tiring vets, something even an average college-level coach would've known better than to do, and that drops him way down the list.

4. DOUG COLLINS

No higher than fourth? Not when you have Michael, Scottie, Horace, and Paxson, and then Jerry Krause deals Charles Oakley to the New York Knicks for Bill Cartwright. Collins got the Bulls to the edge, so close that they could look over the rim and see the real fire.

But he had problems with Phil and even Tex Winter, to the point of banning Winter from practice at one point. And if Michael doesn't hit The Shot over Craig Ehlo in Game 5 of that first-round series, the Bulls are out and never beat the Knicks and go to six against the Pistons in '89. You've got to love a head coach who gets picked up and thrown over a scoring table by a Detroit Rick Mahorn, but after that he was fired. Rightly.

3. JERRY SLOAN

Sloan was an original Bull by virtue of the 1966 expansion draft from Baltimore. He was Johnny Kerr's roommate with the Bullets in 1965, and Kerr made sure to get him when the Bulls were started the next year. Sloan accepted the head job at alma mater Evansville in 1977 but changed his mind and took a job as Bulls assistant. The entire Evansville team and coaching staff were killed in a plane crash that fall.

Sloan was named Bulls head coach in April 1979. The front office handed him forward Larry Kenon, the Memphis State star whom Bill Walton had humiliated in an NCAA semifinal. Sloan still managed to win 13 of the last 15 games in his second season for a playoff run that included beating the Knicks before losing to the Celtics. By then Sloan had to deal with Kenon and Orlando Woolridge, who missed training camp but management still wanted on the court.

When the Bulls hit 19-32 in February 1982, Sloan was fired. Then he went on to be a scout and assistant for the Utah Jazz and the head coach who led them to the Finals in 1997 and 1998—against the Bulls.

The Bulls had a great coach and blew it.

2. JOHNNY KERR

First Bulls coach. Sold the concept of NBA basketball in Chicago. Owner Dick Klein wanted Ray Meyer to coach the

Bulls but the Baron of Belden Avenue wasn't an idiot, thank you very much.

And Kerr did more with less than maybe any coach in NBA history, let alone the Bulls. He coached the team in 1966–67 with an expansion-team roster made up of players their teams didn't think were worth protecting, basically the number eight man on every roster. The Bulls won 33 games and they made the playoffs in that first year. No other team before or since has done that.

This was a coach who carried coins in his pocket so he could call the newspapers after games to report details at a time when it was still an open question whether or not pro basketball really had a place in Chicago.

Try to put Kerr in some perspective: Not long after he signed as the Bulls' first head coach, owner Dick Klein told him they were going to have a parade downtown to build up some interest. St. Patrick's Day stuff? Bud Billiken? Hardly. The "parade" was one flatbed truck with Klein, PR guy Ben Bentley (later to become part of the landmark "The Sportswriters" radio and TV show), Kerr, and a live Bull.

Think Jackson chafed sometimes under the Jerrys? How about Kerr getting a note handed to him, from Klein, letting him know how many turnovers the Bulls had in the previous quarter.

He wasn't their coach for long; Kerr left to coach the expansion Phoenix Suns. But it was on Kerr's shoulders that a lot of others stood as they reached for the stars.

1. PHIL JACKSON

Jackson won all those championships and there is no truer measure of greatness than titles. Period. And he did it with some of the greatest players in the history of the game in Jordan and Pippen, plus Dennis Rodman. He's Sparky Anderson and handled basketball's Big Red Machine. (Sparky once refused to take a lot of credit for the success of that team, explaining, "The thing I had to do was make sure Bench or Rose or Morgan didn't trip over me on the way up the dugout steps to the field.")

Jackson gets high marks for simply not blowing a good thing with his own massive ego. He let the Jordan Rules play out, mollified when he needed to placate, and was fortunate enough to have a collection of talent focused more on winning than on individual accomplishments, even Jordan ultimately, who understood that all the really good things come from winning. Jackson simply had to keep Jordan from tripping over him on his way to the court and the basket.

Most telling of all, perhaps, was Jackson's winning championships both with Horace Grant and Dennis Rodman as his power forwards. He won both with Bill Cartwright and Luc Longley in the pivot.

This is a little like evaluating John Wooden or Bobby Knight, my two all-time all-timers for college coaches. In Wooden's case, he won with a guard-based offense (Gail Goodrich, Walt Hazzard). He won with a center-based offense (Kareem, Walton). He won with a forward-based offense (Sidney Wicks, Keith Wilkes). The greatest college coach ever. Period.

Jackson won with Michael. Won with Bill Cartwright and Luc Longley. Won with Grant. Won with Rodman. Won 55 games without Michael and nearly took out the Knicks except for a phantom foul call.

Great assistant coaches were allowed to do their jobs. Star players could be stars. Jackson was to the Bulls like Auerbach was with the Russell Celtics, then the Havlicek Celtics. The best.

ON COURSE

One Round on a Chicago-Area Golf Course. Which Do You Play?

80 First, a caveat. To make the Finals a course has to be one everyone can play. That's not because of any aversion to elitism, snobbery, or exclusivity, but because very few country club courses have to compete with the conditions that public links do.

It's a lot easier to maintain bent grass and such if membership's deep, often corporate, pockets fund the landscaping budget. Private courses don't get nearly the play totals and accompanying abuse that public tracks get and some of Chicago's best get occasional USGA or PGA money coming in to modify and upgrade everything about the grounds so that the pros will show up. Besides, golf associations pick courses not simply because the courses themselves are better tracks, but also because of how they can handle crowds and host an event. In other words, it's easier to look great and be in great shape if you've got serious money.

So in Chicago, Medinah Number 3 doesn't make the list of "best" even though it has hosted U.S. Opens, PGA's, and a Ryder Cup. It is a great course, with long, mature trees, and as one golf friend put it, "Every hole is a double bogey waiting to happen."

Butler National doesn't qualify because of its members-only status, even though it rates a top-40 ranking on *Golf Digest's* list of Top 100 courses. Classic course, good enough for Western Opens, but it's babied, just like other club courses, so how tough can it really be? Besides, it's too flat to be totally interesting. Beautiful, yes; interesting, not as much.

Olympia Fields has hosted nearly a dozen national tournaments on its North course, which is my personal favorite because of some of the winding holes, elevation changes, and requiring some shots you just don't have to hit at a lot of other courses. Kemper Lakes is going private, so one of the country's most overrated tracks is excused.

But enough about the non-qualifiers; I just wanted you to know that they were fairly evaluated before being passed over.

My best course in Chicago could be Indian Boundary, a Forest Preserve patch. But that'd be just a sentimental pick: I'm partial to the first course where I ever broke 80.

It could be Glencoe Golf Club, which is nestled down in a green low area along the North Shore and is one of the coziest courses to play anywhere in the area.

Seven Bridges in Woodridge used to be a country club; now it's public and a place where there are more water crossovers than holes. The front nine is one of the best around Chicago; the back, however, is anything but. The General out in Geneva is a good place to go if you have too many balls in your bag. The Glen Club in Glenview will be a contender when it ages a bit.

Second runner-up to the top three is Pine Meadow, which opened in 1986 as *Golf Magazine's* Best New Public Course in America. It has just the right amount of water in play to make you shoot with your head as well as your sticks.

But the numbers three, two, and No.1 are just in a class by themselves.

3. BULL VALLEY, WOODSTOCK

Bull Valley is one of the most purely beautiful tracks in the Midwest partly because of the spectacular result the designers achieved by doing...nothing. The glaciers did a fine job of landscaping and Dick Nugent and the late Bruce Borland didn't try to outsmart the Grand Designer. This is a course that was built to fit nature, not the other way around, and the natural grasses, water, wetlands, contours, and trees make this a monster at 7,300 yards, but a pretty one.

Nugent and Borland designed Bull Valley and did everything right. Every Bull Valley hole is distinct and most are potentially lethal. But not too many places make intelligent play, managing risk, and good execution so satisfying.

"Slope" isn't simply a number on the scorecard; it's something that's in play on enough fairways to make you put the Big Dog back in the bag and use the three off the tees.

2. COG HILL NUMBER 4—DUBSDREAD

Dubs makes every Top 100 list and deserves to. It hosts Western Opens and keeps its shine even with the great-unwashed rest of us traipsing through as often as we can afford the $135 drop. Cog Number 2 is also a favorite among some of those surveyed for this section.

Dubs has those truly majestic trees that make it almost— almost—pleasant to walk in among them, if you weren't looking for a little white ball. This is long enough to have you hitting every club in the bag at one point or another. And if you don't play smart, you will play a long, long time.

Dubs nearly got my No. 1 on sentimental reasons. I hit a 4 iron into the cup on Number 2 on the fly in what was my closest call to an ace. The shot exploded the hole, dirt flying everywhere, and the ball came to rest about two inches outside the crater that had been the hole.

Maybe if Dubs hadn't spit that shot out on me....

1. HARBORSIDE, STARBOARD COURSE

This is the best round of golf you can play in Chicago in absolutely the least likely place in Chicago. The tips are 7,166 yards, 132 slope, 75.0 rating; not the hardest course, just the most fun to play.

The reason is all around you. It's wide open so the wind makes you think about every shot. The setting is majestic in its own way, looking at some of the industrial steel might of America not all that far away. The fairways roll and pitch, with mounds of natural prairie grasses just beyond a normal rough if you really go wide. And some water.

The hole that seals it is number 17, Buccaneer's Cove. You go 174 yards over a corner of Lake Calumet on the right such that if you're short or right, you're wet. If you're left, you can be in the high grass. A little long and you're coming back out of a trap looking at the lake if you pick it a little too clean. It's not an island green, just gorgeous and like nothing else in Chicago.

OK, so Lake Calumet isn't the Pacific. But this is Chicago's Pebble number 18. This is a course built on landfill. It has to work hard to look great, and it does. That makes it a winner.

MISMANAGEMENT
It Starts—and Sometimes Ends—at the Top

81 Chicago teams haven't had all that many flirtations with championships. Sadly, when they have, too often they have been undone, not always by an opponent's home run, a ball through the legs, or a lucky bounce on a rim or goalpost (those are a debate all their own). They have been undone by the minds at the top. Or rather, the lost minds.

Charley Grimm may have been Jolly Cholly in popular lore but he boobed away any chance at the '45 World Series for the Cubs when he had Hank Borowy pitch an inning in Game 5, come back and pitch the final four innings of a 12-inning Game 6 and then start Game 7. Detroit scored five in the first in that final contest and The Curse of the Billy Goat was off and running.

Black Hawks coaches like Billy Reay and Mike Keenan were regularly outcoached in playoff situations.

Al Lopez was outmanaged by Walter Alston in the 1959 World Series, failing to pinch-run for slow-footed Sherm Lollar in a situation that cost the Sox a winning run. Lopez left Gus Wynn in way too long in game 6 and pitched to Charley Neal when he shouldn't have.

Leo Durocher was the Cubs' manager in '69. The Mets may have played well but Durocher couldn't get his team where it needed to be to hold off the Amazin's. But he doesn't make the list of all-time coaching or managing goofs that helped keep Chicago title-less for a whole lot longer than it should have been.

How different might Cubs history have been had Dusty Baker not sat on his hands during the Mark Prior meltdown against the Marlins?

Those were cases of mismanagement. But they weren't the worst.

4. NORTHWESTERN AND GARY BARNETT OUTCOACHED IN THE ROSE BOWL, 1996

The Wildcats were the feel-good college football story of the year, maybe in all of sports. They had upset Notre Dame and then, after a loss to Miami (Ohio) and subsequent NU coach Randy Walker, ran off eight straight games. They had Darnell Autry as their featured running back, D'Wayne Bates was on his way to an NFL career, and linebacker Pat Fitzgerald was the national defensive player of the year.

They were better than USC pretty much everywhere, except at the one wide-receiver position played by Keyshawn Johnson. Barnett, who was too busy looking at the UCLA job and interviewing instead of scheming a defense to stop Johnson, got pantsed by USC coach John Robinson. Johnson caught 12 passes for 216 yards, a Rose Bowl record, and the Cats fell 41-32, with help from a couple of late turnovers.

3. JIM FREY OUTMANAGED BY DICK WILLIAMS AND SAN DIEGO, 1984

First of all, nobody knocked down Steve Garvey for the whole series. He did the Cubs in with a home run off Lee Smith that you knew was coming sooner or later, the way the Cubs mishandled this series.

Frey was handed a 2-0 lead in the NLCS and then got stupid. After the Cubs went up on the Padres, Frey started managing for Game 1 of the World Series before he'd won the pennant you need to get there.

Rick Sutcliffe pitched and won the first game on October 2 but pitched only 7 innings of a 13-0 game that was 11-0 after five. The Cubs won the second the next day. Then Dennis Eckersly lost Game 3 in San Diego.

Frey then held Sutcliffe, the hands-down ace of the staff, hoping to get by with Scott Sanderson and hold Sutcliffe for Game 1 of the World Series. Sanderson had a bad back and an even worse day in Game 4, which ended with Steve Garvey's homer off Lee Smith in the ninth. Stupid.

2. MIKE DITKA STARTS DOUG FLUTIE IN THE 1986 PLAYOFFS

Ditka had angered a significant chunk of his '86 team when he gave Flutie star treatment after the smallish QB was brought in as security with the questionable health of Jim McMahon and Mike Tomczak.

Personnel chief Bill Tobin was against bringing in Flutie. But Ditka and GM Jerry Vainisi made the move. The Bears won a few closing games with Flutie starting; they had won games with just about everybody starting that 14-2 year, giving up an NFL record-few points. Then Ditka elected to start Flutie against the Redskins in the divisional round of the playoffs, even though coaches and players knew Flutie still didn't know the offense.

The Bears got off to a 7-0 lead with a Flutie TD pass to Gault. They even led at halftime 13-7. Washington wasn't doing much against that defense. But Flutie tried to force a throw in the third quarter, Darrell Green intercepted, and the Redskins were on their way.

Flutie was woeful: 11-for-31 passing, 134 yards, 2 interceptions. Adding to the misery of the moment was that, because of Flutie's playing time, the sixth-round draft choice the Bears gave up to get Flutie bumped up to a third-rounder. And Michael McCaskey, who also disliked the Flutie acquisition, cited that as one of the reasons he fired Vainisi days after the Washington debacle.

Richard Dent voiced what most of the team felt: "We'd have won the Super Bowl again with Steve Fuller."

1. DICK MOTTA BLOWS THE 1975 NBA WESTERN CONFERENCE CHAMPIONSHIP

The Bulls led the Golden State Warriors 3-2 in the conference finals when Motta, a very good coach in so many ways, was outcoached by Al Attles and a chance at a championship was lost.

Motta was a conservative coach at heart and was not big on going with young, less-proven players in crunch situations. So in spite of double-digit leads in both Games 6 and 7, Motta played his starting five of Tom Boerwinkle, Bob Love, Jerry Sloan, Chet Walker, and Norm Van Lier more than 40 minutes every game while Attles was playing his tenth and 11th men to rest his starters.

Game 6 was at the Chicago Stadium and the Bulls lost 86-72. Then out on the West Coast it happened again: double-digit lead, starters wear down, Bulls lose. It was the end of the Motta "era" and the final gasp of that great—overused—starting five.

WHY, MICHAEL, WHY?

Why Did Jordan Retire the First Time?

Michael Jordan gave his reasons for quitting the first time. Nobody believed him.

Michael quit in October 1993, after the Bulls' third championship and not long before they were to convene for training camp heading into the next season. He'd come back for three more titles. But why did he really leave the game that first time?

He was at the absolute peak of his powers in 1993. He had been named the MVP of the NBA Finals for the third straight year. He was the NBA's scoring leader, averaged 41 points in the Finals, the highest mark ever, and had been the centerpiece of the true "Dream Team" that used the 1992 Olympics as its showcase.

But the night of October 5, word began to circulate that Michael was leaving the game. The next day a press conference was held at which he confirmed that he was indeed through as a Bull.

The preceding couple of years had been filled with almost as many apparent lows as there were highs for the man who was now the most-recognized face in the world, and one of the highest-earning athletes in history. But were they enough to contribute to his leaving at the summit, the way Jim Brown had walked away from football or Lance Armstrong from the Tour de France?

What is the real reason Michael quit and passed up a chance to win four, five, maybe eight straight NBA championships? Here are some theories.

TO SPEND TIME WITH THE FAMILY

That was the reason given by Michael, and it was also the silliest. Jordan made his declaration an even bigger joke when he signed a minor-league contract in March 1994 with the White Sox's Nashville affiliate. He eventually played, badly by pure baseball standards, for the Birmingham Barons in the Sox's chain amid a firestorm of debate over whether or not he was usurping a roster spot that should have gone to a deserving kid who actually intended to play baseball.

People don't play major league baseball as part of spending more time with their families and they surely don't play minor league ball. Jordan hit .202 in his one season for Birmingham; no word on how many games he brought his kids or Juanita to.

This is the easy reason to dismiss.

AS A COMPROMISE WITH THE NBA TO AVOID A MASSIVE GAMBLING PROBLEM

Jordan was a playuh, no question about it. Friendly gaming nights at his house or those of buddies included cards, pool, and other games of chance, with huge sums sometimes changing hands.

But it was the gambling elsewhere that emerged as a serious matter and which attracted the interest of the NBA and authorities.

In March 1992, three Jordan checks to a bail bondsman named Eddie Dow for a total of $108,000 were found in the briefcase of a man who was murdered. That brought the gambling issue out into the open. Later in the year Jordan testified under oath that he had written a $57,000 check to a man named Slim Bouler, a convicted cocaine dealer, in part to cover gambling debts. Before that Jordan had been maintaining it was for a business loan.

The situation gathered dangerous speed in March 1993 when he spent the night before a playoff game gambling in an Atlantic City casino. Then Richard Esquinas wrote in his book, *Michael and Me: Our Gambling Addiction—My Cry for Help* that Jordan lost $1.25 million to him at golf, negotiated the loss down to $300,000 but then reportedly only repaid $200,000.

The NBA was concerned enough to tell Jordan to exercise care in his associations. A story emerged that the league had done its five-month investigation and that

Jordan was looking at a suspension, or worse, for gambling issues. Jordan's "retirement" then was whispered to be a compromise: go away for a while, Michael, and we all avoid the stink of a bigger problem. Two days after Jordan's retirement speech, the league announced that its investigation had found nothing of significance.

That doesn't wash. Even though it couldn't have helped but find something of significance (there certainly was enough to find), the NBA was not going to bounce its worldwide signature identity, the greatest single seat-filler in its history. The league could have paid all Jordan's debts from petty cash.

And give the media some credit as well as some blame in the Michael saga. The *New York Times* got the story of Jordan going to Atlantic City to gamble. The *Chicago Tribune* and other Chicago papers had multiple reporters from news-side as well as sports, assigned to the team. Reporters have missed things in history and looked the other way on some, but to think that so many hounds sniffing would have turned up nothing when they were looking hard for anything is less believable than some of Jordan's explanations for things.

BECAUSE HE WAS JUST FED UP

This is the real story and probably is a little bit of all of the above. It did not come all at once.

229

Michael told *Tribune* colleague Melissa Isaacson, who covered him for many years, that he was bored with practices that had him working with people like Rodney McCray, whom he disliked, and the challenge was gone. What had once been intensely competitive practices, crucibles of fire that spawned the classic Bulls fire, became a lot of people lying around on training tables, getting some treatment—nothing like what Jordan needed to keep his edge. He was fed up with what he'd been through with the media and the whole gambling business.

Tribune basketball writer Sam Smith's book, *The Jordan Rules,* was an exposé that revealed in devastating detail that Jordan was self-centered, selfish, and not all that glowingly popular with teammates.

The murder of his father came crashing in on top of all that and took away from him a father, friend, partner, and more. The media handling of that infuriated Jordan. Then right in front of him was the chance to give baseball a try.

As Melissa wrote in her book, *Transition Game*, Jordan had been telling people indirectly all through 1993 that he was leaving or at least considering it heavily. Dean Smith, teammates, Scottie Pippen—they all had signs that the exit could happen.

The point is that if it were an NBA deal or some specific incident, there would have been far, far less of the long, long goodbye. Jordan told Melissa that halfway through the '92–'93 season he knew "this was it."

That obviously wasn't it. His departure speech left more questions than answers and the rest of the decade after his comeback was a mess that included the acrimonious dissolution of the Bulls, the issues between Phil Jackson and Jerry Krause with Jordan in the middle, and ultimately his stint with the Washington Wizards. Jordan went from the summit to being the brunt of truly venomous attacks from the media for what certainly looked like a whole lot of hypocrisy on his part, all of which made it easier and easier to believe the worst of Michael and therefore his reasons for leaving.

Some insiders felt that Jordan leaving was even a gentle up-yours to the NBA for all of its investigating, which Jordan could have taken as badgering a guy who had given the NBA the world, or at least a lot of its money.

A mess, to be sure. But Jordan didn't leave just because of the gambling.

FOLLOW THE MONEY

Is It Time to Change College Coaching? And How?

Dick Vitale did an interesting look at college coaching versus NBA coaching for ESPN.com not too long ago. He compared the two jobs, how practice regimen differ, what each area deals with in personnel, how the college coach has to deal with academics, alumni, and fund raising, how the NBA coach can't make over a roster as much as he'd like, and how the college coach can totally morph the roster in a few years if he doesn't have what he wants when he takes a job.

But the college-hoops commentator completely missed the one huge point he was making: that college coaches are compared to NBA coaches in the one major way that helps subvert everything about the college game and experience.

Winning.

Sometimes in life we get exactly the world we ask for. College coaches are run out of jobs and towns because they fail to win, treated exactly the same as pro coaches despite having rules and constraints that the NBA and NFL don't have. If the college guys break those rules, they get NCAA sanctions. If they don't, some get crucified if they don't win, even in an organization that insists on referring to the "student-athletes" while it is milking the kids for every advertising and marketing dollar it can.

Put someone in a city and job with the chance to take care of themselves and their families for life. Ramp up the pressure. And then profess shock and outrage when some of them bend the rules to keep those jobs? Who's really the problem?

Local media began ranting for the firing of DePaul basketball coach Joey Meyer in 1997, one city columnist even reaching the heights of hypocrisy as to lament in a eulogy after the death of Meyer's father Ray that the Blue Demons "were forced to fire Meyer after a 3-23 season." Forced? By whom? Another city newspaperman wrote that DePaul had won just one NCAA game since 1990 and "that's pretty sad." If that's sad, the writer has had a pretty sad-free life.

In 13 seasons as Blue Demons head coach, Meyer put together a record of 231-158 that included six 20-win seasons, seven NCAA bids, and three NIT appearances. DePaul won a Great Midwest Conference championship under Meyer. Sad?

After Ron Turner was fired as head football coach at Illinois, one line was that the "program begins the long climb back to respectability." Respectable? By what standard?

Turner was 35-37 in his eight seasons. The Illini went to

two Bowls, but were 9-25 over Turner's last three seasons so...gone. Sad.

What Notre Dame did in firing football coach Tyrone Willingham while he still had a contract, what DePaul did to Meyer, what Illinois did to Turner—that's sad. Some of the media pushed for those to happen and obviously so did college administrations and, ultimately, fans.

Nowhere in the stories surrounding any of those incidents was there anything more than cursory comments about character or graduation rates or anything that matters. In fact, "graduation rate" is one of those things that is never a story, when it's really the only story that matters.

So it's time to fix that. The NFL has a pool of money that pays players based on performance, specifically the amount of playing time in relation to what they were paid. For some it is nearly as much as their base salaries. The NCAA is a pool of money and can fix a lot of what is wrong in its games by creating a pay bump for coaches based on graduation rates of their athletes.

Go one step further: Allow colleges additional scholarships based on the percentage of athletes they graduate. The coach benefits, the program benefits, and, most important, kids benefit, for all the right reasons.

The money in college sports is too big to change the course that ship is sailing. So why bother trying to force something that isn't going to happen? Instead, make it worth everyone's time and effort to make a course correction.

TAKING OFFENSE

The Dream Bears Offensive Team

The Bears are the most distinguished football team in the world: numbers of championships, numbers of Hall of Fame players, founded by the founder of the NFL, Papa Bear.

The defense has drawn most of the acclaim and notice of the last half-century—not surprising given that the last two NFL championships won by the franchise were defense-based, in 1963 and 1985.

But of the one-side-of-the-ball-only Bears in the Pro Football Hall of Fame, 12 of them are offensive players to six on defense. That means that some very, very good players do not make the all-time Bears Dream Team on offense. This unit gets 12 players to allow for using a fullback sometimes. But it only gets one wide receiver.

84 QUARTERBACK: SID LUCKMAN

What about: Jim McMahon? If you had to win one game, like a Super Bowl, I want Jimmy Mac. His passes may have been end-over-end sometimes but he

235

knew where to throw them. No quarterback in Bears history ever had such a complete sense of defenses, and few have ever inspired teammates the way McMahon did. He made them all better. One game, McMahon is probably your boy.

Yeah, but: There is only one Bears quarterback in the Hall of Fame and that's Luckman. At a time when the NFL had quarterbacks like Sammy Baugh, Cecil Isbell, Bob Waterfield and Paul Christman, Luckman was All-Pro five times. In an era that was really just discovering the forward pass, Luckman threw 7 TD passes and 433 yards in one 1943 afternoon.

McMahon threw for 300 yards once in his career. The Bears lost that game, at Denver in 1987, a loss that cost him being the cover story of *Newsweek* that week. Luckman did it three times and the Bears won all three. The Bears won four NFL titles with Luckman to McMahon's one. Luckman was so good that the owner of the Detroit Lions stirred up an investigation with hints that Luckman was in with book- ies and undesirables, just to try getting him out of the way.

It's Luckman's huddle.

85 RUNNING BACKS: WALTER PAYTON AND GALE SAYERS

What about: Red Grange? Well, he was from Wheaton and the U of I. And he did help launch true pro football when he signed with Halas. But he's a might-have-been NFL'er and really did more for the Bears as a DB after his knee injury.

What about: George McAfee? McAfee went into the Navy during WWII for four years of his prime but still averaged a touchdown every 16 times he carried the ball. Walter was one every 35 times, Gale one every 26. Only Gale and Beattie Feathers among Bears running backs topped McAfee's 4.9 yards per carry. If not for Gale and Walter, this is probably your featured back.

What about: Willie Galimore? Oh, could he run. He was The Man for the '63 Bears. If he isn't killed in that '64 car accident in training camp with Bo Farrington, the Bears probably repeat and Galimore is remembered the way Sayers is.

Galimore and Rick Casares—greatest combined backfield in Bears history? You take Walter and Matt Suhey or Roland Harper, I'll take Willie and Rick, same O-line and let's play. You probably take me but it ain't easy. Galimore still ranks seventh all-time in Bears rushing, averaged 4.5 yards per carry and had 26 rushing TDs, 10 receiving, and he was splitting time with Casares and Johnny Morris in the backfield a lot of the time. Do the Bears draft Sayers after '64 if Galimore is still with them?

Yeah, but: The only debate is whether your number one feature back is Walter or Gale. That's its own debate.

TIGHT END: MIKE DITKA

What about: Forget it. Nobody else even close. He was the first tight end elected to the Hall of Fame, still ranks fourth all-time in receiving yards and catches, and 1 of every 9 catches was for a touchdown. The guy averaged 14.3 yards per catch, .1 more than Johnny Morris, more than Curtis Conway, and .1 less than Marcus Robinson, the other portrait of Bears deep besides Willie Gault. And block?

Scary good.

LEFT TACKLE: JIM COVERT

What about: Lionel Antoine? 'Twine was a truly dominant giant on the offensive line, the third-overall pick of the 1972 draft out of Southern Illinois. But he only played six seasons total and was brought down by injuries—only two years with all fourteen games and 68 total—or he might have become one of the greats, particularly once Walter arrived to make everyone a little better up front.

Yeah but: Lots of good tackles to pick from but it has to be the absolute best taking care of Luckman's blind side. That's Covert, who practiced every day against Richard Dent and about whom Dent said, "After practicing against Jimbo, games were easy."

Covert was the left tackle on the NFL's Team of the Decade for the 1980s. That included Hall of Fame possibilities Gary Zimmerman, Lomas Brown, and Joe Jacoby. But Covert was the best, a combination of run blocker and pass blocker that has rarely been seen in the NFL.

His back injury and the Bears' stumbles of the late 1980s obscured how really good he was. Covert was 280 pounds, had protected Dan Marino at Pitt, and was why you spend the number 6 pick of a draft on an offensive lineman.

88 LEFT GUARD: STAN JONES

What about: Mark Bortz? Couple of Pro Bowls, absolutely ferocious. Dan Hampton described Mark Bortz as a cyborg that you would have to destroy to stop. He was as tough an offensive lineman as anyone who lined up next to a center; just ask Randy White, who may be in the Hall of Fame but who was vaporized by Bortz when the two met in '85. "Manster?" Sorry, Randy. The Manster was the guy blocking you.

Yeah but: Jones virtually brought weightlifting to the NFL at a time when the prevailing wisdom was that working out made you muscle-bound and not as agile. No, seriously, people did think that. Not Jones. He was a tackle when he came to the Bears, then switched to guard and was selected to eight Pro Bowls.

Jones was about 255 pounds and it was muscle. The Bears *averaged* 206 rushing yards per game in 1956! Jones was a bad-ass. He moved to defensive tackle in 1963 and the Bears won the NFL championship because of the defense.

89 CENTER: TIE: JAY HILGENBERG AND OLIN KREUTZ

What about: George Trafton? "Brute." This was an original Decatur Staley who put four Rock Island Independents players out of a 1920 game in the first 12 plays. The next time the Bears went to Rock Island, Halas gave the $7,000 of gate receipts, in cash, to Trafton, figuring that "if trouble came, I'd be running only for the $7,000. Trafton would be running for his life."

What about: Clyde Turner? "Bulldog." He gets some votes because he was good enough to play guard, tackle, and linebacker, and even running back. He led the NFL with 8 interceptions in 1942 and was All-NFL six times.

Yeah but: Nobody wanted Hilgy. He was undrafted and wasn't even sure he wanted to play for the Bears if they didn't think enough of him to draft him. Too small. Not really all that athletic-looking, not an NFL body-type.

But Tom Thayer, the guy to his right for most of the 1980s, has a picture of a goal-line scene, a Bears touchdown, in which 21 players are on the ground. The one still standing is Hilgenberg, a college wrestler who understood leverage and used it ruthlessly. He wasn't more than 270, never dominant brute physically, but was the center of one of the NFL's greatest-ever offensive lines.

Hilgy went to seven straight Pro Bowls. Even when the Bears collapsed in 1989, his peers voted Hilgenberg to the Pro Bowl.

And Olin—forget the last name; he's on a first-name basis with his teammates, and it's usually "F***in' Kreutz" to the rest of the NFL—Kreutz is the best pass-blocking center the Bears have ever had, is pure old-school, and is one guy you want on your side if matters turn surly. Kreutz plays about 20 pounds bigger than Hilgenberg and will probably equal or exceed Hilgy's trips to Hawaii, particularly if the Bears keep winning.

90 RIGHT GUARD: DANNY FORTMANN

What about: Tom Thayer? Chris Villarrial? Thayer started for the '80s Bears, and Villarrial was a vastly underrated starter, a mauler, and quiet tough guy on a series of bad teams who annually graded out as the Bears' best blocker.

Yeah but: Fortmann spanned eras. The Bears pioneered the T-formation but that was during Fortmann's career, meaning he did his blocking for two different offenses.

Fortmann was All-NFL six straight years, from 1938–43 and the Bears had five first-place, two second-place, and a third-place finish in his eight-year career. Easy pick.

91 RIGHT TACKLE: JOE STYDAHAR

What about: Big Cat Williams? A warrior who locked up with Reggie White in some memorable battles in the 1990s and more than held his own against maybe the greatest defensive lineman in history.

What about: George Connor? The guy was great everywhere, played tackle on offense and defense at 6'3", 240, and was fast enough ultimately to play linebacker. He's in the Hall of Fame and was All-NFL on both offense and defense in 1951 and 1952. Since he was more legendary on defense, he'll be over on that side of the ball.

What about: Keith Van Horne? 'Horne was 6'8", 290 pounds in his prime, and the acclaim heaped on Covert and Hilgenberg didn't leave a lot of spotlight for anyone else. And this was one of the true characters and personalities of the '85ers.

The Bears played Philadelphia Eagles teams with Reggie and Raiders teams with Howie Long, two Hall of Fame left defensive ends, a total of seven times. They won six of them. Somebody was blocking those guys—'Horne.

Yeah but: Joe Stydahar was an All-NFL left tackle for the four years ending with the 73-0 championship game, then back for another championship in 1946 after two years in the service for WWII.

Because Covert was more experienced at pass protection, and because you have to have two tackles, Stydahar goes at right tackle. The Bears' first-ever draft choice. Plus, c'mon: a tackle with the name "Stydahar." I'll take him.

92 WIDE RECEIVER: JOHNNY MORRIS

What about: Curtis Conway? C-Way was incredibly fast, a touchdown scorer, and not fully appreciated because of the endless carousel of quarterbacks throwing him passes.

What about: Ken Kavanaugh? Tough to not go with a guy who plays two seasons, including the '40 Monsters, gives the next four years to his country in WWII, and so only catches 162 passes for his career—and scores 50 touchdowns! He averaged 22.4 yards per catch but just didn't catch enough balls to start for the Dream Team, and Jim Keane was the receiving leader every year from 1947–50.

What about: Harlon Hill? Hill was the Bears' passing game in the mid '50s, led the Bears in receiving from 1954–56, and was the first Bear to pile up more than 1,000 receiving yards in a season, and he did it in '54 and '56 when he also scored 12 and 11 TDs. Not bad for a guy from Florence State Teachers College. Now that was somebody doing some scouting.

Yeah but: Because this team has Ditka, Payton, and Sayers, it only needs one wideout. That's gotta be Morris. He came into the league as a halfback, split time with Galimore while Casares was the primary ballcarrier, and still averaged 4.5 yards per carry his first three seasons.

Then somebody must've told Halas that the kid was coholder of the world record in the 50-yard dash (5.2 sec.) and so Halas put him out where he could actually run 50-yard dashes.

Besides, he did the Mike Ditka Show in '85 for Channel 2. That counts for something.

93 FULLBACK: BRONKO NAGURSKI

The Bears have always had good fullbacks, some great.

What about: Roland Harper? Matt Suhey? Walter could not have had better escorts in his backfield than Harper and Suhey, who were superb lead blockers. But they weren't really impact players in their own rights.

What about: Rick Casares? The linchpin of the offense from 1955–59, a five-year stretch in which he made the Pro Bowl every single year. He went about 220 pounds and was a bruiser with a flair. Casares averaged 4.1 yards per carry for his career, had 34 TDs and 123 receptions in those first five years, and drove Halas crazy.

Halas was fining players for failing to be at assigned weights. Casares was too far under so he taped a wrench to his stomach to add the necessary poundage. Too much, and Halas was on to him. The Old Man fined him $25 for being a pound over.

Casares once got on the team plane carrying three suits. Halas fined him $500 on the grounds that anybody who takes three suits for a one-day trip has to be up to no good.

Yeah but: The Bronk was in his own class. He threw for touchdowns with a jump-pass and played eight years before needing the money that pro wrestling promised, yet still ranks 10th in Bears career rushing. He came back in 1943 when the Bears were short of players because of WWII and played primarily at tackle. But when the Bears needed help in the 1943 championship game against the Washington Redskins, Nagurski moved back to fullback.

His high school teams never won a game and legend is that the coach at Minnesota recruited Nagurski when he saw him plowing a field—without a horse. Nagurski at 240 pounds averaged 4.4 yards per carry. How would he look in front of Walter or Gale?

BONUS!

Picking an All-Star team is one thing. Picking the three best Bears offensive units of all time is something else. The 1995 group may be one of the best Bears teams to have nothing to show for its offense: three 1,000-yard men: Rashaan Salaam rushing and Curtis Conway and Jeff Graham receiving. Erik Kramer's passing marks from that season still dot the record book and the 378 offensive points.

The problem is, three Bears offenses were better.

3. 1965 BEARS

The team of Gale Sayers's rookie year had not only Gale, with his 6 TDs against San Francisco and 22 for the season. That offense also had Johnny Morris and Mike Ditka catching 89 combined passes and scored 391 points in a 14-game season.

Forgotten was quarterback Rudy Bukich throwing 20 TD passes against only 9 interceptions behind a line that allowed just 24 sacks. Bukich's 93.7 passer rating is fourth-best ever by a Bears quarterback and included 8.46 yards per attempt.

2. 1985 BEARS

The defense held the spotlight but the offense was the greatest one-year Bears scoring force in franchise history. McMahon, Walter, Covert, Hilgenberg, and the rest scored 420 points, more points than the combined offense-defense-special teams total of any other Bears team.

Of the nine Bears who went to the Pro Bowl after that season, five were from the offense. In the first five games of the '85 season it was the offense that bailed out the defense primarily. Walter's 4.8 yards per carry were the second-most of his career. The team had the most yards and first downs of any Bears team and the group is ranked in the top three of more offensive categories than this book has time to list.

1. 1941 BEARS

In the last season before WWII, Sid Luckman ratcheted up an offense that scored 56 touchdowns while he was compiling the third-best passer rating in franchise history (95.5) and netting an average 9.9 yards every time the Bears attempted a pass. And that was in 11 games.

Six members of the offensive unit are in the Pro Football Hall of Fame.

CUBS OR SOX?

Chicago's Hatfields and McCoys: What's Your Problem?

Can you just be a Chicago baseball fan or do you have to be either a Cubs or Sox fan? What is that, a trick question?

It actually might have been possible to be a fan of both once upon a time, but not really since the start of interleague play and annual series between the two teams. You can't very well root for ties. Besides, "fan" is short for "fanatic" and it's asking a lot for zealots and disciples to serve two masters with equal dementia.

But after a long, long time of almost benign disinterest, something turned an in-city fan rivalry into something with an edge that wasn't always there. Who, or what, is really at fault for effectively splitting the city along baseball-team lines with the level of venom that too often infects the whole thing?

The fact is, the White Sox gave away Chicago with the 1919 scandal and then with management taking the game onto hard-to-find TV stations in the 1970s. Curiously, the Cubs have done the same thing in recent years, but that's another issue.

Sox ownership moved the team from free to cable TV while the Cubs didn't make their move to the tangle of cable outlets they now use until much later. So ironically, the team with the image of snob appeal was really the one who made it easier to be a TV fan than the one who was going for the cable money at a time when not many Chicago fans even had access to cable.

Cubs center fielder Juan Pierre grew up in Alabama. He was a Cubs fan because he watched their games on WGN.

Sox fans scoff that Cubs "fans" are just out at Wrigley Field to get drunk. But what were Sox fans doing in all those years when the team was owned by John Allyn and Bill Veeck? Comiskey Park was nothing more than an outdoor tavern.

Jerry Reinsdorf and Eddie Einhorn tried to change that. Golden boxes and premium seats were set up, which cost some of their blue-collar fan base.

It's too easy to lump it all into some notion of North Side versus South Side, along racial, class or whatever lines somebody chooses. That doesn't work. Too stereotypical. The Cubs-Sox jokes are clichés: (from a website) A Cubs fan is more likely to drive a BMW. A Sox fan is more likely to break into that BMW. A Cubs fan will watch HBO's Oz and talk about its "gritty theme" the next day at the water cooler. A Sox fan has probably served time in "Oz" and sees it as a love story.

And it doesn't work to say simply that Chicago has always been a Cubs town baseball-wise. In the 20 years prior to 1985, the Sox drew 23.6 million fans. The Cubs pulled in 25.1 million over the same stretch. Not a significant difference: 75,000 a year. But from 1985–89, when the Cubs were winning two division titles, the Cubs drew 10.6 million to 6.4 million for the Sox and the swing was on.

The Cubs never drew as many as 2 million fans in a season before 1984. Then they went over that number in five of the next six years, even pulling in 2 million in 1988 when they were 77-85.

Acrimony picked up in 1983. The Sox won the division by nearly 20 games, while the only excitement for the Cubs was manager Lee Elia going off on the fans who paid to come to Wrigley Field. The 1983 All-Star game was played at Comiskey Park also.

Cubs fans were generally not enthusiastic about the Sox but the general attitude was that it'd be good if the Sox could beat Baltimore and get to the World Series, since "our team's never going to win anything."

In 1984 the Cubs lost 14 straight in the Cactus League, Bill Buckner and Jim Frey were fighting, and Frey eventually got rid of Buckner for Dennis Eckersley and opened the job for Leon Durham. The Sox started decently but La Marr Hoyt and the rest of the pitching staff spiraled down. And even though the Sox were actually in first place at the All-Star break, and the Cubs were behind the Mets, in the second half the Cubs opened up a lead while the Sox went into a tailspin.

The Cubs made the playoffs and Sox fans were grumpy. Tony LaRussa was hired by a local station as a guest analyst and he was clearly not enjoying the Cubs' success. And when the Cubs faltered, Sox fans aired their venom and delight that the Cubs had fallen.

In 1989, Sox fans were calling Will Clark their hero after he battered the Cubs out of the NLCS. In 1993, Cubs fans began to return fire and the rhetoric escalated.

The Cubs marketed their ballpark; the Sox went exactly the opposite direction and built a new Comiskey that was the antithesis of the retro ballparks that are such hits in Baltimore, Cleveland, Boston...and Chicago. The Cubs' biggest offense is squeezing advertising and marketing dollars out of their venerable home; the Sox in their new park put up a screen in centerfield that bombards the sensibilities with games, commercials, and other video bric-a-brac that is not what most paying customers go to ballgames for.

The Sox's owner flirted with moving his team to Florida. Not the way to Chicago sports fans' hearts.

But there really is no good reason why you can't be a fan of both the Cubs and Sox other than pointing to the outrages of the past. It's like the Hatfields and McCoys. Nobody can honestly recall when the feud really started, particularly since the teams didn't start playing each other until the advent of interleague play.

REMEMBER TENNIS?

Where Did the Boom Go?

95 Chicago was one of the epicenters of the national, even international, tennis boom in the 1970s. The area turned out top junior talent like Andrea Jaeger, and the proliferation of indoor clubs not only made it a year-round sport with lotteries waiting lists for court time, but also attracted quality teaching pros who could work more than just summers.

Less than two decades later, some of those indoor clubs had turned into warehouses, tennis departments in sporting goods stores had shrunk, and the boom was long gone. How did it happen, especially in Chicago?

The summit was in 1974, a year after the Billie Jean King-Bobby Riggs match, when Jimmy Connors had his greatest year, winning Wimbledon and the U.S. Open. U.S. tennis was at the top of the world. But then even Chicago started to lose interest.

What did it was the fact that the game was never really easy. And once the game lost its kitchy status, it was an expensive way to spend an hour for a lot of standing around, given the way a lot of folks played it.

Construction economics then came into play. Clubs built very early, even before the boom, were in good shape because their costs had been less. But the ones built after 1973 in particular, tended to need higher court occupancies to hit their break-even points. Once the craze started to ebb, those places were in trouble.

Prince came out with the oversized racquet, but not even that helped, especially when racquet prices moved above $100. That was fine for the serious player, but it was a heavy money drop for a lot of casuals who started turning to other activities and health clubs for exercise.

Ironically, the better the technology got, the more boring the game got, which squeezed a little more life out of the sport. The numbers of players went back up in the mid-1990s with Andre Agassi and Pete Sampras making it an American tennis world. But it didn't last.

By then the erosion that aerobics and health clubs had started was accelerated by spin classes, pilates, yoga, and the cost of racquets, now into the $200s.

And the game just didn't have "It" anymore. Tennis was no longer trendy. Connors was dubbed the "Belleville Basher" by commentator Bud Collins, which made him an Illinois guy. But after he, John McEnroe, Agassi, and Sampras were in eclipse, it wasn't the same game to watch and follow, at least not for the average American and Chicagoan.

And spin classes were easier.

TEAM BUILDERS

Built to Last or to Finish Last?

No one, Chicago or otherwise, is or was more of a builder than George Halas. Let's put him in a different category all by himself. Halas built the Bears and the NFL. Nobody else built a league.

Bill Veeck comes closest, building what amounts to the modern-day game of baseball in a lot of respects, not including using a midget as a pinch-hitter. He was the one responsible for planting the ivy on Wrigley Field walls and introduced the whole concept of honoring fans, a lesson more than a few owners should relearn, Chicago and otherwise.

Honorable mention belongs to Dallas Green, who built the Cubs that went to the 1984 NLCS and the 1989 team that reached the playoffs. Green constructed the first Cubs team with a trade for Larry Bowa and Ryne Sandberg, another for Dennis Eckersley, still another for Rick Sutcliffe, and brought in virtually every starter on the '84 team.

With him in charge of the Cubs, the farm system developed Shawon Dunston, Mark Grace, Greg Maddux, Jamie Moyer, and Rafael Palmiero—the core of the '89 team.

But because there wasn't a championship at the end of the construction process, Green falls just short of the top three:

3. KENNY WILLIAMS, WHITE SOX

Too soon to rank him with the best? Hardly. Williams has been Sox GM for five years and built a team that won a World Series. But he did more than that. Williams changed their entire personality and the White Sox's place in Chicago along with it.

Williams signed Ozzie Guillen to manage the team, the biggest imprint of all. That made over the team from the laid-back era of Jerry Manuel and put a chip on the shoulder of an organization that flirted with great but was never going to reach it.

Williams went into free agency, but instead of bringing back an Albert Belle, he brought in outfielder Jermaine Dye, reliever Dustin Hermanson, pitcher Orlando "El Duque" Hernandez, Japanese infielder Tadahito Ichuchi, and catcher A. J. Pierzynski. He also let go of fixtures like Carlos Lee and Magglio Ordonez and went for Scott Podsednik, the National League's 2004 stolen-base champion.

Williams brought in pitcher Freddie Garcia and signed him and key members of the pitching staff to long-term deals, returning to baseball basics of building a team around pitching. Williams had the guts to deal away Aaron Rowand, an everyday center fielder, for Jim Thome, a DH.

And it didn't just start with Williams becoming GM. He was the club's director of minor league operations from 1995–96 and was promoted to vice president of player development for four additional seasons (1997–2000) and under him the White Sox were named 2000 Organization of the Year by Baseball America, USA Today, and Howe SportsData.

The Sox had four losing seasons in the five before Williams became GM. They have not had a losing one since. He can build me a team anytime.

2. JERRY KRAUSE, BULLS

Krause's legacy will be the way he kept throwing himself on the Jackson-Jordan-Pippen fire and ultimately blowing up the Bulls. Hey, come on, what's one little hickey?

The reality, though, is that Krause, who never played basketball or any other sport, did build the Jordan Bulls even if he didn't draft Jordan. And he did it more than once.

255

Without what Krause did, Jordan is Kobe Bryant, a high-wire act that scores his 50 and politely exits the playoffs when the real teams start playing. Krause drafted Horace Grant and Scottie Pippen in 1987, which built around Jordan.

Then Krause made the bold stroke of trading away forward Charles Oakley for center Bill Cartwright. Krause replaced Doug Collins with Phil Jackson to coach the Bulls in 1989 and the Bulls had an NBA championship two years later.

Unfortunately, Krause was angering Jordan along the way. Oakley was Jordan's best friend on the team and heard about being traded, not from Krause, but from a TV report. Krause also had drafted Brad Sellers in 1986 instead of Jordan's choice, Johnny Dawkins from North Carolina.

By the time Jordan retired and returned, Grant was gone. Krause, who'd brought in Toni Kukoc from Europe, gambled on a deal for Dennis Rodman and the Bulls were off again.

Did Krause contribute to the demolition of what the Bulls had? Definitely. Because of Krause, or at least what Jordan and Pippen spread about him, the Bulls were off the lists of teams a lot of free agents would consider.

But a key to the success of the mid-1970s Bulls was the acquisition of forward Chet Walker from the the Philadelphia 76ers. The Bulls' scout who pushed the deal: Jerry Krause.

1. JIM FINKS, BEARS

Finks built the 1980s Bears. 19 of the 22 starters in Super Bowl XX were drafted during the Finks regime.

Late Bears chairman Ed McCaskey had a plan to place Finks in charge of the Bears and groom Michael to take over the franchise when he was ready. Finks instead wanted his own shop and left in 1983 to become president of the Cubs. That step lasted only a year, but that year was 1984, the year the Cubs won their division and missed the World Series only by blowing a two-game lead in the playoffs to San Diego.

Finks built the Minnesota Vikings of the 1960s around the "Purple People Eaters" and won eleven division titles and made four Super Bowl appearances in the 14 years of his stewardship as general manager. He also hired Bud Grant as the head coach.

He resigned in 1974 to take over the Bears and used the same formula to build a team for Chicago.

In 1986, Finks took over the New Orleans Saints, a team that had never had a winning season in its nineteen years. The Saints won 12 games in Finks' second year.

Finks died in 1994 of lung cancer and was elected to the Hall of Fame in 1995. He gave Chicago the greatest football team of all time and did it just about as well in two other places. No one better.

THE *CHICAGO* *TRIBUNE* AND THE CHICAGO CUBS

The Best Thing or Worst for Chicago Baseball?

 This is really two issues in one. One has to do with ethics, the other with baseball, and those two unfortunately too often have little to do with each other.

Chicago Tribune columnist and colleague Rick Morrissey wrote in April 2006 that the *Tribune* should sell the Cubs, that "a newspaper has no business" owning a baseball team. Rick could not be more correct.

Rick could well have argued too that the paper, which bought the Cubs in 1981 for $21 million, should divest itself of its 31 percent share in the Food Network or the WB Network or WGN radio/TV. It is difficult to make people believe that there is no relationship between the paper's business interests and its coverage of those interests.

The hard part here is where to draw a line. The local newspapers advertise in local stadiums, which is giving money to an entity the paper covers. The other papers in town do the same thing. And newspapers certainly can accept advertising money from teams and the stations that broadcast the games. So... .

While Rick is right about the need to sell the Cubs, and it will happen eventually, when it makes financial sense for the paper, one thing that doesn't wash is others' criticism of the Cubs under *Tribune* stewardship.

The Cubs went into 2006 with the sixth-highest payroll in baseball. While the Black Hawks can be vilified for failure to spend money, the Cubs under the *Tribune* cannot. The *Tribune* went out and landed manager Dusty Baker for $14 million in his initial four-year contract and it paid Sammy Sosa in a style to which all of us would like to become accustomed.

The Cubs have rarely had it so good on the field either. After the run of success through the late 1930s, the Cubs had exactly two winning seasons from 1941 to 1960 (1945-46). From 1961 through 1980, they had seven, six of those in the 1967–72 run with Ferguson Jenkins, Billy Williams, and a core of players that wasn't free to go anywhere.

In the nearly 25 years since the *Tribune* bought the team, it has had eight winning seasons, including 2001, '03, and '04, and that has been in the age of free agency when players are free to leave and because of that are anything but free.

259

They haven't gotten to a World Series since 1945? Of the next 62 years since that season, 36 were before the *Tribune* bought the team. Blame Leon Durham, Alex Gonzalez, Mark Prior, Kerry Wood, even Steve Bartman if you want. But not the Tribune.

The Tribune is criticized for drawing money out of the Cubs and for commercializing the team's ballpark. Naming rights for the Cubs' ballpark could be the next flash point with fans. Wonder if the last guy to do that took the same kind of heat?

PEEVES
These Are a Few of My Favorite Things...Not!

ORGANIZED KIDS SPORTS

Organized kids sports are part of what is ruining sports in Chicago and elsewhere.

It isn't that Little League or soccer leagues or grade-school basketball are bad by themselves. It's certainly better for a youngster to spend some hours at a ballfield hitting a ball with a stick than playing the same games with a joystick. It isn't even the abuses that come in the form of psychotic parents or Rockne-wannabe coaches driving the kids.

It's that the organized sports turn into the only sports the kids play, and that's not good on a couple of levels.

Instead of dads and moms playing catch with their sons and daughters, off the kids go to baseball leagues that are the only baseball they play. Call it athletic daycare; turn your kids over to the coaches.

The coaches are better at helping the kids learn how to play the games? That isn't completely true, on two counts.

Playing a little hoops or catch with your folks isn't about learning how to throw a two-seam cutter; it's about time with your kids while they still aren't embarrassed about admitting they have parents.

But the second thing is that kids don't learn how to play sports if it's only organized practices and games. It's work. It's a job. It's somewhere you gotta be, for practice, for games. You sign up, you gotta do it.

The baseball leagues now are for kids six, seven years old. It used to be that the youngest you could be in Little League was nine; now you're a vested veteran by the time you're that old. Then the parents running the thing are trying to start traveling teams to get the better players off by themselves and supposedly just playing better, other traveling teams.

A big part of why so much talent in basketball comes from poorer areas is because the kids don't have organized leagues holding them back. You go to the park, you learn to play the game, or you don't get to play. You'd better get better or find something else to do.

The flood of great baseball players from Latin America isn't coming from Little Leagues. Besides the obvious fact that baseball is better in areas where it can be played year-round, it's coming from parks and places where kids play baseball. You learn some bad habits just playing in the wild with any sport but you also learn to play the game tough and that is putting a core in place.

Who is likely to be the better player: the one who hung out at the park and played pickup games or the one who only came through the organized program? Which is sweeter: the hothouse tomato or the vine-ripened one?

WHAT HAPPENED TO THE WHITE GUYS?

I had an interesting talk a few years ago with Shannon Sharpe, a great tight end of the Denver Broncos who should wind up in the Hall of Fame. We were both in the lobby of the Broncos's headquarters waiting for people and got to talking about Ed McCaffrey, Sharpe's teammate with the Broncos and an NFL anomaly: a white wide receiver.

Sharpe was both angered and tickled at how opposing defensive backs would start arguing with each other over who got to cover McCaffrey. "I got the white guy!" "No, I got him!" And then, after McCaffrey'd caught a handful of passes and scored once or twice, Sharpe laughed at how the arguments changed into, "Hey, YOU had the white guy!" "No, I didn't, YOU did!"

Sharpe's point was that nobody respects white guys at certain "athlete" positions (receiver, running back, defensive back) and questions whether or not they can even play there, just the way assumptions a quarter-century ago were that blacks couldn't play quarterback, center, or other "thinking" positions. They were wrong then, Sharpe said, and they're wrong now.

The problem was, and is, that stereotypes form and, once they're in place, they stay. They're safe. Michael Jordan said some years ago on *Late Night with David Letterman* that "There's white guys who can play and nobody gives them a chance." Somehow if they're European, they get a different look than if they're American.

A problem with all of this, besides depriving young athletes of a fair chance, is that we as fans get less of a sports world to enjoy. Baseball before Jackie Robinson was fine; lots of nice players. How much better would it have it been to watch if Josh Gibson, Buck Leonard, Satchel Paige, and others had been allowed to play the Major League game?

Anytime you close your doors to a significant population group—and that's what is happening with the "new segregation"—those in the group lose. So do we all.

CHICAGO: GOOD SPORTS CITY OR A BUNCH OF PUSHOVERS?

Chicago is a great town in which to be an athlete. Chicago wants to love its teams and players and you have to be pretty bad as well as pretty obnoxious not to get a hug from Chicago fans.

Yet somehow Cubs fans are saps for going out to Wrigley Field when critics claim management is just interested in their money and not putting a championship team out there for them to watch. Bears fans are boobs for taking their snowmobile-suited selves out to Soldier Field and suffering through November and December games that haven't mattered in a lot of years. Hawks fans who give Bill Wirtz $75 for a seat to watch his teams are suckers.

No. The games we watch are entertainment. If you subscribe to the symphony and the series isn't the best, you're patronizing the arts. If you do a season's subscription to the Goodman, and half the plays are bad, you're patronizing the arts.

If you're a season ticketholder for the Cubs, you're a pigeon? No. Take your son and daughter out to the park and enjoy baseball. Having a good time on a Saturday afternoon is not a character flaw.

DYNASTY DENIED

Who Killed the '85 Bears?

They were the greatest football team in history and yet were gone after one Super Bowl. They weren't gone as a great team; they were 14-2 in '86, 11-4 in '87, 12-4 in '88, and put up 11-5 in 1990 and 1991 when some of the '85ers were still good enough to do damage.

So why only one Super Bowl? Who, or what, ultimately killed the 1985 Bears?

THE PLAYERS

In the end, some of the very elements that made them great proved to be their undoing. Personality, ego, talent— all of them fell over each other and fused into a ball that, instead of rolling over everything as it did in '85, had too much envy, jealousy, and selfishness to roll as well as it needed to in the years that followed.

Some players felt they took their feet off the gas at times after '85, so that instead of overcoming problems, they exacerbated them. The problem between Dan Hampton and Jim McMahon, two of the most central of figures, split some of the team and nobody healed that or other wounds.

In short, they had it and let it get away.

MIKE DITKA

As Richard Dent said, "He was the reason we won one Super Bowl and the reason we didn't win three." He was the emotional leader of the team and he was also the leader in losing the "we" focus of the team. Da Coach didn't miss any tackles or blocks. But he didn't do the core of the team any favors with his decision to start Doug Flutie with a second Super Bowl within reach or with his endless spectrum of outside distractions. That ultimately undermined his ability to demand of players that they take the high road of making the team and each other No. 1. A shame, really.

MICHAEL MCCASKEY

The team president certainly had his legions of detractors, and few individuals did more to alienate players than Michael. Mike Ditka wasn't his hire and wasn't his choice even to stay on after the first couple years; the Bears just kept winning and there was no way to dump Ditka.

Michael got rid of GM Jerry Vainisi. He got rid of Jim McMahon, let go of Wilber Marshall, Otis Wilson, and others, and took some of the heart out of a team that had plenty of it at one point. If ownership is supposed to help build a team, this was a case of the opposite.

JIM MCMAHON

It wasn't just McMahon's play; it was his lack of play. McMahon finished 1984 and 1986 on the sideline with serious injuries that can't be blamed on him, although more than a few teammates argue to this day that if McMahon took better care of himself preparing for seasons, he would have had an exponentially better chance of surviving or avoiding some of the hurts that eventually brought him down.

Don't deify McMahon either. He stunk up Soldier Field in the 1987 playoffs by throwing 3 interceptions to the Redskins—one more than Flutie did the year before. And in the '88 NFC championship game, he didn't complete half of his passes, didn't throw a TD, and was picked off again.

VINCE FOR BUDDY

Buddy Ryan left after the Super Bowl to take the head coaching job in Philadelphia. The statistics the next season under Vince Tobin were better, but the attack mindset that Ryan had fostered was not there. Hampton's observation: attack dogs had been turned into sentries.

THE NFC

The problem with the Bears after '85 wasn't all the Bears. They had the misfortune of playing in, and being part of, the Golden Age of the NFC. The conference was replete with Hall of Fame coaches—Joe Gibbs in Washington, Bill Parcells in New York, Bill Walsh in San Francisco—and Hall of Fame players. The Washington team they lost to in the '87 playoffs and the 49ers they lost to in '88's both won the Super Bowl.

The Bears simply didn't have to fall very far every year before they were set upon by packs of dogs almost as tough and mean as they were to start with.

THE REAL REASON...

is that there isn't one single reason. That team was so good that it took all of those reasons to bring it down. Blame one, blame all.

AND TOMORROW?

The Ones to Remember

100 It's unusual for even a down era (Chicago knows about these) not to produce at least one or two greats, All-Stars at least, maybe even Hall of Famers. A handful of athletes performing in Chicago now will be remembered with the greats of other eras.

BEARS: CEDRIC BENSON, RUNNING BACK

Benson's career start was as dismal as Gale Sayers's was spectacular. But before it finishes, Benson will threaten all of the records, including some of Walter's. He began his rookie season with a holdout, and then got only table scraps of playing time left by Thomas Jones and Adrian Peterson and missed most of the year with a knee injury.

But Benson was the Walter equivalent at Texas, with a workload such that the only question was whether or not it used up too much of him. He is in a Bears offense that wants him to be a load-bearing wall. If he can approach Payton's longevity of 13 seasons, he will leave the game as the number three back in Chicago behind only Walter and Gale.

SOX: BRANDON MCCARTHY, PITCHER

McCarthy went into the 2006 season without a starting job after the 2005 seasons had by Mark Buehrle, Jose Contreras, Jon Garland, and Freddie Garcia, plus the addition of Javier Vazquez. He will not be waiting long.

McCarthy is a dead wringer for Jack McDowell, a one-time Sox ace whose eccentricities and injuries ended what looked to be a budding superstar career. McCarthy has an easy delivery and has one of the top pitching coaches in the game in Don Cooper. Ozzie Guillen found a roster spot for him in the bullpen and when the door opens, he'll step through it and wind up as the second best behind Buehrle or Garland on a great Sox staff.

CUBS: MICHAEL BARRETT, CATCHER

Barrett spent the first six years of his career in Montreal and quietly arrived in Chicago after the circus that was 2003. Before the Cubs he'd hit over .265 just once; since the trade he hit .287 and .276 along with his two best home run years (16).

Barrett has been in some of the shadow from Derek Lee and Aramis Ramirez in addition to the pitching staff he catches. And while he may not reach the numbers of Cubs great Gabby Hartnett, Barrett's next ten years will leave him as one of the best backstops in Chicago. If the Cubs become a force in the National League, Barrett will become a perennial All-Star.

BLACK HAWKS: NONE

Kyle Calder, Tuomo Ruutu, Radim Vrabata—nice players but they will not threaten the roster of all-time Hawks.

COACH OR MANAGER: LOVIE SMITH, BEARS

In his first two-plus seasons, Smith is starting out faster than Mike Ditka and building his team, with GM Jerry Angelo, the same way Ditka and Jim Finks/Jerry Vanisi did: defense and smash-mouth offense. Keeping Smith may prove pricey; good ones are always expensive. But the fans love him, players play for him, and before he's done, the shock will be if he doesn't put another Lombardi Trophy next to the one Ditka won.

INDEX
by Subject

INDEX
by Name

287

ABOUT THE
AUTHOR

Chicago Tribune writer John "Moon" Mullin has covered the Bears since the closing days of the 1985 era and the farewells of Mike Ditka and players from that historic team. He has won writing awards from the Pro Football Writers of America and Associated Press Sports Editors, in addition to an Emmy award for his "Bears Insider" segment of the FOX-TV Bears pregame show. Mullin's writing has been nationally syndicated, and he is the author of *The Rise and Self-Destruction of the Greatest Football Team in History: The Chicago Bears and Super Bowl XX, Tales from the Chicago Bears Sidelines*, and *Tennis and Kids: The Family Connection* (with Jim Fannin).